BIG O'S

Sex Coach Book 2

M. S. PARKER

Belmonte Publishing, LLC

This book is a work of fiction. The names, characters, places and incidents are products of the writer's imagination or have been used fictitiously and are not to be construed as real. Any resemblance to persons, living or dead, actual events, locales or organizations is entirely coincidental.

Copyright © 2018 Belmonte Publishing LLC

Published by Belmonte Publishing LLC

ISBN-13: 978-1985132252

ISBN-10: 1985132257

Reading Order

Thank you so much for reading Big O's, the second book in the Sex Coach series. All books in the series can be read stand-alone, but if you'd like to read the complete series, I recommend reading them in this order:

1. Sex Coach
2. Big O's
3. Pleasure Island (releasing late spring 2018)

1

Raye

When I asked my boss about getting more overtime, I hadn't quite planned on staying so late that I'd end up getting caught in the midst of the New Year's Eve revelers. That was what I got for offering to let everyone else with a life enjoy the festivities.

Which was fine. All I had to do was restock, straighten, and handle the end of the night paperwork. It was monotonous work, especially since I was on my own, but sometimes, I preferred it that way. Especially here in the store. It wasn't that I minded my co-workers or even the manager. I liked them all, but people and me...well, I'd never quite figured out how to make myself click with them, and sometimes, the downtime away from others cleared my head.

I'd had plenty of it over the past two hours, cleaning up the shop and restocking for the New Year's Day sale that would start in...oh, maybe eight hours. And that was *late* for a New Year's Sale, some people thought.

The hours didn't suck as bad as they did on Black Friday, but they weren't banker's hours either.

Fortunately, I didn't have to come in until noon.

I swung by the bathroom on my way out, and after using the facilities, I automatically checked my reflection. A petite woman with bright red hair and blue eyes stared back at me, the shadows smudged under those eyes a mark of too many nights spent working or studying or both. I was cramming as many classes in as I could at NYU while juggling both school and my job.

To say that I was exhausted would be putting it mildly.

After one last pass through the shop to check the lights, I headed for the employee entrance that let out at the small alley in the back, pulling on my winter coat along the way. I hated that alley. Even though there was a security camera and other people often getting off or going into work, it was still too isolated for my liking.

Turning up the collar on my coat, I checked the doors and the alarm system before turning to head down the alley toward W. 35th and the crush of people jamming Times Square just beyond.

It was my first New Year's in New York City, but I wasn't going to join the revelry.

I was heading home.

Fighting my way through the bodies packed elbow to elbow took some time, but since it wasn't quite midnight, I was making some headway.

Somebody wolf-whistled, practically right in my ear, and I ignored them. Another block or two and things would loosen up. Not much, but at least I'd be able to walk freely. Most of the people were fighting to *get* to Times Square. I was almost positive I was the only one fighting to get out of it. It might have been easier if I'd just stayed another hour or two, but I'd prefer not to walk the streets completely alone if I didn't have to.

Of course, I'd have to wait until five or six in the morning for *alone* to even be a possibility tonight.

Finally breaking free of the crush, I shoved my hair back from my face before jamming my hands back into my coat pockets and began to walk.

Somebody wolf-whistled at me again.

I ignored it.

When it came a second time, it was a little harder to ignore, mostly because it sounded closer, but this was New Year's Eve and everybody and their brother was plastered three sheets to the wind. Drunks, as obnoxious as they were, were *normally* harmless. The best thing to do was just ignore them.

That was what I told myself right up until my arm was caught in what felt like a giant vice. I found myself jerked to a stop and a big, leering man peered down at me. "Well, look at you, sweetheart. Where you going in such a hurry?"

Even though my heart had begun to hammer, I gave him a pointed look, then lowered my gaze to the hand gripping my arm. "Away. If you don't mind?"

"Maybe me and my buddy could join you. Seems we ain't got anybody to kiss at midnight," he said and broke out into loud peals of laughter as if he'd told the funniest damn joke he'd ever heard.

My belly roiled, but I kept the nerves I felt from leaking out and showing on my face as I suggested, "Maybe try kissing each other."

Jerking my arm away, I pivoted on my heel and began to walk even faster.

"Hey!" he hollered out behind me.

I deliberately stepped into a clutch of people and twisted, thankful that most of them were quite a bit taller than me. Being short had been the bane of my existence for most of my life, but sometimes, it did come in handy.

I put my legs to good use and swung east, heading in a different direction than I'd intended. It would still take me home, although it would add a few minutes more to the commute. The main thing, I was going a different route than those assholes and that was what counted.

When I heard the footsteps and a shouted, "Hey, honey! Hold up!" panic started to chitter inside me.

I didn't *hold up*. I walked even faster, just this side of a run.

Nerves were quickly fading into panic, but I held it at bay. They were drunk, and they'd get bored once I proved to be more trouble than they were worth. Maybe I should swing back to Times Square, find one of the cops–

Yeah, right, a jeering voice inside me said. *Fat lot of good that would do you. Just get home!*

I wasn't even halfway there, and I knew the subway would be packed this time of night. I could always try to flag down a taxi, but that would mean *stopping* my headlong rush to get away from these guys and...

Shit.

A hard hand clamped around my upper arm, and once more, I was swung around to face the guy who'd hassled me earlier. His breath smelled of stale beer and fried food, an altogether unappealing combination that made my stomach spin and flip even more than it already was.

"Where you running off to?" he demanded. "We was talking to you!"

Were! The word leaped into my addled brain, but somehow, I didn't think correcting his grammar was the ideal route to take here.

I jerked against his hold, but his grip was punishingly tight. "Let me go," I said, trying to make my voice stern.

"No...I wanna talk to you."

The look in his eyes had nothing to do with *talking* though.

His friend leered at me as I looked around, trying to figure out what to do. The panic that had been whispering inside was now a full-throated yell, and I thought about calling for help. I was afraid it would be useless. The air was full of people's shouts, music from nearby parties, and for some insane reason, although there were people all around, hardly anybody seemed to really be *there*.

"Let me *go*," I said more insistently, jerking my arm.

Instead, he hauled me in closer and dipped his head. "You're a pretty little thing. I bet you taste as sweet as a strawberry."

I turned my head as he got closer, his fingers close to bruising the bone.

But his mouth never touched mine.

Quick as a wish, he was yanked away, and I gulped in a breath of air as I stumbled a few steps back, smacking into the rough brick of the nearby building. A big, towering figure stood between me and my would-be attacker. "You're going to back the fuck off, or I'm going to break your arm off and feed it to you an inch at a time," he said, his voice flat, the deadliest neutral I'd ever encountered.

"Hey, why don't you back the fuck off?" the man said, puffing out his chest. "We saw her first."

I never even saw what he did, he moved so fast. There was a blur of movement, then Beer and Nacho Breath was bent over at the waist, his face red. My rescuer turned to look at the other guy, a man he towered over by almost a foot. He took a step in that man's direction. "You want to try a round?" he asked in a menacing tone.

The man shook his head wildly and took off running. A minute later, his friend staggered off after him, huffing and puffing, wheezing as he tried to suck in air.

The guy turned to look at me. "You okay?" he asked, his voice softer now.

"I'm..." Licking my lips, I nodded at him. "I'm fine, thank you." I glanced in the direction the men had gone and added, "And thanks for that."

He took a hesitant step toward me, gesturing to where I was rubbing my arm through my thick coat. It ached a little, but it wasn't anything bad. I'd probably have a bruise from where that asshole had been pawing at me. It could have been so much worse.

"You're rubbing your arm. Sure, you're okay?"

Looking down, I stared at where my hand was cupped over my upper arm, feeling a little dazed. Blood roared in my ears. *Reaction*, I thought dully. It was the reaction settling in, that was all.

Swallowing, I tipped my head back to look up at him.

He'd gotten closer.

When had he gotten closer?

Dark, shaggy hair hung in his eyes. I couldn't make out the color in the dim light, but I wished I could.

His gaze dipped to my mouth as I licked my lips again and my heart started to hammer in my ears.

Abruptly, the chaos and noise from the street I'd left behind grew deafening, and I jumped.

"Easy. It's just…" His eyes dipped to my mouth again. He shrugged. "It's New Year's. Happy New Year."

He looked at my mouth again.

Without thinking, I looked at his.

And then his mouth was on mine.

I sucked in a sharp, startled breath.

The brush of his mouth against mine was light, almost gentle. He didn't try to force his way past my open lips, and I caught just the faintest hint of his taste, something I couldn't define.

But desperately wanted to.

Which meant I shouldn't.

2

Kane

Her mouth was every bit as soft as I thought it would be.

That was my first thought. My second thought...*Kane, what the hell are you doing, man?*

I was kissing a total stranger on New Year's Eve, that's what.

And it was a normal, sweet, innocent kiss...then it was over. So over, and not likely to be repeated because even as I contemplated doing it again, she jerked back and glared at me.

"What the hell?" she demanded. Without waiting another second, she hauled her hand back and let it fly, slapping me across the face.

There wasn't a lot of power in the blow, and I wondered if she'd ever hit anyone before, which was a stupid thing to be wondering since I'd clearly pissed her off. What I should have been wondering was how to make an apology.

She was gone, though, ghosting through the crowd on feet

so fast I'd be hard pressed to catch her. I was long-legged and big, but she was *fast* and moving at an all-out run.

A few people turned to look at me, which led me to realize they'd seen the whole damn thing.

Great.

Just great.

What in the hell had I been thinking?

Easy answer.

I hadn't been thinking. At all.

Shaking my head, I turned on my heel and headed back through the crowd. I'd just dropped off the keys for a car I'd finished for one of my regulars. He was the manager at a hotel on W. 35th Street and had promised a nice tip – and delivered – if I'd bring the keys to him tonight. Since I was still struggling to pay off what I owed on the garage, so it would be mine free and clear, I never ignored a request when it came with the words *nice tip*.

The tip had indeed been nice, and I'd already hit an ATM, depositing the cash so I didn't have to worry about getting mugged. It wasn't really a big concern in my mind. Most muggers went looking for somebody who came off as being far less trouble than I'd be, and while I wasn't the tallest guy I'd ever come across at six-two, I was one of the roughest bastards in the area. Heavy with muscle, tattoos roped my arms and marked my hands. A scar bisected my left eyebrow courtesy of a fight where my opponent had gone for a knife – it could have taken the eye if he been just a little faster than me.

Fortunately, I'd been the faster one, and he'd ended up with that buried in his thigh. *He* was lucky I hadn't gone for that big artery there. But I hadn't wanted him dead.

My looks probably had something to do with how people tended to fall away when they saw me in a crowd, and made it a little bit easier to cut through the masses as I headed for the subway. I deliberately chose one a little farther away from Times Square because I didn't want to wait for the crowds to ease up.

The plan worked well enough, and it was only a little after one when I got to the party some friends in Brooklyn were throwing.

Briefly, I wondered if the cute redhead I kissed had made it home okay.

I hoped so.

Briefly, I wondered if maybe I should have caught up with her and made sure she *had* made it home.

But that *really* wouldn't have gone over well after I went and smacked the kiss on her. I didn't understand the slap though. I'd felt something the second I looked at her. I could have sworn she felt the same tug I did, but maybe I just needed to get laid.

Music blasted through the windows as I approached the house. Nobody would think about telling them to turn it down, and nobody would think about calling the cops.

It didn't mean the cops wouldn't come by here and tell these guys to quieten down, but as soon as the uniforms left, the music would go right back up.

I knew the drill. I'd been to parties like this.

The house belonged to Russell Carpenter. He went by Rusty, although whether the nickname was because of his red hair or because he hated his first name, I didn't know, nor did I care to ask.

I'd known Rusty since before I'd gone to prison.

We'd both run in separate gangs then, but we'd never caused each other problems, and we didn't now. He and some of the guys in his were some of my steadiest customers, although they came in late, paid in cash and never wanted anybody but me working on their cars or bikes.

As I entered the house, ears already vibrating from the music, I peeled out of the jacket I'd worn and hung it up on the coat rack, trying to bury it under a layer of other coats so it might still be there when I left.

If not...well, it wouldn't be the first time I'd lost one at a party like this.

"Oh...you're here..." A soft, feminine voice purred up at me, and I looked down to see Calie Smalls giving me a seductive smile.

She was taller than a lot of women and must have been wearing a pair of stiletto heels because now her mouth was just an inch lower than mine. When she would have leaned in to kiss me, I eased back.

Calie and I had an on again and off again thing going on between us. Lately, it had been in the on switch quite a bit, which might explain why she kept sidling closer, but I hadn't come to see her.

"Hey." I managed a smile for her, but before she could loop her arm through mine, I said, "Nice seeing ya. I need to go say hi to Rusty. Happy New Year, Calie."

I lost myself in the crowd and didn't look back, not even when a low crash reverberated behind me, and a bunch of hooting broke out. A piece of furniture had likely just been broken.

This was why I didn't ever want to have parties at my

place. When it came to guys like this, if only *one* thing got broken, it probably wasn't even considered a party.

Rusty was in the back of the house, smoking a joint and nursing a bottle of beer while his girlfriend leaned up against him. He met my eyes and lifted the beer in greeting then pointed over to the far wall. I craned my neck around and saw the cooler, nodding my thanks as I moved to grab a beer for myself. I snagged another one and lifted it, showing it to Rusty. He mouthed something that might have been, "*Fuck, yes.*" I had no idea but took the bottle along. If he didn't drink it, I'd need it in a few minutes.

One of the guys saw me and got up, vacating the chair without me having to say a word. I wouldn't have, I would have been fine standing with my back to the wall, but I took the seat. It was mostly turned to the wall, like a lot of the chairs and it gave me an almost full view of the room.

That was how I preferred it.

Seated next to Rusty, I nodded at his girlfriend as I passed him the beer.

His girlfriend, Bernadette – Bernie to all of us – saw me and swayed forward to wrap her arms around my neck in an overly enthusiastic hug. She wasn't the flirtatious type unless she was plastered so I didn't think much of it, just eased her back toward Rusty. "Had a bit to drink, Bernie?" I asked her.

She snorted and laughed. "A bit? Nooooo..." Then she fell back against Rusty and said, "I'm tired, baby. Let's go to bed and fuck."

He grinned down at her. "We've got company, baby."

She wiggled her eyebrows and giggled. "They can come watch!"

He patted her cheek, then shifted on the chair where he

sat so she could curl up against him better. The two of them had been together for as long as I'd known them.

"How's that bike coming along?" Rusty asked as Bernie snuggled into his heavy frame. He stood almost four inches taller than me, and Bernie, at five-six, looked almost delicate next to him. She buried her face in his neck, and I had no doubt she'd be asleep in no time, never mind the noise and chaos going on around her. And Rusty would just sit there holding her.

For some reason, the thought hung there with me as I thought about the bike one of Rusty's guys had brought me the other day. "Need a few more parts. They've got to be ordered in. Already placed the order, but with the holidays, things are moving slow."

Rusty rolled his eyes and muttered, "Fuck the holidays. I want my bike."

"You might be able to get it quicker if you took it to a bigger garage," I offered.

"I don't want a bigger garage."

I knew he didn't.

Off to my right, two women broke out into a screaming argument, and I grimaced as the splatters from what was probably beer hit the side of my face and neck. I was going to smell like the inside of a brewing vat by the time I left here.

"You find yourself a pretty girlie to kiss at midnight?" Rusty asked.

Shooting him a glance, I said, "What?"

"Midnight...kissing in the New Year."

"It's ringing in the New Year," I told him.

"Whatever." He rolled his eyes, his gaze on the girl fight carrying on next to me. I was paying it a fair amount of attention myself, watching from the corner of my eye. When the two women practically tumbled into my lap, I shifted automatically, shielding them from accidentally striking Bernie, who had started to snore.

I rose, letting them fall from my lap. One of them hit the table which set the bottles on top to wobbling. They continued to fight right up until the bottles fell and the domino effect had beer, cocktails, and wine pouring down on the two screaming and scrapping women.

They stopped, half choking.

"If you're done," Rusty said in a level voice. "Can you do something about this fucking mess you just made?"

3

Raye

As I closed the door behind me, I realized something.

My lips were still buzzing.

It had taken me almost forty minutes to get home – it was normally a twenty-minute trip, both the subway ride and the walk, but tonight it had been double.

So just over forty minutes since some big, sexy stranger with a scar slicing his left eyebrow had smacked his mouth over mine and kissed me.

It had been a quick, light kiss really, now that I think of it.

And it had been the New Year.

Maybe I shouldn't have slapped him.

I didn't know.

What I did know was that my mouth was buzzing.

I hadn't kissed anybody in recent memory who'd actually had the ability to make *anything* buzz. That made this pretty...well...I couldn't call it epic, except it kind of was.

And I'd *slapped* him.

He'd helped me, dealing with the two creeps who'd been up to no good, then midnight strikes and...okay, maybe I'd been gawking at him a little. It might have seemed like a moment, now that I think of it. Not that I'd understand what a moment really felt like.

A kiss on New Year's Eve was a simple enough thing, wasn't it?

Strangers kissed strangers on New Year's Eve, right?

It wasn't a big deal, but I'd gone and made something of it.

He hadn't been grabbing at my ass or my boobs or anything.

"Just a kiss," I murmured.

I might have felt exceptionally silly if I let myself think about it too much. It would be hard to do that though. Every time I tried to clear my mind, I was left thinking about the ever-fading buzz on my lips.

I licked them, fleetingly wondered if I could catch a taste of him like I had when he'd actually *been* kissing me. But if any taste had lingered, it was long gone now.

"You shouldn't have slapped him," I told myself. And it was the truth.

But hindsight was twenty-twenty.

NEARLY A HALF AN HOUR LATER, I stood under the hot spray in my minuscule shower, letting the water beat down on me. My apartment was tiny, barely big enough to be called that, and I was actually lucky to have this much space. I'd been living in an area half this size, forced to share a bathroom, but my current manager's sister worked in real estate, and they'd helped me find this place. Friends from the store had helped decorate and improvise with the vertical space.

Sadly, there was nothing to be done about a tiny, cramped bathroom.

I fit in there just fine, if I didn't do a lot of turning around. If I'd been anything other than what some people called *fun-sized*, I had no idea how I'd manage in the little shower.

As the heat billowed around me, I thought again about the guy who'd come out of the crowd to chase away my harassers and a tingle raced through my entire system. It wasn't unpleasant.

I hadn't been able to *stop* thinking about my kissing hero, and the more I thought about him, the more surreal the event seemed.

I wished I hadn't slapped him.

I wished I had kissed him back.

If I had, what would have happened?

I must have been more tired – or more dazed – than I realized because I found myself cupping a breast in my palm as I relived that short kiss and let it play out in my mind to a better one, a longer one. One where I opened my mouth, and he slid his tongue inside to taste me.

I'd kissed a few guys who seemed like adequate kissers and a couple who were even pretty good at it. I think he would have qualified for really good. He hadn't tried to mash his mouth to mine or choke me with his tongue.

I groaned, closing my eyes. Now I was fantasizing about opening for him and taking his tongue into my mouth, sucking on him as he cupped one of my breasts.

That tingling sensation spread, and I let my hand slide lower.

I found the folds between my thighs, which were damp – and not only because of the shower.

Curious, I rubbed myself, and while I felt something that *seemed* like pleasure, I didn't know what else to do. Nothing felt *right,* and the more I thought about it, the more awkward this whole situation seemed.

Frustration grew inside me, replacing that wonderful tingling sensation, and as the pleasantness faded, I smacked my head back against the tiled wall of the shower.

There was something broken inside me.

The part that was supposed to *enjoy* all of this just... didn't.

"Maybe you're thinking about it too much," I told myself as I pushed off the wall and finished up the shower.

It was possible, I guessed.

Anything was possible...like having some big, tattooed sexy stranger swoop down out of a crowd to chase off some roughnecks, then linger long enough for a kiss.

Heaving out a sigh, I turned off the water and reached for a towel. Since clearly, I wasn't going to be able to relax via self-induced orgasm, I'd dry off and pull on some PJs. I wasn't ready to sleep, but I had other plans in mind.

Classes started in a little over a week, and I wanted to get a head's up on the courses I was tackling for the next semester. So far, I'd been able to hold up my GPA, and none of my scholarships were in jeopardy. Even so, I wasn't the sort to take any of that for granted, especially since I was carrying a heavier class load this time around.

Fifteen minutes later, clad in flannel pajamas, with a cup

of tea next to my elbow, I cracked open the top book on the stack waiting on the table.

It wasn't as good as lying back and fantasizing about some tall, dark, and sexy stranger, but if all that was going to do was end up with me frustrated, I'd rather study.

At least I'd feel like I accomplished something.

4

Kane

A hand smoothed down my thigh, and judging by the way things felt, that hand was attached to a naked woman lying between my legs. A mouth kissed the head of my cock, and I shuddered at the sensation.

"You're awake," a familiar voice said. And those words were followed by a giggle.

Calie.

I opened my eyes and craned my head upward to see her sprawled between my legs. She grinned up at me and took my cock into her mouth before dragging her head up, then down.

Blearily, I looked around, and it was pathetic that part of me could still focus on logical shit while she was giving me a blowjob, but the fact of the matter was…I could.

And it wasn't that she wasn't good at it.

I just wasn't…invested in anything but the outcome.

If I closed my eyes, it made it easier to get to the end goal, too. Closing my eyes made it easier to think about the hot, wet mouth as it slid down my cock, taking me deep, all the way to the back of her throat in a practiced glide before sliding back up and holding the tip of my penis between her lips for a teasing moment before starting it all over again.

She kept that pace up for several minutes before shifting away to close her mouth over my sac, and I arched up with a grunt as she fisted her hand over my dick and began to pump.

Calie moved up, taking the head of my cock once more, and I could feel her head bobbing up and down. I needed to stop thinking about *Calie*, because every time I did, the interest waned a little...and wasn't that a bitch when the woman had my dick in her mouth?

I deliberately blanked my mind and focused on the sensation, reaching down to fist a hand in Calie's hair. It came as something of a surprise when I found myself wishing the chin length strands of reddish brown were a brighter shade of red...and a lot shorter.

The cute girl from last night.

My dick stirred, and the waning interest wasn't waning anymore.

Calie purred, the sound vibrating down my shaft, but I shoved out thoughts of her. It was the rudest damn thing to do, but deflating while she was giving me head wasn't very polite either, I figured.

I didn't *entirely* let myself fantasize about another woman while I was there in bed with a different woman, but every few moments, the girl from last night made an appearance.

It was frustrating, and I tightened my hand in Calie's hair, half-thinking to pull her off. She gasped a little and said, "More."

Hell.

I let her finish me off, and when she curled up next to me, I laid there with my eyes closed, feeling like a bigger asshole than normal. But I hadn't asked her to stay the night. My head had been full of the cute redhead for hours, so I was almost *positive* I wouldn't have asked her to stay the night – I never did.

Calie arched against me, and I felt the slick glide of her cunt grinding against my thigh. "I'm kinda hungry over here," she said in a little girl voice that was no doubt meant to turn me on. It didn't.

Climbing out of bed, I grabbed a pair of jeans from the foot and shot her a look. "It's morning. Why are you here?"

"Because you didn't kick me out?" She giggled and sat up, sitting with her legs crisscrossed, showing off the pink, wet folds between her thighs.

I kept my gaze focused on her face. "You know the rules. I don't like it when people spend the night."

Her lashes drooped over her eyes, and she lifted one shoulder in a shrug. "You didn't seem to mind just now."

"I rarely mind it when a woman decides to give me a blowjob," I said bluntly. "That doesn't mean you can break the rules we established when we first hooked up. We talked about them, remember? I don't stay the night at your place, you don't stay the night at mine. Remember that talk? We've had it a couple of times now actually."

Her lids flickered, and her full mouth tightened with annoyance for the briefest moment, but I didn't let it get to me. I never made any pretenses about who or what I was, and she knew it.

She rolled onto her hands and knees in the next moment and started to crawl toward me. "Why are you so afraid of a commitment, Kane?" she asked, her voice soft, almost gentle. "It was just one night. We both had fun. It shouldn't be such a big deal after how long we've been together."

I almost laughed but told myself it wasn't going to help anything.

Grabbing a t-shirt, I hauled it on, ignoring the small pains in my back that let me know she wasn't lying when she said we'd had *fun*. She'd scratched the hell out of me. I could feel it.

"I'm not afraid of commitment, Calie," I pointed out. "I just don't want it." Especially not from her. She was...clingy. And it was dawning on me lately, how manipulative she was. I didn't care to have anybody pulling my strings, but nobody was going to do it using sex and slow, sultry smiles. I'd stopped letting my dick make decisions for me a long time ago, and I wasn't about to go back down *that* road. "As to us being together...we're not. We fuck. This isn't exclusive."

Something hot flashed in her eyes.

Aw, hell.

Cocking my head, I studied her face. "You do remember that I told you from the beginning this wasn't exclusive, right? We can see other people, fuck other people, we don't spend the night with each other, and we use protection, period."

When she didn't answer, I turned on my heel and strode into the small bathroom attached to my bedroom.

I breathed out a sigh of relief when I found two used rubbers in the garbage can. When I came out, she was sitting in the middle of the bed, a pillow clutched to her middle. "You gloved up," she said peevishly. "I told you that you didn't have to. I'm clean, and it's not that time of the month."

"I've been with two other girls in the past month. For all

you know, *I'm* not clean." I was – I got checked every month. A friend of mine from the joint had managed to go his entire time there without getting sick with HIV, hepatitis, or any of the other shit that could grab guys like us, but then a month after he got out, he hooked up with a girl from before his time inside, and voila. He ended up with HIV. It made me nervous. I *always* gloved up, and I got tested regularly.

Her eyes widened, but I didn't know if it was because of the *not clean* comment or because I told her that I'd been with girls other than her. "I made it clear that this wasn't exclusive," I said again, grinding the message in.

She stood up on the bed, glaring at me. "Why you gotta be so mean to me? Don't you know how I feel about you?"

"Whatever you think you feel..." I shook my head. "You might want to stop feeling it. I'm not ever going to feel the same way, Calie. It's time for you to go."

She blinked back furious tears, although I had no idea if they were real or not. I couldn't say it mattered much to me either. She was working me on some level, and I wasn't going to have it.

Especially not after that crack claiming she'd told me I didn't have to wear a rubber.

That had been rule number one, and if I'd been drunk enough last night not to remember her coming home with me, then I'd been way too drunk for her to go planting her ass at my side and inviting herself over for a sleepover she knew I wouldn't agree to if I was sober.

It pissed me the hell off.

"It was just one night!" she shouted at me as she jumped off the bed. "What's the big deal?"

"The big deal is I don't do *one nights* – at all." I glared at her as she went to swing the pillow at me. "And I already pointed out that it's time for you to go. I've got stuff to do, and I need to get to it. I've got plans for dinner with my family later."

Immediately, her face changed, softening. A smile curled her lips. "You should have said so. Now I know why you're so grumpy. You always get uptight when you have things going on. Why don't you let me help you?" She bit her lip, an attempt at shyness that just didn't do it for me.

I knew her. She wasn't shy.

Another flicker flashed through my mind – the redhead from Times Square.

The nervous glint in her eyes, how she wouldn't look straight at me for the first few seconds.

"Maybe I could even come with you," Calie was saying. "I've never even met your family. You hardly ever talk about them."

"No." I held up a hand, cutting off anything else she might say. "I don't talk about my family for the same reason I don't spend the night, Calie. I'm private. My bed is mine, my home is mine, my family is mine."

Her face tightened, the chill coming back to her eyes. She turned on her heel and took a few steps to where her clothes lay in a pile. "Well, *fine*. Be an asshole, Kane!"

I rolled my eyes as she continued to shout and mutter at me, and once I'd shut the door behind her ten minutes later, I wondered if maybe it was time to just stop seeing her altogether. The sex was fine, but it wasn't good enough to merit the headache that was starting to accompany it.

5

Raye

Warm hands cupped my breasts.

Big warm hands.

A warm mouth covered mine.

I had my hands buried in a head of thick hair, and without even looking, I knew it would be shaggy and dark. Black? Brown? I had no idea, and I didn't care. I cared about the fact that he'd kissed me again, and this time, I'd had the courage to kiss him back.

Where were we?

Music flowed around us, and a familiar voice echoed in my ear.

Pulling back from the stranger, I looked over my shoulder and saw my manager from my job.

Okay.

This *had* to be a dream.

She smiled at me, then nodded at him. "Now *that* is what I call a keeper. But I bet he can't pick out lingerie worth a damn."

In the next moment, she was gone, swept up in a dance by some guy in a mask. I looked back at the stranger, and then we were dancing. "Is this a dance?" I asked, confused.

"It's whatever you want it to be. Do you want it to be a dance?"

I shook my head, but my feet were moving along with his, moving in time to the music floating in the air like a dream. *We* floated in the air, weaving our way through tables and mannequins dressed in elegant lingerie and masks – and the mannequins were dancing, too.

"I don't think this dream is what I want it to be," I said faintly, staring at the mannequin I'd decked out in a lace bra and thong set, along with a sash that read *SALE* in glitter. She had a mask made of glitter and was dancing with one of the guys who worked at the Asian place just down the street. He always made my drinks good and strong and winked at me.

"What do you want this dream to be then?"

Whipping my head around, I looked up at the stranger who'd kissed me.

"I want to be back on the street where we met."

In a blink, we were.

And the street was empty. There wasn't a soul around us.

"What now?" He studied me with intense, dark eyes as he stroked his hands down my arms.

"Would you kiss me again?"

"The last time I kissed you, I got slapped," he pointed out.

"This is my dream. It won't hurt you if I slap you," I told him.

"Do you want to get slapped? Even if it's in somebody else's dream?"

That was some logic I didn't want to ponder. So, I didn't. It was my dream. It could be whatever I wanted it to be. I rose up onto my toes and pushed my fingers into his hair. Right now, this could be a dream about kissing him. This could be a dream where I was brave enough to do all the things I wanted.

It could be a dream where I was whole instead of broken inside.

I WAS STILL TRAPPED in that place between dreams and wakefulness when my phone started to ring. Reaching out, I smacked around on the nightstand for it. I didn't know if I planned to answer it or silence it. The dream still lived large in my mind, and the thought of talking to anybody would shatter the pleasant haze.

But before I knew it, my mother's voice was filling the room.

Okay, I wasn't dreaming that. "Mom?"

"Hi, baby!" she chirped, her voice overly bright and cheerful, and not just because it was...

I blinked and looked around. What time was it? Way too early for the chore it could be talking to my mother, that was for certain.

"Honey?"

I frowned in the direction of her voice. She had to be up to something. The honeys and the babys never came this early otherwise. Dragging myself upright, I tried to force my brain to work, but it was a difficult task. A quick look at the clock told me why. It was barely after ten.

It had been somewhere between three and four before I fell asleep, so that put me at about six hours of sleep. That normally wouldn't be a big issue, but I'd been up since nine the previous day.

"It's awful early, Mom." Rubbing at my eyes, I wondered if I could put whatever this was off until my brain was more equipped to handle a call from her, but it wasn't very likely.

"It's not that early in New York...why, I'm wide awake, and I'm three hours behind you!" She laughed brightly, and the sound of it made my head hurt even more.

"I was up late, Mom. I didn't get off work until close to midnight."

"Then I bet you were out partying." She giggled next, and that sound wasn't any better. "I know how you are."

My belly churned. She sure as hell didn't know how I was.

"I'm juggling a heavy class load and a job, Mom. I don't have time to party. I barely have time to sleep," I pointed out.

"Oh, I know...you're such a busy thing. You never have time to call me." The syrup in her voice thickened as she added, "But I'm so proud of you."

Uh-huh. I didn't say that out loud.

"What did you need, Mama?" I asked, keeping my tone free of the skepticism I felt.

"Oh, I just wanted to call and wish you Happy New Year's, Raye. That's all." She paused a moment, then added, "You know, I've been going through some stuff up in the attic. Some of your old school things and the like."

"That's nice, Mom."

"You could sound more enthusiastic…you're never going to believe what I found."

Knowing my mother, it could be anything from the medal I got in the third-grade spelling bee to an article clipping from the time I'd like to forget. There was just no telling.

"What did you find?" I asked dutifully as I dragged myself upright and crossed my legs.

"It was the craziest thing, baby…I saw it lying there in the box and I just…well, I couldn't believe it. I know I've seen it before, but it never really connected. Staring at it, I was thinking, *how could this be here all this time and me never really notice?* It was just one of those things, ya know?" She huffed out a breath as she finally came to a pause.

"What was it you found, Mama?"

"A picture!" she replied brightly. "Raye, I found a picture of your daddy."

My heart squeezed.

I didn't *know* my dad. Not his name or even what he looked like. I was the product of an affair between my mother and some married guy. Mom told me he didn't want anything to do with me, so if that was what he wanted, I didn't want anything to do with *him* either. What little I did know was that he and Mom hooked up while he was married. She got pregnant, but he was out of the picture by the time Mom knew. She kept me and raised me all without ever saying much of anything about him.

Oh, it wasn't like I didn't *ask*. When you're five years old, and all the other kids talk about their dads, it's only natural to ask about your own. But when I did, she always brushed me off, and when that didn't work…she yelled. Or she cried.

It wasn't until I was a teenager that she finally admitted to the affair and told me a few scant details about him, including the fact that he didn't want a relationship with me.

"Why are you telling me this now?" I asked slowly. "I'm twenty-one, Mama. Well past the age when I need a daddy in my life. He's married and didn't want anything to do with me, remember?"

Maybe he changed his mind, a soft voice whispered.

It didn't matter, though. Even if I was maybe a little curious, I didn't want to be the reason some guy and his wife had some trouble. That just rubbed me wrong, even if I was the innocent party in all of this. Well, me and the wife.

"Honey...I didn't tell you who *else* was in the picture. There's a little boy. I think you've got a *brother*!"

It was a good thing I was sitting down because those words would have put me back on my ass.

"What?"

"Listen, I'll text you a shot of the picture...just hold on..." Her voice got fainter, and I sat there, my heart pounding in my ears. A moment later, she came back on the phone. "You should have it any second."

Another few seconds passed, and a faint ping sounded in my ear to let me know I had a text.

I lowered the phone and let my thumb hover over the button.

"Do you see, honey? Your eyes...look at how similar your eyes are...oh, you're both so beautiful!"

Mom's voice came to me distantly, and I finally hit the button and swiped the screen. As the image downloaded, I closed my eyes.

Mom said something, but the words made no sense, and I finally lifted the phone again, forced my eyes to open so I could look at the picture.

It was of a man who probably had been in his early thirties, give or take, when the picture was taken. There was a boy standing next to him. Maybe there was a resemblance. Mom had loved to go through my old picture albums, so I had a good idea of what I'd looked like as a kid. There could be a resemblance. His hair stood up in spikes on the back of his head, a pale blond compared to the reddish-gold mine had been. My mom was a natural redhead.

Rubbing my eyes, I studied the picture once more.

It didn't go away.

"I think his name is MJ."

I frowned at the picture on the screen. "I thought you told me that my father's name was Leland."

"That's your father's name. The back of the picture has the words *Leland and MJ*," Mom said with a loud, inappropriate laugh. "It sounds like you're stunned."

"That might be because I *am*."

She started to talk again, and I closed my eyes, bringing up the image on my phone in my mind.

It wasn't until a few more moments had passed that I realized Mom had said something.

Then the reason for her call became clear.

"I'm kind of tight on money, honey. And I know you're working at the fancy boutique there. Is there any way you can float me a loan?"

I closed my eyes.

Of course, she couldn't have just been calling to tell me

Happy New Year's or with this news about my supposed brother.

Not *my* mother.

6

Kane

"Uncay!"

Uncay, as far as I could tell in my limited understanding of two-year-olds, meant *Uncle Kane*. Small hands patted my knee, and I bent over to sweep one of two twin girls up in my arms. As she was over here wanting to be loved on and not trying to climb the walls, I knew I had to be holding Zoe. Rose would find a way to fly off the roof by the time she was five. At least that was what I'd told her father, my younger brother Nathaniel.

It had turned him an all-new shade of white, probably because he realized I just might be right.

Zoe, on the other hand, was content to cuddle up against me, with her head tucked under my chin as I made my way through my mom's now-crowded living room.

I had too many siblings for us to keep crowding in like this, but somehow, we managed, week after week. All major holidays. Anytime somebody close was getting married or died.

We managed.

Zoe wiggled up closer and pressed her lips to my cheek, and my heart squeezed a little. She was the sweetest thing.

Her brothers, Connor and Grant, spied me and came shrieking my way. I held up a hand, and they both stopped the shrieking. "Remember to keep the volume level to a dull roar, dudes," I said.

"Yes, sir." Connor, the older one, hugged my hip while Grant grabbed my left thigh and hugged it, then they were both gone again.

"Hey, man."

I looked up as one of my brothers stepped into the room. Eddie grinned at me and Zoe. "Looks like a pretty lady caught your eye," he teased.

"The prettiest." I nuzzled her curls and caught sight of Rose peeking around the corner at me. "Well, one of the two prettiest. I don't think you can figure out which one's prettier. It's too hard to tell."

Rose grinned and came running at me. I shifted her sister and knelt just in time to catch her, then I had both arms full of sweet-smelling, little girl warmth.

Eddie laughed. "Man, if some of the guys from your old life could see you now, they'd just die."

I scowled at him. If I was sure Mom wouldn't see me, I might have flipped him off, armload of twins or not. "Where's Ricky?" I asked, deciding to distract him instead. Rick was his boyfriend, and the two of them rarely went to an event, even something as simple as a family dinner, without the other.

"He got stuck working a double." Eddie rolled his eyes. "Staffing cuts and now half the employees at his place are pulling doubles to make up for it. How does that save the city money, you tell me?"

"Find a politician and ask him," I advised. Rick was an EMT – they'd met on the job and had been together for a while.

"Dinner's almost done," he told me, coming over and liberating Zoe. "I'm taking this little doll."

Zoe went to him with a beatific smile, and I was left with Rose who immediately turned inscrutable, big dark eyes on me. "Unca Kane," she said in a serious, little adult voice.

She'd managed to get most of the syllables in there. She'd be reading by the time she was three. And if they weren't careful, out for world domination by age six. "Come on, let's go see what Grandma is doing."

"Out kichen," Rose announced, almost getting *kitchen* perfect – and she knew the rule. Nobody was allowed in Grandma's kitchen when she was cooking. The rule had been the same when I was little. Mom would make all of us clean up, but she didn't like stepping on toes when she was busy whipping up a feast. Not that I minded. All I did was get in the way.

"Okay. We'll go find your mom and dad," I told her.

That seemed to content her, and we found her parents, Madison and my brother Nathaniel on the fire escape that my mom used for her small container garden. "No making out until after dinner," I said, snaking a hand through the window and smacking Nathaniel on the back of the head.

He glanced at me through the glass and mouthed, *Fuck off*.

I grinned at him.

Dinah, one of my two sisters, was in the kitchen with my

mother, the only other person allowed in the sacred space. According to my mom, Dinah was the only person who *'got her rhythm.'* Which I understood. The two of them moved like they were a matched set when they were cooking. It made sense. Ever since Dad had died and I'd had to step up and help Mom out more and more, Dinah had done the same, in her own way. She'd been the one who took over the cooking and the cleaning when the multiple jobs Mom had held had her working late into the night. In retrospect, I should have been more like Dinah, instead of taking the path I'd taken. But hindsight was twenty-twenty and all that bullshit.

My sister caught sight of me and nodded, a faint grin on her face at the sight of Rose nestled up against me. "I see the rottens have found you already. Which one you got?"

"The soon to be ruler of the universe," I answered.

Rose tapped her chest. "*Rosie,*" she said indignantly. She didn't like it when people didn't recognize her for her genius alone.

Mom heard me and paused in the middle of whipping mashed potatoes to come over and kiss me. "How are you, baby?"

"I'm good."

Rose lifted her rosebud mouth for a kiss. "Kiss me!" she demanded.

Mom laughed and obliged.

Rose added as Mom walked away, "Unca Kane not baby."

"I'm not even going to bother explaining," Mom said, waving a distracted hand. Her voice sounded a little strained, and I shot Dinah a look.

She mouthed *later*.

I bit back a sigh because chances were I'd already figured out what the problem was. The same reason Mom's voice often sounded distracted or grim these days.

There was one brother I hadn't seen yet. I could have asked, but instead, I put Rose down and patted her diapered backside. "Why don't you go find your sister?"

AUSTEN, my youngest sibling, was locked inside his room. He didn't answer the first knock, so I tried again – harder.

He all but ripped it off the hinges then, a belligerent look on his face that faded when he saw me. "Hey, man! How ya doing?" he asked, reaching out to pull me into the room.

It was the expected disaster a seventeen-year-old boy's room was likely to be, maybe even worse.

I sidestepped an empty bag of chips – at least I hoped it was empty – and a pile of clothes. "Mom asked you to clean this up anytime recently?"

"She's always after me to clean it up," he said with an unconcerned shrug. "I figure if it bothers her that bad, she can do it. *I* don't care."

"Mom works forty hours a week to make sure you get decent clothes and food in your belly," I told him, biting back an angry retort. "You can do a bit to help out."

"Hey, I can buy my own clothes. I got money." He went on the defensive, jabbing a thumb at his chest.

"And are you going to be able to buy the uniforms you need for school? New shoes? A coat for winter?" I swept a hand around, spied the shoes Mom had busted her ass to buy him for Christmas, and that just made me angrier. "Come on, Austen. She wears herself out trying to take care of you."

"I don't ask her to!" he half-shouted. "Shit, if you're going to be on my case too, why the hell you in here?"

"I wanted to say hi to my brother, see how you're doing." Folding my arms over my chest, I stared him down. "Obviously, you're being an arrogant little shit who doesn't give a fuck about anybody but himself."

His face fell, as I'd expected it to when I gave him that look. He hated it when I came down on him, and it made me feel like shit having to do it, but if he was talking like this to me, how was he talking to Mom?

"Look, man..." He shifted from one foot to the other. "You know that ain't true. I just...I got suspended for fighting, and Mom's all worked up about it. She thinks I'm gonna get expelled if it happens again and she was crying an' all..." His voice trailed off, and he stared off at a space on the wall behind me.

"Are you?" I replied.

"I...I dunno. Maybe." He sounded like an unhappy little kid now, and I fought the urge to go give him a hug.

"Then maybe it's time you stop doing whatever shit you're doing and get your act together."

"YOU WANT to tell me what's going on with Austen?"

It was hard to find any privacy in the apartment, but I managed to catch Mom in the hallway when she took one of the twins to her room to change a diaper. With the pungent odor of that hanging in the air, I hoped this would be a short conversation, but I'd smelled worse shit in my life.

Mom made a face at me and put Rose down, then glanced around.

"Did he talk to you?" she asked softly.

"No. Well, not really. I know he's had some issues with fighting apparently. Said he might get expelled." Studying her face, I hesitated a moment, then asked, "Is it that bad?"

"I don't know," she replied, sounding more helpless than I'd heard her sound in a long time. "I want to say no, but it's the second time he's been in a fight this year, and he hurt the other kid pretty bad."

"What was the fight over? Who started it?"

"I have no *idea* what it was over." Mom rolled her eyes. "Boys fight over anything, it seems. But the school did admit that the other boy started it. Austen just...ended it." She gave me a bleak look and shook her head. "He's got to get that temper of his under control. And some of the kids he's hanging with..."

The words trailed off, but I didn't need her to finish to surmise there was some trouble there, too.

"Anything else?"

"Isn't that enough?" She wagged the small bag that held the diaper and said, "Now, I'm tired of breathing in Rose de Poopie Pants so I'm going to throw this out. We can talk about your brother later, okay?"

She smiled at me, but the strain was still in her eyes.

Yeah, we'd talk about it later.

"HE'S SKIPPED SOME CLASSES LATELY," Nathaniel said over a beer.

I was sitting on the fire escape while Nathaniel leaned outside, the two of us catching up. We'd spent Christmas together, but with the kids, that day had turned into holiday chaos, and before Christmas, my brothers, sisters, and Mom had been busy with getting ready for the holiday.

I guess I'd been busy in my own way, but I kept my shopping to a minimum. I had gift buying down to an art and started back in August, so I didn't have to spend more time around people than needed once the Christmas rush got here.

But any time people got busy, so did their cars and that meant more work for the garage.

I had only a few employees, and when things got too crazy, it meant longer hours for all of us. I was getting a bigger client base, something I was glad to see, but sooner or later, I'd have to hire part-time help.

Between the holiday rush and my garage, I just hadn't seen my family as much as I wanted, so the news about Austen was just that – news. "He's skipping classes," I muttered, shaking my head. I lifted the beer to my lips and sipped. "What's going on with him? He's a senior. A few more months and high school will be behind him. He doesn't gotta worry about it anymore."

"Senioritis?" Nathaniel offered. "Hell, I don't know. He's...angry at things sometimes."

I'd noticed. He'd had an attitude with almost everybody although he'd been nice enough to the babies. He'd even been a bit of a shit to his nephews, and usually, he was great with them – and they adored him. Because they adored him, they'd forget all about him being a little asshole today, but I didn't like seeing him act that way.

Rubbing my forehead where a headache was trying to form, I debated on whether I should talk to Austen again.

Nathaniel must have been reading my mind because he bumped his beer bottle against mine. "He's going to work it out, Kane. You were in worse trouble when you were his age, and look at you now."

"Yeah, but think about how much trouble I had to *get* into and how much shit I had to go through before I got my act together," I pointed out.

"True." Nathaniel winced and lifted his bottle to his lips.

I did the same, draining my beer in three swallows.

"Just give him some space for now," Nathaniel advised. "Maybe he just needs to realize he's being a little dick."

"Maybe."

7

Raye

"Man..."

I all but had to pick my jaw up off the floor as I finished reading the last in a series of articles I'd found online.

I was almost positive I'd found my brother.

I'd used one of those free ancestry websites to look up Leland Jakes and found his son's name, then did a google from there.

Had I ever hit the jackpot once I added in *Texas* along with *Matthew Jakes*.

He'd been involved in a car crash some years ago where he'd been accused of killing his mother. Several other guys had been in the car, including the son of some politician, Washington McCrane.

But the doozy of all of them was an article written by one Michelle Nestor that had been picked up by the Associated Press. Years after his release from prison, this woman, Michelle Nestor, breaks a story that my brother – wow, that was weird, even just *thinking* it – hadn't been driving the car at all.

The person driving had been the politician's kid, and Mr. Big Time Politician had covered everything up to avoid the bad press.

Now McCrane was in jail, and Matthew's name had been cleared. The article mentioned that the son had died a few years earlier. It was all...surreal.

I dug in deeper, trying to find more on Matthew, but there really wasn't anything outside of those articles and the myriad links to people finder websites. If I had to, I could *try* one of those, but how many of them were scams? I'd have to research it and find one that was reputable and reliable. I didn't want to go digging around in people's lives if I didn't have to.

"Why couldn't you make it simple and have a Facebook profile?" I mumbled.

It was possible he did have one, but it was set to private. None of the Matthew Jakes I'd found looked to be the right guy, and I wasn't about to start hitting up random strangers.

After another hour of fruitless searching, I went back to the article written by Michelle Nestor.

Reading it through, I studied the quotes she'd taken and the brief part of the article that focused on the time she'd spent talking with Matthew. "You know him," I mused. There was a...familiarity about the entire article.

Okay, if I couldn't find him myself, I'd reach out through her.

My face burned hot as a flame when I googled *her* name.

A lot of hits came up, and almost *all* of them were focused on sex.

Big O's

My toes curled into the carpet as I clicked on one of them, and an article on oral sex popped up.

My mouth was dry by the time I was done reading it – other parts of me were decidedly *not* dry.

She had a way of writing that was hella sexy.

I found an article that had actually been written about *her,* and how she'd gone from an unknown name to an overnight sensation at the magazine she wrote for, all starting with her interview of a... "Son of a bitch," I whispered. "A male *prostitute?*"

She went from writing an exposé about the politician who set my brother up to writing sexy little pieces inspired by talks with a *gigolo?*

Except that wasn't the only stuff she wrote about. There was a piece on sexual harassment in the workplace. Another on campus rape. I clicked away from both of those, uncomfortable topics.. It looked like she wrote the gamut when it came to women's interest.

But the only real investigative type piece that I could find was the article about Matthew and McCrane.

"Weird," I muttered. "How did you even find out about him?"

There was no answer in my quiet little apartment, and I sighed, zooming my mouse in on the search bar so I could type in *Michelle Nestor website.*

It took me to her LinkedIn page, and I had to go through the hassle of setting up an account I wouldn't use to get her contact info, but finally, I had it.

I copied it, pasted into the *to* line of a blank email, then leaned back and pondered on what I should say.

It took nearly an hour to get the words right, but I felt it had to be *perfect*. It wasn't like I could just drop her a note, saying...

*Hey, I read your articles about sexual harassment and oral sex. Oh, and the one about that guy Matthew Jakes? Um, so...*crazy *story, but I think he's my brother and I'd like to meet him. Can you hook us up?*

Once I finished, I leaned back and read it through – again.

Before I could let myself start the line of self-doubt and questioning, I sent the email off.

"Okay," I whispered, shoving back from the kitchen table that doubled as my desk. "You went and did it. Now it's out of your hands."

I blew out a hard breath and looked back at the laptop. How long would it take for her to answer?

Oh, shit. What if she *didn't* answer?

I dropped my face into my hands and groaned.

She did answer. Less than an hour later, actually.

I heard the little *swish* announcing a new email and all but tripped over my feet running over to the table.

I hadn't mentioned anything about Matthew and I being related when I reached out to her.

That wouldn't be the most ideal way to broach this, so I simply acted like I'd read the article and had a few questions, and asked if she'd be open to meeting for drinks?

Surprisingly, the email reply was a *yes*.

Slumping in my seat, I read it repeatedly to make sure I hadn't missed anything.

She could meet...*tomorrow*.

The place she named was unfamiliar to me, but I rarely

got out and about. If it wasn't near NYU or the boutique, I wasn't likely to know about it.

I hurriedly emailed her back before she could change her mind – she still might and then what was I going to do?

This time, her reply was almost instantaneous. Eleven o'clock.

Tomorrow, at eleven o'clock, I was going to meet the woman who'd helped my brother clear his name.

And then all I'd have to do is convince her to help me out, so I could meet him.

8

Raye

I changed my clothes four different times.

By the time I was satisfied with the way I looked in the mirror, I'd spent nearly an hour getting dressed. Also, I realized with a grimace, I was wearing the first outfit I'd tried on.

Talk about being indecisive.

It was only a little after nine, too. I'd already done my hair and make-up. The trip uptown would only take a half hour, although I planned to leave at ten and be a little early.

Better early than late, always.

I made myself wait until ten to leave, although I was itching and chomping at the bit to get there. Showing up at ten o'clock wasn't going to make her show up any sooner.

I made myself take my time walking to the restaurant and even ducked into a lingerie boutique – not to shop. It was a competitor, and we liked to keep up with the competition. After wasting about ten minutes inside and deciding their displays weren't as good as ours, I cut out and finished the walk to the restaurant.

I got a table just a few minutes before eleven and was watching for Michelle. She had a picture on her LinkedIn profile, so I knew who to look for, a redhead with a great smile. She looked too innocent to be writing all those *hawt* articles. Part of me wished there wasn't something so messed up inside me, wished I wasn't as shy as I was when it came to things of intimacy and the like.

When she came in, I recognized her right away and lifted a hand to wave.

She gave me a hesitant smile as she approached. "Are you Raye?"

"I am." I rose and offered my hand. She shook it quickly before slipping out of her coat and draping it over the back of the chair. "It's so cold out there." A bright laughed escaped her. "Granted, it's January in New York City. Of course, it's cold, but sometimes, it's like it cuts right through me."

"Tell me about it." I smiled at her. "I hate this kind of cold."

We made small talk for a few minutes as we waited for the waiter and placed an order for drinks. I had juggled the budget, and if I took my lunch all week instead of treating myself once or twice, I'd be okay to buy the drinks and an appetizer, so I asked if she was interested in nachos.

Her eyes gleamed. "When am I not interested in nachos?"

I laughed. "A girl after my own heart."

After the server disappeared, Michelle focused her blue-green eyes on me. "So, what did you want to ask me? It's been a while since all of that went down."

"I know. Really, I wanted to ask you about..." I bit my lip

as nervousness began to rattle inside me. "It's about Matthew Jakes."

A change settled over her face. It was subtle but undeniable. Her eyes became more guarded, and a faint tension tightened her muscles. She still smiled, but it was less relaxed, one of those blank polite smiles that could hide a million emotions.

"Oh?" She reached for the ice water and took a sip, shifting subtly in her seat as she did so. "What do you want to know about him? As I said, it's been a while since I wrote that series."

"I..." The change in her attitude was unsettling, and I wasn't sure how to handle it. As my nerves got worse, I glanced around, wishing the waiter would hurry up with our drinks so I'd have something other than the water. "This is going to sound kind of crazy, but I have...well..." That damn server still hadn't shown up. I reached for the water, although I was still freezing from my walk from the subway. I took a sip to wet my throat, then met her eyes once more. "I think Matthew Jakes is my brother."

She blinked.

Slowly, she straightened in the chair.

She shook her head and cleared her throat. "I'm sorry," she said softly. "But can you repeat that?"

I did, and she blew out a hard breath. "Maybe you should give me a little bit of the back story here."

"Okay." The server finally showed up with our drinks, and I greedily grabbed the Irish coffee I'd ordered. Sure, it was before noon, and I was having a drink, but it wasn't every day that I reached out and tried to find my brother, right? Folding my hands around it, I waited until the server walked off, then I met her gaze once more. There was still a world of speculation in the blue-green, and I could sense her guard was up, but at least she was still listening.

"It's kind of...awkward, okay?" Huffing out a breath, I took a sip of the coffee then put the cup down. The heat of it seeped into my hands, and it felt so good. "I'm originally from Illinois. I was born there. I'm here in New York going to NYU. My mom called me the other day and...well...." My face reddened. Shit. Now, I had to explain. "See, I never knew who my father was. My mother told me when I was a teenager that she had an affair with a married man, but she didn't find out about me until after it ended. When she told him about me, he said he didn't want to have a relationship with me and...well, it was just Mama and me. I've never known anything else about him." I'd spent the past few minutes checking out the swirls of whipped cream on my coffee, but now I made myself look up at her.

To my surprise, there was compassion on her face. "I guess that wasn't easy."

"I never thought about it much," I said honestly. "It's just what I knew."

She nodded to indicate she understood, and I continued. "During the call with my mom..." Reaching into my bag, I pulled out my phone and went to the gallery, opening to the picture of Leland with the little boy that I thought was Matthew. I flipped the phone around and showed it to Michelle.

Her eyes widened as she took the phone, then they softened. She reached up and traced a finger of the screen. "Huh," she murmured under her breath.

She continued to stare at the picture, and I had the weirdest feeling she forgot I was there.

"Michelle?"

She started at the sound of my voice. "Sorry. Ah, my mind was wandering," she said, a faint blush rising to her cheeks. She returned the phone. "What's the deal with the picture?"

"Mom sent it to me. She told me that was my father. His name is on the back, along with *MJ*. I did some digging around online and found that my father is supposed to have a son...*Matthew Jakes*." I took another sip of coffee, a bigger one, needing it to bolster my courage, even though the coffee was still scalding hot. "I read about the accident. I know he went to jail."

Focusing on her, I added, "And I know how you helped discover that it was that politician's son who was actually responsible. He got his name cleared because of you."

Her cheeks flushed. "It wasn't just me." She licked her lips, clearly flustered.

"But it *was* in part because of you." My throat tightened, and I had to fight back the urge to reach out and grab her in a hug.

She opened her mouth, then stopped, smiling at me. "Yeah, I guess."

Her gaze fell back to the phone, and she sighed. "I guess maybe the two of you should meet, huh?"

9

Kane

An ugly scrape marred the back of my knuckles. Okay, it might qualify as more than a scrape. If I had much sense, maybe I'd go get it looked at because it might need a stitch or two.

Instead, I prowled through the first aid kit that Eddie and Rick had helped me stock and pulled out something called a butterfly bandage. It took another couple of minutes of holding pressure to it before it stopped bleeding long enough to slap the bandage into place, but once it was done, it looked like it had managed to close it enough so that only a little blood seeped through. I covered that with a bigger bandage and went back to work on the truck that had appeared in my lot during the middle of the night.

I'd expected it.

It had come from Ringo, one of the guys I used to run with before I'd gone to prison. Of course, Ringo had been the one to suggest I go on the run that had landed me in prison.

Shit.

"Don't think about that mess," I told myself. Ten years stood between me and the stupid boy I'd been when I'd taken the job to run some drugs to Mexico via Texas. I'd gotten caught, arrested, and summarily sent to prison for possession with intent to sell. Since I'd had a record in New York, they hadn't given me much of a chance, and I'd taken the deal rather than risk a heavier sentence.

After five years, they'd let me go, and I'd come back here, back home to New York.

I'd started working in a garage, avoiding that old life, but there were still reminders of it. Reminders in the form of trucks belonging to Ringo that kept showing up. Sometimes I wondered why I kept any kind of contact with those guys. Every time somebody like Ringo came around, I found myself thinking about how different my life might have been if I hadn't done that run through Texas.

"What's the matter, Kane? You forget how to handle a wrench?" came a lazy familiar drawl.

The sound of that voice made me smile, and I turned around, grinning at the tall, lean blond standing in the doorway. "Hey, you son of a bitch."

Jake King came striding toward me, and the two of us met in the middle of the garage, greeting each other with a quick hug and a slap on the back.

Pulling back first, Jake pointed a finger at me. "You stood me up, you bastard. You were supposed to come by the house for New Years. You chicken out?"

"I sure as hell did," I admitted honestly. "I don't do champagnes and canapes." I was almost positive I'd pronounced it wrong and watched as Jake shook his head, his grin widening.

I didn't take it personally. "I told you that when you called me to ask if I'd be coming over."

"I know, I know. That's why I asked Michelle if she minded if I had a guest over for dinner sometime this week. That way, you and I can ring in the new year the right way." He winked at me. "With beer and a good action flick."

"That sounds more like it." I considered what I had on schedule the next day and figured I could come in an hour or so later in case the night ran late. Although Jake was no longer in his previous line of work, he still made his own hours, and it didn't matter to him if he stayed up until one or two in the morning occasionally. Even though I was self-employed myself, garage owners who had hours like that were either shit-faced with exhaustion all the time, or they just didn't sleep. "How is Michelle?"

Jake had been seeing this girl for close to a year now, although I hadn't met her until late spring or early summer. She was a doll, no doubt about it, and she didn't seem to mind that I was about as rough as they came. As far as she was concerned, friends of Jake's were friends of hers.

"She's fantastic." Everything about him changed as he talked about her and I couldn't deny a little bit of envy.

It wasn't likely I'd ever end up finding somebody who accepted me the way Jake had with Michelle.

The two of us had both done time in prison, but Jake wasn't rough around the edges like I was. Hell, I wasn't rough around the edges. I was rough all over, and I knew it.

It turned out that Jake's stint in prison had been all for nothing because he'd been framed. How he managed not to be bitter about it, I didn't know, although Michelle probably had something to do with it. Maybe being able to go home to a woman with a summery smile who looked at him like he'd hung every star in the sky made all the difference in the world.

Shrugging off the melancholy, I gestured for him to join me as I got back to work on Ringo's truck. "You got time? Have a seat." I scanned him up and down, taking in the expensive sweater and jeans that had probably never seen a speck of grime on the threads and snorted. "If you weren't dressed so pretty, I'd tell you to get your hands dirty. That's assuming you remember how."

"I've forgotten more about cars than you ever knew, dickhead," Jake said. He looked the truck over and shook his head. "I thought you were trying to take in more imports and shit. This thing is a hunk of junk."

"I know. It's a job for a friend."

His eyes slid to mine, and I knew he didn't need any hints to figure out exactly what kind of friend Ringo was.

"You so sure it's a good idea to keep any kind of contact with those...friends?" Jake asked after a moment.

"Let it go." I dropped down onto the rolling stool I used while he grabbed a folding chair and joined me.

"Hey, I'm just being a friend. If you were in a car, heading straight for a ditch, I'd tell you to steer away from the ditch," Jake pointed out. "This just seems like a bad idea."

I bit back the smart-ass response that immediately jumped to my lips because he wasn't entirely wrong. Sometimes, one of the guys brought me a vehicle that was in...questionable shape. I always figured if I didn't know anything about it, I was free and clear, so I never asked, and I didn't let them tell me anything either. But I doubted it was as simple as that, if I was being honest with myself.

"You've thought about it," Jake said softly.

"Hell, all I'm doing is fixing up a banged-up truck," I told him, irritated now.

"And how'd it get banged up? Looks like it hit something – another car, maybe?" Jake held up his hands and looked at me. "Hey, I ain't trying to start anything. I got your back, always have."

That was the truth. The two of us had been tight in the joint. That hadn't changed, even though he'd gotten out a year before I had. The two of us had both ended up in New York City about the same time, and he'd helped me land a job at the garage where I'd worked up until I bought this place.

He'd left the garage before I had to pursue an, um, alternate line of work, and while I'd missed having him around regularly, I couldn't blame him for not wanting to get up at the crack of dawn and listen to that old bastard who'd constantly ridden our asses. That was why I'd been dead set on getting my own place.

I'd done that, just a couple years ago.

Was I jeopardizing what I had because I just couldn't sever that connection to a past that was better left in the past?

I didn't know.

"You ever miss your old life?" I asked him, staring hard at the truck.

"What old life? I've had a couple by now."

I cracked a grin and looked up at him. "The one you gave up for Michelle, I guess. You sure as hell can't miss living behind bars, and it goes without saying you miss what you had with your mom and dad, although nothing will bring that back."

His eyes took on a far-off look. Jake's mother had been

dead for years, and his father had disowned him. "Nah, man. I don't miss prison, and you're right. I'm not getting back that time before Mom died. I wish I could sometimes…wish I hadn't been that stupid kid who'd gotten wasted at that party, but you can't turn back the clock." He scratched his chin. "Even if I could, I don't think I would."

"Why not?" I asked, curious. If I could go back and save my dad…

"Because the road I've been on led me to where I am, and I'm not giving up Michelle." He shrugged. "Not for anything. So, to answer your original question…do I miss whoring? Not even a little."

His blunt words weren't any shock. He'd never tried to pretty up the occupations he'd chosen after he left the garage. He'd somehow slid into a life where women – beautiful, wealthy women – were happy to pay him for sex, and he'd gotten to where he was in serious demand for it, from what I could tell. There had been a time when the two of us barely had time to get together for more than a quick beer every few weeks, his fucking dance card had been so full.

"Ain't that something," I muttered, shaking my head. Bemused, I studied him, and he still had that goofy grin on his face. "You slept with beautiful, rich women for money and you don't even miss it. You had the *life*."

"Nah. That wasn't the life." Jake shook his head. "What I've got now? That's the life."

JAKE SURPRISED me by finding a pair of coveralls to slip into, and the two of us spent the afternoon getting that old, beat-up truck back into shape. Ringo wouldn't like it, but Ringo didn't have to know, and I knew if there was anybody I could trust to keep their mouth shut over something, it was Jake.

"So, I figure if I charge you my going rate..." Jake said as he stripped out of the coveralls, "you'll be owing me from now until...hell, maybe next New Year's Eve. Sound, about right?"

"Why don't you suck my dick?" I suggested.

"Sorry, man. I don't do that anymore. And I never took on guys." He gave me a solemn look. "But I do know a few who do. Want their number?"

I threw a shop rag at him, and he dodged it with a laugh. "You want to go back to your room and shower?" he asked, looking me up and down. "You're a fucking mess."

I flipped him off on my way to turn off the *open* sign and make sure everything was locked up. The woman I employed part-time to help with the books and run payroll only came in the latter half of the week, and Bryce Tanner, my only full-time guy, worked from five in the morning until two in the afternoon, so for the past few hours, it had just been me.

To be honest, I preferred it that way, but my garage wouldn't ever grow if I only took on the work I could handle on my own.

Besides, there was no way in hell I was going to handle contacting insurance companies and all those other headaches. That was what Sandra Parr had been hired for.

"Why don't you come on back?" I told him. "You can watch TV while I clean up."

He complied, ambling along next to me with a loose-hipped gait that made me think he must have been a cowboy in Texas, but he'd just been a kid, an all-around jock who'd been everybody's best friend up until he'd made a stupid mistake. He'd paid for it and then some. But hell, it was amazing how he'd turned his life around.

While he kicked back on my old, beat-up couch, I retreated into the tiny bathroom to scrub off the dirt. As I did that, I mentally tried to figure out when I'd done laundry last and what I had to wear that wasn't just grease-streaked blue jeans and beat-up old band shirts or graphic T's with rude suggestions on them.

JUST OVER AN HOUR LATER, we stepped through the brightly lit, oversized loft apartment where Jake now lived with Michelle. It was more than twice the size of the apartment where my mom lived with Austen, and everything about it screamed class and money. Just like the sweet lady who lived there with one of my best friends.

But as he called out for Michelle, there wasn't any answer.

"She must have gone out," Jake said, tossing his keys down on the small wooden table that looked like it belonged in another century – and not the 1900s.

He gestured for me to follow him into the kitchen. "Come on. I'll go ahead and start dinner since she's not here. We always eat around seven, so she'll be here soon." He frowned and pulled out his phone to check it. "She hasn't texted me so she's probably just out shopping." He rolled his eyes. "She's falling in love with shopping."

I chuckled. "Aren't all women in love with it?"

"She didn't use to be." He shrugged and went over to the sink to wash his hands. "She plans the week out when it comes to food. Today's supposed to be pasta. That okay with you?"

"Any food I don't have to cook is fine with me," I answered. This was turning out to be a good week. Two home-cooked meals that I didn't have to go to the trouble of cooking.

Not that I had much ability in the kitchen other than nuking a pizza or making macaroni and cheese.

I'd just managed to pull up a stool to the kitchen island where Jake had put some water on to boil when the door to the apartment opened.

Michelle's voice rang out, and a grin split my buddy's face. "She's here."

"Is that a fact?" I responded with a straight face as he cut around the island to head for the living room.

I got up to follow him but stopped dead.

Michelle wasn't alone.

And the petite woman with flame-red hair standing next to her?

It was the drop-dead gorgeous woman I'd kissed on New Year's Eve.

10

Raye

I so wasn't sure this was a good idea, but I was already here.

Michelle and I had spent the afternoon together, dropping into stores as we talked, and she shopped. After she asked where I worked, we dropped by my boutique, and inside, she hadn't been like a demon with a credit card. She'd been like a kid in a candy store...with a credit card.

I was in awe.

Or at least I had been.

Now I was feeling a little sick as I stood behind her, holding the few bags I'd talked her into letting me carry.

She shot me a grin as she opened the door. "Relax. It's better this way. Get it all over with in one shot, okay?"

"And what if he doesn't want to meet me?" I asked in a hurried whisper.

"If I thought that was the case, you wouldn't be here."

"But...how well do you know him?" I demanded. Then it dawned on me that she was unlocking the door – not knocking on it. "You live here. Are we going to his place next?"

"This...*is* his place," she admitted softly. She made a face and chewed her bottom lip for a second. "I wasn't sure how to cop to that part. We're...uh...the two of us have been living together for the past six months or so."

My mouth fell open in surprise, but I managed to snap it shut just as she pushed open the door. "Hey, Jake...we're here!"

Jake...?

A tall, lean blond appeared in the door, a smile curling his lips as he looked at Michelle. That smile lit up his entire face, and I fell a little in love just looking at it.

I wanted somebody in my life who looked at *me* like that.

Movement behind him caught my eyes, and I glanced past him. Although I'd successfully managed to shut my mouth a few seconds ago, I found my jaw hanging open all over again.

It was the big guy who'd saved me on New Year's Eve.

The guy who'd then kissed me.

The guy who I'd been daydreaming about ever since.

Oh...and the guy I'd slapped.

Oh, *shit* – what if *he* was Matthew? Talk about *awkward*! Maybe I'd misunderstood Michelle. If that guy was my brother...my belly twisted violently at the thought, but as the blond stepped forward, Michelle reached back and took my hand. "Come on," she whispered.

She tugged on my hand persistently, pulling me forward and I went, still holding three shopping bags in my right hand. She'd dropped hers near the door, freeing her hands to hustle me deeper into the apartment.

"Jake, there's somebody I want you to meet," Michelle was saying.

Heat suffused my entire face, and I uneasily looked at the blond in front of me before shooting another look at the tall, dark stranger looming in the background.

"Raye, this is Matthew – MJ – Jakes. He goes by Jake now." Michelle winced, and I looked from her to Jake and saw that his mouth had gone tight. "Don't look at me like that, baby. I've got a reason for telling her. She's..." Michelle looked at me. "Do you want to tell him, or should I?"

Matthew...

I stared at the tall blond in front of me, stared into his blue eyes. Eyes a lot like mine, I realized. And the shape of his nose. Even the shape of his chin. *He* was Matthew, not the other guy. My knees might have melted in relief, except everything in me had gone rigid the moment he shifted those blue eyes my way.

I couldn't speak.

Michelle was waiting for me to answer, and I couldn't speak.

"I guess I'll tell him," Michelle said lightly. She squeezed my hand in support, then looked back at Matthew. No. Jake. She said he went by Jake now. "Honey, Raye...Raye tracked me down because she wanted to talk to you. She thinks she's your sister. And..."

Michelle pulled out her phone. She'd had me text her the picture my mom sent me, and I guess that was what she was showing him.

His mouth parted as he stared at the screen.

"Where did you get that picture?" he asked, his voice rough.

"Raye's mama sent it to her. She said it was her father."

Jake looked at me, shaking his head. "I don't understand."

To my horror, tears flooded my eyes, and all I could do was stare at him. *Again.* "I...um..." I finally squeaked out a few words after Michelle looked at me, waiting. This part had to come from me, I realized. I understood the reason, and it made sense, but I couldn't tell him yet. "Can I get some water?" I asked desperately. "Please?"

MICHELLE POURED me a glass of wine instead. I would have refused. I hated most wines unless I cut them with Sprite or something. They always made me feel like I'd shoved a handful of crackers into my mouth. But I was desperate for something to loosen my throat, and wine would probably do a better job than water would. Taking a gulp of it, I braced myself for the chore of swallowing – and hating it – only to be surprised by the sweet, fruity taste of the pale golden liquid.

"Wow," I said, the band around my throat loosened either by surprise or by the booze. "That's good."

Michelle laughed. "I don't do dry wines. You looked like you were preparing to eat a mouthful of sour grapes."

"I was." I made a face at her, then took a second, smaller sip. After that, I put the glass down and made myself look at Matthew – *Jake* – standing across the island from me.

"This is awkward," I said softly. "I'm sorry."

"Just tell me," he responded. It wasn't said in a rude voice, just a...direct one.

I got the feeling I was dealing with a blunt, no-nonsense sort of guy. I could appreciate that. Typically, that was how I preferred to face things. Just then, I could use a bush to beat around.

"My mom had an affair," I blurted out, just to get the worst of it over with. "It was with a married man. He...he traveled some because of his work. He lived in Texas, but he met my mom on a business trip when he was in Illinois. His name was Leland."

Jake's mouth tightened slightly, but he didn't say anything, gave no other reaction.

"I didn't find out about that until I was a teenager. Whenever I'd ask about my dad before that, I'd just get these vague answers." I didn't offer any of them because it didn't matter just then. But I could remember the hurt I'd often felt on days when parents could come to field trips or to school parties, and nobody had been there. Mom always had to work, and...there was no father. "Finally, she told me about this guy she was with. She didn't find out about me until a few weeks after it ended, and when she told him...well..."

I hesitated for a moment, uncertain, but Jake pressed. "Well, what?"

"He told her he didn't want anything to do with us. I guess he had one family. He didn't want a second."

"That doesn't sound like my dad," Jake said, shaking his head. "He and Mom always wanted another kid."

"But that was your mom, baby," Michelle said gently.

"It doesn't matter," Jake snapped, then softened his tone. "He's not the kind of guy who'd brush off his responsibility like that."

"And how about how he treated you?" Michelle stared at him.

I sensed a world of unspoken words between them and felt more out of place in that moment than I'd felt all day.

Finally, Jake shook his head. "I'll figure all of that out later." His gaze came back to mine, speculation lurking there. "You're sure this guy your mom was with...it was my dad?"

"That's what my mother says," I answered weakly. I gestured toward the phone he still held. "She called me the other day, said she'd found a picture of him. She texted it to me and told me that on the back, his name was written down..." I looked away for a second, gripping the stem of the wine glass in my hand. Finally, I looked back at him and added, "And yours. MJ."

At the name, he flinched slightly and shook his head. "That's not me anymore. That kid died a long time ago."

"But it was you," I said, clinging to his words.

"It was," he allowed.

I was dimly aware that the big guy was still watching us and part of me wanted to turn on him, tell him to go away. Why was he here? Listening to this private conversation? But this wasn't my home. Jake and Michelle lived here, and if they didn't care, I had no right to say anything.

Yet I had the feeling that Jake had forgotten about him.

He continued to eye me narrowly for the longest time, then finally lifted the phone with the picture still on display so he could study it. "My mom kept a copy of this picture on her dresser for most of my childhood. It was taken when I was in first grade," he said softly. "Bring Your Dad to School Day. We were supposed to bring our dads in and...well, show them off. And I did. We had matching suits and Mom spent about ten minutes trying to make my hair stay down. You can tell it didn't last."

"Yeah."

He shot me a look, a faint smile on his face.

"So, I've got a sister."

"I think so." I bit my lip, reluctant to let myself do much of anything just yet. Did this mean he believed me?

"And Dad doesn't know," he said slowly.

I shook my head.

In the next moment, I was caught up in a tight hug. A watery laugh escaped me.

Jake was hugging me. My *brother* was hugging me.

I didn't even know how to process that.

I still clutched my wine glass, and if I didn't think it would make me look like a lush, I might have tried to drink a little more of it, just to steady myself. Instead, I wrapped my free arm around his neck. Over his shoulder, I saw the other guy watching us and making no attempt to disguise it.

"This is unbelievable," Jake said, lowering me back to the floor and taking a step back.

I managed a watery smile. "I know."

He glanced around, then frowned as he caught sight of the other guy. "Man, Kane, I'm sorry. I totally...anyway. Raye...it is Raye, right?"

I nodded at him.

"Raye, this is my friend, Kane Jonson."

Kane. As the big guy nodded at me, I tucked that name away in my heart like a secret.

Kane continued to stare at me.

"Kane, as you heard...this is Raye." Jake was grinning at me, looking like he'd won the lottery. "Raye's my sister."

"So, I heard," came a deep, rumbling reply.

The sound of his voice sent a shiver down my spine.

Now that I was no longer caught up in a bear hug, I lifted the wine to my lips and emptied the glass.

11

Jake

She was a pretty little thing.

Hesitant and shy...sort of. But there was something ballsy about her, too. How much guts had it taken to come here and meet Jake face to face?

For all she knew, he would have laughed in her face and thrown her out on her ass.

Some people might hear they had a brother and they'd only care about it if they stood to gain from it. Calie's face came to mind, all her bold, brash ways and I found myself a little irritated by the fact that I'd even ever associated with somebody as cold as I knew Calie could be.

Then there was Michelle, elegant and confident. If she'd been in Raye's shoes, I thought she would have reached out, but not in person like this.

She would have sent an email or written a letter. Something polite, like she was, and...aloof. Yeah, that was the word.

"How did you track me down?" Jake asked.

I tuned in on that part of the conversation as Jake led her

over to the island, taking up the seat where I'd been sitting a little while ago. I wasn't worried about it. It was easier to lurk on the fringes, and I didn't want Jake to get it in his head to ask me to leave yet. I was...hell, the only word to describe it was *intrigued*. I felt stupid getting intrigued by a woman, but I was.

This slim woman with the short red hair and the big blue eyes was intriguing. She wasn't like some of the rougher women who ran with the guys I knew from my old life, and she wasn't the smooth elegance that defined Michelle Nestor.

I didn't know how to define her yet, and I wanted to. I wanted to understand more about her, so I could classify her and put her in a neat little space in my head, and maybe stop thinking about her.

"I started googling you," she admitted, sounding sheepish as she met his eyes. "I..." Her gaze fell away, and she said softly, "I read about your mother, and what really happened. I'm so sorry."

No beating around the bush for her, I thought. She just came right out and said it.

I liked that.

Jake's mouth went tight, the way it always did when he was hiding his emotions. He just nodded and said, "Thanks. It's been a long time."

"Finding out you got used like that...that wasn't a long time ago. It had to be like reliving it all over again," she said, voice gentle.

"It was," Jake admitted.

I slid my gaze toward him, a little surprised to hear him admit it. He'd never told me that. But then again, I'd never thought to ask. I would have thought being cleared of the crime would...well, not change things. I didn't know how I expected him to feel, I suppose. He'd never really understood that he was innocent. Not until years later. He'd been drunk on that terrible night and hadn't realized that somebody else was driving the car that killed his mother. Hadn't realized he'd been wrongly accused. Framed.

Finding out he was innocent hadn't brought his mom back. But knowing he hadn't been the one to kill her had to make things...hell, I'd think it would make it better.

But this girl with the sad, too-wise eyes had figured out something that hadn't ever occurred to me.

All of it had brought the hurt back.

An awkward silence stretched out, and I was thinking about leaving. This wasn't the night for an action flick or even just hanging out.

But before I could suggest it, Michelle looked at me. "You still planning on joining us for dinner? Jake texted earlier, said he was dragging you over."

"Uh..."

Raye's eyes slid my way.

"Seems like this is a weird night to do it," I said finally.

"Sit your ass down, Kane," Jake said without looking at me. He crooked a grin at Raye. "He's the closest thing I got to a brother. Guess you'll end up getting to know him sooner or later. Might as well start now."

I wasn't so sure I wanted to be considered something like a brother to Jake now, even though it was the truth.

But if Jake and I were like brothers, was it right for me to be thinking about how Raye would look naked?

No.

Jake would rip my head off.

Hell, *I* should rip my head off. A girl like her didn't need some roughneck like me ogling her. Thinking about getting her naked. Wondering what she tasted like or what kind of sounds she made when I...

My phone buzzed, dragging me out of my reverie and I grabbed it from the island. I'd been staring at Raye, I realized.

Raye had noticed, too.

Her pale skin had flushed pink, and she had jerked her gaze away, locking her eyes on Jake.

Good thing the phone had rung before Jake noticed.

That was the last thing I needed.

It was a text from my mother, asking me to call her.

"I need to make a call," I said to the room at large and slid out of the kitchen into the hallway.

I'd been there often enough and felt comfortable enough to slip into the room that Michelle used as her library. Surrounded by books and the scent of lavender and vanilla, I made my way over to a window as I brought Mom's contact info up and hit dial.

She answered almost immediately.

"Hi, Kane. Are you busy?"

I thought about the dinner I'd been asked to join. "Not if you need me."

"You've got plans," she said, worry in her voice.

"Nothing's ever more important than you, Mom. You know that."

She sighed. "I hate this, but I need your help. Austen and I had an argument earlier, and he left the house. Honey...I think he went to one of those underground street fights with that boy, Jonas. You remember Greg Haynes who lived across from us?"

"I remember him." I also remembered his kid. Jonas was a punk. He was also a couple of years older than Austen, and I'd seen him running with the wrong kind of crowd. I had a feeling he had gotten involved with one of the new gangs that had popped up, and that was the last thing my kid brother needed to be involved in.

"Well, I overheard them talking, and Jonas was telling him about these fights. I shouldn't have lost my temper, but that boy is a rude little shit. I knocked on the door and asked what they were up to. Anyway, we got into an argument after I told Jonas that Austen had school work and couldn't have company. Jonas mouthed off to me, and I told him to get out of my home and not come back. A few minutes later, Austen left, too! Kane, those street fights are trouble...I don't know what to do!"

"I'll handle it, Mom," I told her, staring outside at the slow drift of snow that had started to fall.

It had been a while since I'd been to the part of town where Jonas had probably taken my brother, but that didn't mean I didn't still know my way around. "I need to go."

I had a few phone calls to make.

RUSTY HAD GIVEN me two places to check. To my surprise, he offered to hit the one closest to his place, but I'd passed.

If Rusty went in and found Jonas and Austen, he'd suggest they leave. Austen wouldn't know Rusty, and he'd follow Jonas's cue. Jonas was a stupid little shit and might try to mouth off to Rusty. That wouldn't end well for the punk, and I'd rather my brother not see just how it might end.

Maybe it would scare him straight, but I'd still rather avoid that sort of thing.

The first location was a bust.

Less than thirty people there and none of them were my little brother.

The second location, housed in an empty warehouse well off the beaten path, that was a different story. Almost thirty cars were parked in the lot, and somebody at the door was taking money.

I peeled off the bills needed to get inside. I'd hit an ATM on the way in, knowing I'd need to pony up the entrance fee. They weren't going to listen to a tale of woe about how I needed to find my brother.

As soon as I got inside, I had a feeling he was in there. It was a younger crowd for the most part, and I recognized a few faces belonging to the guys I'd seen Jonas hanging out with.

A couple of guys saw me prowling around, and I knew I was being sized up. I ignored them. Most of the guys in there, I could take blindfolded, but I wasn't looking to fight.

Not unless I had to anyway.

I headed to the rough ring set up in the middle of the floor first, searching for a messy head of hair. I struck out, but off to the far left, I heard hoots and hollers and decided to check it out.

A few kids were staggering toward me, and I rolled my eyes as I stepped out of their way. They'd be puking in a few minutes.

One guy crashed into me, half stumbled back a step, then

glared at me with baleful eyes. "You should watch the fuck where you're going," he said.

I just stared him down.

After a few more seconds, he just sneered and told me to suck his dick before cutting around me to get lost in the crowd. I heard a voice over a crappy loudspeaker setting up the next fight and announcing the odds.

I didn't turn around.

I found Austen near a couple of kegs, his hair standing on end, his eyes bleary from the effects of booze. When I said his name, he craned his head around, searching for me.

Crossing my arms, I said his name again and waited until he finally sighted on me.

A bright grin lit his face.

"Hey, Kane!" He lifted a red SOLO cup to his lips and drank.

If I had anything to do with it, he'd puke his guts up *before* he got into my car.

"You here to watch the fights?" he asked. Then his eyes widened. "Are you here *to* fight? I bet you'd kick *everybody*'s ass."

He said it in a voice loud enough to have multiple eyes come my way. I lifted an impassive gaze and waited for somebody to move in on me, but other than a couple of scoffing laughs, nobody reacted.

"How about you keep your voice down?" I suggested. "And get your shit. I'm taking you home."

"No." Belligerent now, he pointed at me, still holding the cup, spilling out some of the amber liquid in the process. I caught the pungent aroma of cheap beer as it splashed to the floor. "I ain't going home. Tired of being treated like a fuckin' kid. I'm a man, damn it."

"And look at you, acting like one. You're so drunk, you can barely see straight." Looking around, disgusted, I resisted the urge to pick him up and carry him out, but only because I didn't want to risk getting puked on. It might come to that, but I was going to try talking first. "You run off and scare Mom, shirking your responsibilities, that's how a man acts?"

"I..." He frowned at me. "Why's Mom scared?"

I didn't have a chance to answer because his friend Jonas emerged from the crowd and threw an arm around his neck. "Heeeeeyyyy...Austen. Man. Guess what?"

Austen blinked at him. He'd already forgotten me.

"I put your name down for the next round."

Aw, *fuck*.

"That's it," I said, grabbing Austen's cup and throwing it into the nearest upright drum that was close to overflowing with trash. "You and me, we're out of here, kid."

Jonas laughed. "No way, dude. He's up next to fight. He's going to kick ass!"

I caught Austen's arm and bent my head until I was nose to nose with Jonas. "Let go," I said in a flat voice.

Jonas looked at me, then smiled, displaying teeth that were already starting to yellow from nicotine. Shit, he couldn't be any more than nineteen or twenty. "He's gotta fight. Name's down. That's the rules."

"*He* is seventeen years old, you dumbass. If you think you're going to get him in that ring with some dickhead, think again."

Jonas jutted his chin up. "Hey, it's the luck of the draw."

"Then you go take his place."

Jonas's eyes flitted away, but his grin never wavered. "I can't. I put money on the fight. I'm not allowed to take his place."

I shot out a hand and grabbed the punk by the front of the shirt, never letting go of Austen, who'd started to weave on his feet. "The day my brother steps in that ring is the day I put you in a pine box, kid. Now wipe that shit-eating grin off your face before I do it for you."

Jonas's face pale the tiniest bit, but as I let him go, a voice came over the loudspeaker. And it said my brother's name.

Lights shown all around, clearly searching for him.

Jonas threw up his arms and waved them, shouting, "We're over here."

"You stupid fuck," I snapped at him as the light hit Austen and me.

People started to shove at Austen. He promptly went to his knees and puked, a mess of beer and mucous splattering on the floor.

Jonas laughed, a sound that rang out like caged coyotes. "He's still gotta fight...or you can have fun busting your way out of here," the boy said.

I turned my head and stared at him. "I ought to bust you you pathetic sack of shit."

Then, turning to my brother, I hauled him up, and the two of us began walking to the circle. Understanding began to dawn in his eyes. Maybe with some of the booze out of his system, he was realizing what sort of shit he was in. I grabbed his shoulders and shoved him into one of the few empty chairs, then shrugged out of my jacket.

Somebody came prowling over to us. He held a microphone in his hand.

"Which one of you is Austen?"

"That depends," I said, staring him down. "Who is your fighter, and does he want to take on a drunk, scared seventeen-year-old kid or is he a man?"

A bunch of hoots broke out because my words had been picked up by the mike.

People started to clap, and a big, muscled guy stepped out to join me. "I would have taken it easy on the little punk, just because I'm a nice guy," he said, grinning at me. "I won't take it easy on you."

"Good." I was fucking pissed.

As I took one step forward, I looked out into the crowd and searched for Jonas's gaze. Once I had his attention, I smiled. Then I focused on the man in front of me and waited.

He swung...fast, low, and hard.

I sidestepped, trapped his arm and struck at his elbow with all the force I had in me. I wouldn't have been surprised to see bone burst through skin.

He hit the ground screaming.

"I think we're done here." As everybody fell silent in stunned shock, I hunkered down next to him. In a low voice, I added, "I find out you're ever roughing up kids in one of these fights, I'll come back for you and break every bone in your fucking pathetic body. You hear me?"

When I stood up, I sought Jonas out once more.

He stared at me with wide eyes and a pale face.

Even from where I stood, I could see his Adam's apple bobbing as he swallowed.

Pathetic little sack of shit.

I GOT Austen home and tucked into bed within an hour.

He stayed there maybe five minutes before he bolted upright and hit the bathroom, on his knees and hurling like a champ.

Mom and I stood in the hallway, listening.

"Thank you," she said quietly.

"No need to thank me." I shrugged, thinking of the shit my brother would have been in if I hadn't found him. "He done something like this before?"

"Run off like that? Or hang out with Jonas?" She didn't wait for an answer, just shook her head. "No to both. He's just...lately, he's so angry. He's so determined, so convinced he's already a grown-up and..." She threw up her hands, a helpless look on her face. "I feel like I'm losing him."

She didn't say it out loud, but there was a subtle tension between us. *Like I almost lost you.*

"You're not going to lose him," I told her. I reached out to her with one hand, and when she took it, I tugged her in close for a hug. She felt fragile against me, but my mother had a core of pure steel. She'd needed it after Dad was killed in the bodega where he'd been working overtime to save money back when she was pregnant with Austen.

Sometimes, I wondered if all that anger he held inside was because he blamed himself.

It was stupid, because it wasn't his fault. But we didn't always think clearly when it came to family. There had to be something that would explain the sullen, simmering anger that lurked inside him lately.

"I'll talk to him again," I told Mom as the toilet flushed.

"What should I do in the morning?"

I don't know if she was talking to me or not.

Meeting her eyes, I asked, "Are you off?"

She'd worked up to regional manager for the small chain of grocery stores she'd been at for years, so I doubted the answer would be yes. She had her weekends and holidays off, but her work week was still often a fifty hour one.

She scoffed. "I'm the manager. If I need to go in late for once, I can."

And she'd bust her ass to make up for it, too.

But I knew nothing I said would change her mind if she'd decided to go in a little later, either.

"Make him breakfast," I told her with a wry grin. "Turn on all the lights, bright and early. Make a lot of noise. And make him breakfast. Bacon and eggs…make the eggs good and runny, too. Make sure he has some ibuprofen or something for that headache. But don't do anything else to help with the hangover he's going to have. Maybe that will teach him. I know he ended up getting his ass good and scared tonight. Who knows? It might be enough."

But I wasn't betting on it.

12

Raye

It was a full day later, and I still couldn't wrap my brain around the fact that I'd met my brother.

Jake had told me a little about his childhood and growing up, stories that had made me laugh even as pangs of wistfulness and envy stirred inside. It wasn't that I was jealous of him, per se. It was just...he had the childhood I'd wanted. I was glad he'd had it. I just wished I could have had it, too.

Through his eyes, I was able to learn a little more about my father, and as the evening grew later, part of me was maybe, a little, more willing to admit that it was possible my mother had lied to me. Maybe she hadn't told Leland about me, or maybe she had. And if she did, maybe he'd wanted a relationship with me, and she wouldn't allow it.

So many maybes. I just didn't know.

Even though they were estranged, Jake offered to introduce me, but I wasn't sure how I felt about it, so I told him no.

For now, at least.

It was enough to know that I *did* have family, somebody

other than my mom, and judging by the way Jake lived, I'd never have to worry that he'd ever call me early one morning, sounding all happy to talk to me, just to turn around and beg for a loan. I could have somebody who wanted a relationship with me *for* me...and not just to use me.

It was a mind-boggling thought.

It had been so long since my mother and I'd had any sort of decent relationship, I couldn't fathom what it would be like to have somebody I could count on in my life.

"Your head is up in the clouds today," a voice behind me said. I turned around and saw my manager eyeing me closely. "Are you okay?" Pauline cocked her head, her cat-eye glasses not quite concealing the gleam in her eyes.

"I'm fine." The urge to babble out my news rose to my lips, surprising me. I liked Pauline. We'd even had drinks together a couple of times, but I wouldn't go so far as to call us confidantes. Maybe it was because the news was *so* different, and felt so...well, *good* compared to the things I normally had going on.

A bell chimed at the door signifying the arrival of a customer. Pauline patted me on the shoulder. "You just keep straightening up tables and stocking. Once your head is on straight, you'll deal with customers. Just don't take too long," she advised.

I nodded numbly, hearing one of my co-workers, Janelle, as she called out, greeting the new arrival.

A man's voice filled the air, oddly familiar, but I kept at the task at hand, not turning around.

Jake had given me his cell number and asked if I wanted to get lunch on Saturday, just me and him. Of course, I'd said *yes,* but now I was wondering if we should.

What would we talk about?

He'd told me all about his family. Would he want to know about my mother? Hell. What could I tell him?

That would be nothing more than a lesson in embarrassment and discomfort. *My mom loves me, but she's...flighty. She brings home these boyfriends who think it's okay to flirt with me. No, nobody ever did anything, but how creepy is it to have the guy who sticks his tongue down your mother's throat turn around and tell you how hot you are in the next breath?*

There weren't any funny, awkward stories to tell him like he'd told me.

I could tell him about the days I'd dressed in my best hoping that just once, Mom would show up for one of the parent/student functions. But she never had. Those weren't funny. Just awkward.

I could always tell him about the time she'd gotten me a goldfish for Christmas. She'd at least tried that time. But the poor thing had been dead by the time I came down to open presents.

Mom's words of comfort... *Well, I tried, honey.*

That was what I'd clung to. She'd tried.

No. Telling him about my childhood wasn't going to be high on my list of topics to talk about. Nor was college. Making a face, I finished smoothing down the rainbow river of silk and lace panties on the table I'd just finished then returned to the back of the store.

Bras were next on the list, so I mentally re-inventoried the store and went to fill a box with what was running low.

I could always talk about school – here at NYU, at least. I'd rather not talk about my time at Texas A&M to anybody. Ever.

With the box full, I slid back outside. Leaving the box on a chair near the stockroom entrance, I took several of the bras and headed over to the nearest table, still pondering things that were safe to discuss with a brother I barely knew. I took care of one side and turned to circle around.

A big body stood in front of me, and I all but crashed into him. Hands came up, gripping my arms.

A dull flush washed over me.

The floor of my belly bottomed out.

The rush of blood roared in my ears.

Tipping my head back, I stared into a pair of eyes I'd thought – had *hoped* – I'd never see again.

Blue eyes stared back at me, a friendly affable smile set in a round face. His hair was still the same bright orange, a smattering of freckles danced across his nose. Chad Gibbons.

Son of a bitch.

Chad Gibbons was here.

My belly started to pitch and roll as he squeezed my arms lightly. "Excuse me there, sweetheart," he said, his voice heavy with the sounds of Texas. "You okay?"

I jerked back, edging away from him. I dumped the bras back in the box I'd brought out and carried it to the back of the store where I almost crashed into Pauline.

"Raye, you really are...honey." The smile faded from her face as she caught sight of me. She took the box away and set it on a nearby table. Then she reached around me and nudged the door to the front part of the boutique shut. "Raye, what's wrong? You're white as a ghost."

She pressed her hand to my cheek, and it felt way too hot against the sudden chill of my skin.

"I think I'm going to be sick," I whispered, lifting my eyes to stare at hers.

She let me go immediately, and I bolted past her, heading to the bathroom.

"Claire's in there!" Pauline called out urgently.

Claire was one of the few full-time employees, and she was currently spending a fair amount of time in the bathroom. She was just over seven months pregnant, so none of us held it against her.

But just then, I was desperate.

Panicked, I whirled on my heel and headed for the back entrance, bolting in the alley that opened out onto W. 35th. Cold air stung my cheeks as I stood there, shaking and waiting for the nausea to pass.

This wasn't happening.

He couldn't be here.

A memory, little more than a vague hint of one really, washed up from the back of my mind. A hand in my hair. I'd worn it long then. It fisted and jerked tight. Voices laughing.

Moaning, I leaned against the wall. A cold wind whipped own the street, and I huddled against the wall with my arms around myself. Had he left?

Why was he here?

Shit, did he *live* here now?

What was I going to do if he did?

That memory circled around and around in my mind like a whirlpool, and the nausea inside swirled with it.

Pressing a hand to the back of my mouth, I fought off the shivers and tried not to cry.

Why was he *here*?

Tears pricked my eyes, and I shoved the heels of my hands against my eyes, willing them back.

It was bad enough he'd made me feel so weak in front of my manager, but damned if I'd let him make me cry.

I shoved off the wall, straightening up.

Get it under control, I told myself.

The memory of his blue eyes staring down at me was all it took to buckle my bid for strength, and I swallowed back a small scream of frustration as I dropped my hands, looking around wildly.

I wanted to run away.

But I'd already done that.

I'd left Texas and come to New York City – almost as far as I could get away and still be in the same country.

And he was *here*.

Panic welled up inside me, and the urge to vomit once more rose, gorge building in my throat.

I sucked in air and took one awkward step, then another forward. *Breathe, Raye,* I told myself. *You gotta breathe.*

I blew out the breath, but it didn't help the nausea any.

Taking another step, another breath, I focused on those simple tasks. Bit by bit, the panic fell back. Bit by bit, the urge to vomit faded.

I'd almost reached the end of the street, so I turned to go back.

And once more, I crashed straight into a big, hard body.

Big hard hands came up to grip my arms.

I panicked and shoved, smacking at the chest of the man who held me. "Let me go!" I said as my throat seemed to close, making it now impossible to really take a deep breath. I yelled at him, although the words came out in more of a whisper this time. "Let me go!"

"Raye!" The sharply-spoken voice was a far cry from the slow, easy drawl I'd expected.

Slowly, I tipped my head back.

It wasn't Chad.

Swallowing, I found myself staring into a pair of deep, dark eyes.

The strength in my legs faded and I all but wilted.

The hands on my arms tightened, and I found myself being supported by one Kane Jonson.

"Are you okay?" he asked.

To my surprise, a nervous laughed boiled out of me, and I couldn't silence it.

13

Kane

After delivering the second car to a client on W. 35th in less than a week, I was starting to think that maybe I needed to start charging for delivery. Not so much because delivering a vehicle was a hassle. But freezing my ass off as I made my way on foot to the nearest subway?

That was a fucking hassle.

The manager of the hotel on W. 35th had tipped me nice, and I could have used the money for a cab, but I drew a hard line about luxuries like that. Of course, plenty of people wouldn't see a New York City cab ride as a luxury – more like a thrill ride, depending on how far you were going.

But if it was money I didn't have to spend, then I wasn't spending it.

I did a mental tally, thinking about the jobs I'd done over the past week. Since it was a holiday week and nearly half of the jobs that had been dumped on me had been deemed *rush* jobs by their respective owners, I'd been able to charge a little more. I had a fairly decent amount I'd be able to put down toward the money I still owed on the garage.

If I kept having years like the last one and kept living like I had been, maybe in another five to seven years, that garage might be mine, free and clear. Maybe. But I wasn't banking on it just yet.

I needed to expand and hire more help, but that would cost money.

"Problems for another day, man," I muttered as a cold wind whipped its way down W. 35th.

I put a little extra speed in my step and reached up to jerk up the collar of my coat to protect my bare neck. I blew into my hands to warm them and wondered if maybe I should invest in another pair of gloves. I was always losing them, but fuck, it was *cold*.

Somebody came careening around the corner just as I reached it, and I jerked to the side to avoid slamming into them, my hands going up to steady the woman who'd almost barreled into me.

She shrieked and jerked back, her face a pale oval, dominated by big, dark blue eyes.

Raye.

"Stop it," she said, the words broken and panicked. "Just... let me..." As she spoke, she slapped at my hands and chest, trying to get away from me.

Fear all but bled from her pores and recognition hit me like a punch straight to the solar plexus.

"Raye!"

She stilled at the sound of my voice, her eyes finally coming up to meet my face, and I saw something in her eyes that made red wash over my vision. Terror.

She blinked, focusing on my face. "Kane?" she whispered, the word trembling as it escaped her.

"Yeah." I tried to smile, not sure if it would help or not. "Were you expecting the boogie man?"

She laughed, but the sound had more of a sob to it, and I wondered if maybe I'd hit the nail on the head.

"Somebody scared you," I said.

She gave a jerky nod and looked around, her eyes half wild.

"Was somebody following you?" If somebody was, I was going to find them and twist them into a pretzel, like I'd wanted to do with the men from New Year's night.

"I..." She licked her lips, then said, "No. It was just..." She sucked in a breath. "You know what? I don't want to talk about it."

I nodded. "Understood."

She started to shiver, and I shrugged out of my coat, slinging it over her shoulders. Cold air stung my skin like a thousand needles, but I wasn't the one standing out there in a cute black dress and heels. My jeans, flannel, and thermal shirt had to be warmer than what she was wearing.

"You work around here?" I asked, trying to get her mind off whatever it was she didn't want to talk about.

"Yes," she said, her gaze flitting over her shoulder.

I caught sight of a door, but couldn't read the writing on the neat little sign next to it.

"You should get back inside. It's freezing out."

But she shook her head, almost wildly. The spikes of her hair tremored with the movement and what little color that had returned to her cheeks washed away. "No!"

"Okay, okay..." Holding up a hand, I looked around, then

gestured to the hotel just across the way. "Come over here then. I know the manager. We can grab a cup of coffee and..." I almost said, *wait for whoever to leave*, but I wasn't going to clue her into the fact that I'd figured out that much. "Think that will work? Can you take a few minutes?"

She hesitated and said, "I shouldn't." Then she glanced back over her shoulder to the door, almost like she expected her boogie man to come rushing out. "But, yes. A few minutes."

Tony saw me striding back inside and frowned, but the expression melted away as he caught sight of Raye. Immediately, a warm smile appeared on his round face, and he came from behind the counter where he'd been talking to one of his employees.

"Raye works across the street," I said before he could ask. "Is there any way we could trouble you for a cup of coffee?"

I didn't exactly fit in with the clientele, not with my rough clothes and tattoos, but I knew one thing about Tony – he couldn't resist a damsel in distress. It wasn't so much that he was a flirt. He was happily married and had been for twenty years. I couldn't come into this place without him telling me something about his wife and his two daughters.

He just loved women.

I could appreciate that about him.

I loved them myself.

And he saw the same thing about Raye that I had seen – she'd probably hate being thought of a damsel, but she was sure as hell in distress.

He smiled at her warmly, as though they were best friends who were meeting up for the first time in weeks. "Of course. Come with me."

Tony led us to a small, semi-private area just off the bar, and after he'd left to get coffee, Raye asked, "Can I use your phone please?"

Her voice sounded a little steadier, which I was glad to hear. But she was still so pale.

As I turned over my phone, I wondered who in the hell had scared her so bad.

She sent a quick text off, then returned the phone. "I just wanted the boss to know I'd be right back," she said, and now, as she looked around, her face flushing with embarrassment, she wouldn't meet my eyes. "I feel so stupid."

"Why?"

Now she did look at me, for a fleeting moment. "A guy like you wouldn't understand."

"I've been afraid before," I said mildly. I was afraid just the other day when I had to go track down my brother. What if I didn't make it in time? What if he got in the same kind of trouble I did?

My words must have surprised her, because she finally looked right at me and after a moment, she asked, "What makes you think I'm afraid?"

I wasn't going to tell her that it was written all over her face. Thankfully, I was given a few seconds to think because Tony appeared, carrying a tray of coffee, cream, and sugar. After putting the tray down, he disappeared. My phone buzzed, and after a quick glance revealed a number I didn't recognize, I turned the phone over to Raye. "Is this your boss?" I asked.

She took the phone and glanced at it, then nodded. "She just wants to make sure I'm okay. I think I scared her." She tapped back a response, a faint groan escaping her throat. "I'm going to have to think of something to tell her."

"Take a drink of the coffee and take a deep breath. Whoever you saw is probably gone by now," I told her.

"What makes you think—"

"Cut the act, Raye," I said, keeping my voice as gentle as I could. "It's not hard to recognize when somebody is afraid of something – and you looked terrified. Unless you suddenly developed a fear of lingerie, it only stands to reason that somebody upset you."

She frowned at me. "Lingerie?"

"I'm in this part of the city a lot. I know what store is on the corner." I grinned at her, feeling a little sheepish. With a shrug, I added, "I'm a red-blooded male. We tend to notice pretty women in lingerie."

Her face went red once more, and she looked away. "Okay. Yeah, I...there was somebody I knew, but I don't want to talk about it."

"Like I said, understood." I thought about the way she'd panicked on the street when I had my hands on her arms, slapping at me as she fought to break away. "You ever taken any sort of self-defense class or anything?"

She paused, the cup of coffee at her pretty pink mouth. I really did like that mouth. And I really shouldn't be staring at it. She lowered the cup back to the table. "What?"

"Self-defense," I said again. "Ever taken any classes?"

"Like karate?" She scoffed and picked her coffee back up, taking a sip. "No."

"It doesn't have to be karate. Just some basic techniques to use in case you were ever cornered."

I already knew the answer to the question, though, and I was determined to change that.

With what looked to be great reluctance, she shook her head. "No."

"You should." Leaning back in the chair, I studied her slight frame, then met her eyes again. "If you know how to get out of a tight spot, you're less likely to panic if you ever get trapped in one. The first step is to not panic. But it's hard not to panic if you don't know how to get out of such a spot."

"I'm five foot nothing," she retorted. "What am I supposed to do if I get cornered by a guy *your* size?"

"Punch me in the throat," I offered. "Or the balls. But the throat would be better because a lot of guys are expecting a knee to the 'nads. Have your keys out when you're walking and keep one between your fingers. Punch somebody in the eye with that thing and they ain't going to be coming after you any time soon – they'll be looking for the remains of their eyeball. It's all about getting in the crucial shot to give you time to get away. But it takes practice."

Speculation entered her eyes. A few seconds passed before she nodded. "I'll look into it."

"Do better." Grabbing one of the napkins, I pulled a pen from the pocket of my flannel. "Here's my address. You can come by anytime after six, and I can work with you. I'm free, too."

She took the napkin, crumbling it up in her fist. "I'll think about it," she said again, shrugging out of the coat I'd given her. "I need to get back to work."

She left me sitting there, but I got up and followed her, watching from the windowed lobby of the hotel to make sure she made it to the door of her work without being disturbed.

I sure as hell hoped she came by and took me up on my offer. Not just because I wanted to see her. As cute as she was, as attracted as I was, the two of us just wouldn't ever work. I probably scared the hell out of her.

But I didn't like seeing that fear in her eyes.

It pissed me off.

"Is she okay?" Tony asked, joining me at the window.

"For now." I hitched up a shoulder in a shrug as the door swung shut behind her. "Thanks for letting us have a minute. She needed it."

"Do you have any idea what scared her so badly?" Tony asked as I shrugged back into my coat.

I drew in a breath, acutely aware of the new scent that now faintly clung to it. "Only that it was a guy," I replied. "She didn't want to talk about it."

The two of us eyed each other, and I suspected he was thinking the same thing I was. Judging by the look in his eyes, he felt as much disgust as I did. I turned away because I didn't want him to pick up on what else I was feeling.

An all-consuming rage.

Somebody, at some point, had hurt Raye.

14

Raye

"You are not actually considering going over there," I muttered to myself as I picked up a bucket of ribs.

Of course, the comment was moot, because the restaurant I'd decided to grab some food at was several blocks out of the way when compared to my place. But it was just down the street from the address Kane had given me.

As I checked the bag to make sure plastic ware and the sides hadn't been forgotten, I tried once more to have a rational conversation – with myself – about what I was doing.

I was going over to a total stranger's place because he'd offered to show me some self-defense moves.

The self-defense moves weren't a bad idea, and in retrospect, maybe it was something I should have done a long time ago.

But going over to a total stranger's place to *learn* them?

Was that a good idea?

He's Jake's friend, one half of me argued. *That automatically gives him points.*

The logical part of me pointed out, *you barely know Jake. So why does that count for anything?*

Okay, so I didn't really know my brother. I barely knew Michelle. But I was a decent judge of character, and I sensed both were good people, the kind of people you could trust. And they weren't the kind of people who'd be friends with sleazebags.

That automatically made Kane okay, by that rule.

But what if they didn't really know Kane?

I'd been going back and forth this way for nearly twenty minutes, ever since I'd left my apartment to get some food. It was almost six-thirty when I started down the block – away from the subway entrance.

Right toward the address Kane had given me.

"I really am doing this," I muttered.

Yes. Yes, I was.

I finally reached the address and had to draw the napkin from my pocket to double check – yep, this was the right place.

It was a garage. The *open* sign was off, and the hours of the place showed that it had closed at five-thirty.

"Okay," I mumbled, stepping back and wondering how I was supposed to get inside. That was when I noticed the bell by the door. Shrugging, I reached out to punch it.

It didn't even take a minute before I heard noise coming from the back of the garage. A tall form, lined in light, appeared in a doorway somewhere inside and my heart fluttered a little as I recognized Kane.

Tightening my grip on the bag of food, I held my breath as he drew closer.

He eyed me through the glass and a slow smile curled up

the corners of his mouth. The smile softened everything about him. I couldn't help but notice that. He looked less... aggressive. Even the scar bisecting his left eyebrow seemed less intimidating. My heart kicked up a few more beats as he unlocked the door.

I thought about how he'd kissed me.

Then I remembered slapping him, and I blushed.

"You came," he said, pushing the door open and stepping aside so I could enter.

"Yes." I moved in past him, feeling the heat of his skin reaching out to mine as I brushed by him. I shivered a little, wondering a bit at the enticing sensation. "I...um...I brought food. I figured we could...eat. I don't know if you've had dinner."

"I haven't," he told me. "But even if I had, I'm always hungry." He smiled as he said it, taking the bag from me. He gestured to a row of hooks on the far wall. "You can hang your coat up there if you want. We'll do this in the bay area."

I had no idea what that meant, but I figured I'd find out. Hanging up my ccat, I turned just as he relocked the doors. He shot me a grin. "If I don't lock up, people will try to come in, no matter if the sign's off and the hours are posted."

Nodding, I stood there, feeling awkward and out of place. I was glad when he gestured for me to follow him.

The bay, it turned out, was the area used for repairing the cars.

"Is this your garage?" I asked, eying the space that looked to have been cleared out just for us.

"Yes."

A heavy mat was spread on the floor, and I glanced at him. "You do this sort of thing a lot?"

"I've got sisters," he replied.

Did some small part of me deflate a little at that answer? Was that why he was doing this?

Why did you want him to be doing it? That logical part of me wouldn't shut up.

Biting my lip, I decided to just ignore it.

"So..." I folded my arms over my chest. "How do we start?"

MY ARMS HURT.

My upper body hurt.

My legs hurt.

"You should start doing push-ups," Kane said, dropping down next to me where I sprawled on the mat, trying to decide if I was ever going to move again.

I heard plastic rustle and lifted my head.

Okay, crap. Even my neck hurt.

It wasn't like a strain or anything, just a deep sort of muscle ache that let me know I'd been working parts of me that weren't used to being worked.

But none of that stopped me from dragging myself into an upright position as he peeled the top of the ribs off and the smell wafted out. My belly rumbled demandingly.

"I hate push-ups," I told Kane, taking one of the plates he offered me. They were plain, simple, and white. I wondered where they'd come from.

"They'll build your upper body strength," he said with a shrug. He had a healthy serving of ribs on his own plate and watched me as he selected one. "The stronger you are, the better you'll be able to hurt somebody if you ever need to use any of this stuff I'm teaching you."

He couldn't have said anything more likely to convince me.

I WAS BACK over at the garage for the third time in as many days. School started back up the following week, and I wouldn't be able to come over as much – I'd already told Kane that, and he said we'd work around my schedule as needed. I was nowhere confident enough that I could use any of the moves he'd shown me yet.

Of course, sometimes I had trouble concentrating on what he was showing me. It wasn't that he was hard to follow, but...well...sometimes he *did* make it hard. Hard to pay attention. Hard to think. Hard to do anything but wish I could be normal, wish I knew how to do something about the heat he caused inside me.

I wished I knew what to do when our hands accidentally touched, and sparks erupted between us.

I wished I knew how to close the distance between us and kiss him, or how to handle the lulls in the conversation when we were eating.

If they bothered him, he didn't let on, but for me, those lulls were emotionally charged, and I wanted, more than anything, to be the kind of girl who could take the bull by the horns and lean over toward him during one of those silences, press my lips to his mouth and just...see what happened.

Last night, he'd ordered pizza for us, and those silences had happened several times.

Tonight, I had Chinese, and I had no doubt those silences would happen a couple more times.

If I wasn't so awkward, so bad at the man/woman shit, I could handle this.

But even the few dates I'd been on had been disasters, and the attempts at sex had been nothing but a study in awkwardness and pain, at least from my point of view.

"Stop worrying about it, or you'll make it worse," I told myself as I rang the doorbell, my arms laden with Chinese food.

Since I didn't know what he liked, I'd ordered three different entrees and had a mess of egg rolls and crab Rangoon. One thing I'd noticed – the man could put food away like nothing I'd ever seen.

My arms ached a little as I went to ring the doorbell. I'd taken him at his word and started doing push-ups.

I could manage maybe ten. When I told him that last night, I'd expected him to laugh, but Kane just nodded. "Next week, do fifteen. Then go for twenty. You'll get up there."

I couldn't imagine doing *twenty* push-ups. The pitiful ten I was doing now took all the strength I possessed.

The door opened, and Kane stepped aside to let me in. I smiled a little easier today, not as nervous as I'd been the first night.

"That smells good," he said, locking the door behind me. He took the bags as I hung up my coat.

"I didn't know what you liked so I got a couple of things." When I turned to face him, I tensed, finding him standing closer than I'd expected. "Ah..." I licked my lips.

His gaze dropped to my mouth, then moved back to meet my eyes.

A rush of heat exploded through my chest. What was that?

A grin crooked his lips. "I'm easy, Raye. I like a little bit of everything. I'm sure whatever you have is fine."

I nodded, feeling like an idiot.

I also felt more than a little hopeless, because another one of those moments had just slid through my fingertips, and I didn't know how to do jack about it.

"RELAX," Kane said, his voice rough in my ear.

It was almost impossible to relax, considering the position we were in.

He held in what could almost be called a lover's embrace, with my back tucked up against his front, both of his arms around me. He didn't hold me too tight, but his arms weren't loose enough for me to escape either. I was supposed to be using some of the techniques he'd shown me to break free.

A crazed mix of fear and want slithered through me, though, which was making it almost impossible to think. And he wanted me to *relax*?

"Remember what I told you," he said, speaking in a tone that was almost soothing despite the rough, raw grittiness of his tone. "A man's gotta be able to see and breathe to do much of anything, so what are you going to do?"

His words jarred loose the proper action, and I jerked back with my head.

He moved his just in time, but he'd told me he knew to

move because he was expecting it. Anybody who came up and grabbed me out of the blue wasn't likely to be prepared for a fight – most predators weren't.

"Good. Now...next?"

I was supposed to stun him enough that he let me go.

I brought up my tennis-clad foot and slammed it down on his instep. He was wearing work boots and had told me not to pull the hit – *you're little, and you need to prepare for this. Give it all you got.*

He grunted, a sound of pain in his voice. "Good one. Next?"

I drove back with my elbow and hit a torso that felt as hard as a tree trunk, but he let me go. I rushed to get away before he could grab me again, which would start the process all over.

"Good job."

As I turned, I found him grinning at me, the grin that turned his dark, brooding face into one that was good-looking enough to take my breath away.

I could pretend that it was adrenaline, though.

15

Raye

My heart was still racing twenty minutes later when he led me into the back of the garage. There was a small apartment set up back there, and I looked around, curiously. "I figured it would be easier to eat Chinese at a table," Kane said, gesturing for me to sit.

I did so, arms wrapped around myself.

He noticed. "Are you cold?"

"No." I had to fight to keep my teeth from chattering, but it had nothing to do with cold and everything to do with nerves.

My skin felt like it was on fire, alive with sensation.

It had been like that ever since the first time he'd come up behind me and wrapped his arms around me.

Odd that *terror* hadn't been the first thing to go through me.

Odd that I wasn't terrified now, alone in this room with him.

But while fear was a shadow in the back of my mind, it

didn't loom over me. Not even when he sat down across from me at a table so small his knee touched mine as we began to help ourselves to the food he'd spread out in front of us.

"You're doing pretty good with everything," Kane said after taking a bite of fried rice.

"Thanks." I shot him a smile and tried to pretend I wasn't nervous as hell.

His gaze lingered on mine a little longer this time.

Throughout the meal, those lingering gazes happened more and more, and by the time we were done eating, I felt like I might come out of my skin. I was the first one on my feet. "Here," I said, voice higher than normal. "Let me help you clean up."

I turned away before he could say anything, arms full of nearly empty containers. Moving to the counter by the fridge, I asked, "You want to keep this for lunch tomorrow? I don't want it."

"It doesn't matter," he said from right behind me.

I jumped at the nearness of his voice and froze when his arms came around me, caging me in where I stood. Trapped. Yet oddly, I didn't feel that way. I felt *surrounded* by him, but not in a bad way.

"Turn around and look at me, Raye," he whispered, mouth right next to my ear.

Tension made me awkward and stiff as I did so, and I tried to tell myself to relax, but unfortunately, there was no coaxing voice to remind me of what came next as I turned to meet his eyes. We weren't out in the garage, and he wasn't teaching some move that might help me avoid an attack this time.

Sensation flooded me, swelling through me so big and overwhelming I didn't know how to handle it.

Everything seemed clearer and sharper as I met his eyes. I could see striations of a lighter brown cutting through the dark chocolate of his gaze and I could make out each individual eyelash. He reached up to cup my cheek, and the callouses on his palm felt exquisite against my skin. I wanted to rub myself against his touch like a cat.

So why don't you?

That soft voice inside me urged me to be bold, but I didn't know how. Didn't know if it was the right time or even if I should.

"What are you thinking?" he asked. "Your thoughts are racing. I can see them all flashing through your eyes, but I can't keep up with them."

My breath hitched in my chest.

Here was my chance. I could tell him what I wanted and let him decide. I thought maybe he wanted me. He'd kissed me before, and the tension in the air between us couldn't be entirely one-sided, could it?

I licked my lips, and when I did, his gaze dropped straight to my mouth, and a strange noise escaped him.

Tell him...

"Will you kiss me?" I blurted out.

His lids drooped low over his eyes, but that didn't quite prevent me from seeing the way the pupils swelled, all but swallowing the dark brown of his irises. A ruddy flush settled across his cheekbones, and he swayed forward just the slightest bit.

But he didn't kiss me.

Instead, he reached up and cupped my cheek.

"Why?"

What do you mean, why?

"Um... because I want you to." I had to fight the urge to pull away from him, and there was also a faint, hysterical giggle bubbling up in my throat, although I somehow managed to keep that held back. He continued to study me, and when he didn't do anything, I arched my back, forcing some distance between us. "Unless you don't..."

He pressed his thumb to my lips. "I've thought about kissing you again pretty much since the first time I did it, even when I didn't think I'd ever see you again. But since that one ended with you slapping me..."

"I shouldn't have done that," I said weakly. "It was New Year's Eve."

"I disagree. You'd just had two assholes hassle you. New Year's Eve or not, I had some seriously bad timing." His gaze swept down to my mouth and heat lashed me from the top of my head to the soles of my feet. "Still...I wanted to do it again. I still want to."

"Then why aren't you?"

"Good question, Raye." His gaze held mine as he slowly lowered his head and brushed his lips against mine.

That was all he did at first, rub his lips against mine.

And he *watched* me.

Unprepared for that, I couldn't tear my gaze from his, held captured by those dark brown eyes as he brushed one feather-light kiss after another against my mouth. A low, vibrating noise emanated from somewhere, and I didn't realize it was me until after I'd moaned a second time.

By then, my mouth had parted, and he took advantage of

it, sliding his tongue out to lick at the small opening. That had me opening wider for him. He tasted so good...

He groaned against my mouth, finally deepening the kiss and his lids drooped all the way closed. As if that alone was all I'd been waiting for, I finally let myself close my eyes and gave into that kiss completely.

He slid one arm around me, pressing his palm against my ass and drawing me flat against him.

Heat exploded through me as his cock swelled against my belly.

It was a reaction I wasn't prepared for. Any time I'd ever felt a man's cock, it had caused a mix of terror and trepidation, although there had only been a handful of instances, mostly on dates gone bad, back when I thought maybe I could *make* myself be normal.

But this was new.

This was...kind of wonderful.

An empty ache centered low in my belly.

It pulsed, echoing through my entire body, and when his cock throbbed, those pulsing sensations started all over, as if in answer to some call from his body that mine sensed.

He boosted me up onto the counter at my back, and I gasped as he tugged me close. With the movement, his cock nestled up against me, and instinctively, I arched closer. That had those pulsing sensations panging that much stronger, and I felt his cock more fully now.

"Can I touch you?" he whispered against my mouth.

"You already are."

He laughed against my lips, and it was a pained sound. "Not what I meant."

I got his meaning a moment later as he placed his hand on

my side, under the hem of my shirt. "I want to take this off and touch you," he said, the words blunt. "I want to touch your tits...taste them. Can I?"

The stark, raw words had me jerking in his arms, and I pulled back, staring at him.

My breath came in harsh pants as I processed what he'd just said and what I felt about it. The answer, I already knew – everything in me was screaming *yes*. But I'd never expected to have a guy say something like that to me, and I didn't know how I felt.

But I think I kind of liked it.

Slowly, I nodded and reached for the hem of my shirt, but he brushed my hands away, guiding them back to my sides. He was the one to peel the shirt off, and when he was done, he tossed it onto the seat just behind him. The kitchen was so small, there was barely room for the table and appliances. If I reached out with my foot, I'd be touching the chair I'd used for dinner.

I didn't understand why the small area and the big man didn't make me feel trapped.

But I felt...safe.

And...*wanted*.

His hands came up, cupping my breasts, and I jolted at the sensation. I'd been braced for...something. An echo of memory tried to take over, cruel hands, pinching, pulling.

But it faded under the gentle motions of Kane's hands, the way he tugged lightly at my nipples through the bra. Then... I gasped as he dipped his head and took me in his mouth, his teeth lightly raking the nipple through the damp material of my bra. He worried and tugged and sucked until my nipple was tight, aching, and full, and everything he did sent a jolt of sensation shooting straight down to... there.

I was wet, something I didn't realize until I started to squirm, and my panties rubbed back and forth over me.

He reached between my thighs.

I froze.

"Easy, Raye," he murmured against my flesh.

But I couldn't.

Tension shot through me, and slowly, Kane raised his head to look at me. I don't know what he saw, but I had a good idea. It was probably the same look I saw on my face on the mornings when the nightmares brought me gasping into wakefulness, and I'd rush into the bathroom and turn on the water, hoping to wash away the nausea and the taste brought on by dreams I never could quite remember.

"It's okay," he said again, his hand now resting flat on my upper thigh. "We can stop anytime you want."

I want...

That was the scared part of me that wanted to shout. The words were even boiling up my throat.

But a bigger part of me needed to fight those words back, and I swallowed hard against them, forcing them back down my throat, locking them away where they wouldn't spill out the moment I opened my mouth.

"I'm scared," I whispered.

"I know." He cupped my cheek again and brought our mouths together. The soft, sweet kiss was seductive, and before I knew it, I was leaning into him, my arms around his neck, my knees hugging his thighs. When he broke away, I tried to follow, but he held me back just the slightest, gripping my upper arms. "Look at me, Raye."

I blinked my eyes and focused on his face, hunger and want humming in my veins in a way I'd never felt before.

"We can stop whenever you want," he said again. "But if you trust me, I'll make you feel like you've never felt before."

I TOLD HIM YES.

I barely remembered doing it, hardly believed that low, throaty-sounding voice was mine, but I told him yes, and he'd picked me up.

Now, I was lying on the couch, half on top of him. He had one hand on my ass and the other cupped the back of my neck.

I moaned against him as the hand on my ass moved to my hip, and he began to drag me up and down against his erection, eliciting an entirely new series of reactions. I shuddered at the feel, going a little wild when he pulsed against me.

He muttered something under his breath, then pulled back.

"I want to take you to my bed, okay?"

I blinked at him, the words not making sense.

Crooking a grin at me, Kane said, "Let me take you to bed. I want you naked, and I want to do things to you, but I can't out here. There's no room."

I had no idea what he meant, but if he kept making me feel like this, he could take me to the moon, and I wouldn't mind.

"Okay," I whispered against his mouth.

He sat up, holding me against him like I weighed nothing. In a series of quick movements that had the world swirling around me, he carried me into another room. This one was dark, and panic filled me. "Lights?" I whispered.

He let go of me, one hand reaching out to the table by the bed and a soft, pale gold filled the room.

"Better?" he asked as he laid me down on the bed.

I nodded, bracing myself as he knelt between my thighs. He'd come down on top of me now, and I wasn't sure if I could take it. He read something on my face and laid a hand on my calf. "We stop when you say stop," he told me.

I nodded, still nervous.

He gave me that same, lopsided smile and reached for the waistband of my jeans. "Can we take these off?"

"Yeah. I guess."

He peeled the jeans away but left my panties on. I was glad I'd put on one of the pretty lingerie sets I'd bought from work as I lay in front of him. The silk and lace set was steel blue, and while the bra wasn't a push-up, it made the most of my curves.

"You're beautiful," he said in a gruff voice, laying a hand on my thigh and stroking down.

I wanted to tell him thank you, but I was shaking hard and didn't want the words to come out a wobble.

He moved, and I tensed even more, even as I tried to force my body to relax. He did lay down – but not on me. He sprawled between my thighs and pressed a kiss to my belly button as he toyed with the lacy waistband of my panties. "So pretty," he murmured.

I lay like a stick under him, and he was telling me how pretty I was. He had to notice I was about as receptive as a doormat.

Not normal, not *normal*, I shrieked mentally.

But if he noticed, he acted otherwise. He eased lower, rubbing his lips over my belly.

I shivered.

He had to notice!

But he just continued to kiss and stroke and rub his way down until he was nuzzling me through my panties.

"Raye?" he whispered.

"Y-y-yes?"

"I want to eat you up," he muttered.

My mind went blank. Eat me...?

"Can I eat your pussy?" he asked.

It was a shocking question, and one that managed to shock the tension right out of me. I went lax as I tried furiously to figure out how to answer that question, but my body had already figured it out and knew the answer. While I was still confused and thinking, my hips were lifting toward him, and he didn't wait for any other answer.

His mouth touched me through the silk and lace, and a startled cry escaped me.

"Raye?"

"I..." Sucking in a breath, I closed my eyes.

"Should I stop?" he asked.

"No!" I shoved my hips toward him again, my body taking over once more.

He pressed his mouth more firmly against me – and this time, my panties weren't in the way. He'd moved them, and I felt his *tongue* licking inside me, around me...he sucked on my clitoris, that mysterious spot that magazines kept saying could make me fly, but I'd never flown, not even once.

Until now.

He sucked on me, and I went straight up into the stratosphere, like somebody had put me on a rocket. It was the sweetest, most unexpected thing I'd ever experienced.

Then, while I was adjusting to that sensation, he pushed two fingers inside me.

It sent me straight to the moon.

I wailed out his name, and without thinking, reached down and twined my fingers in his hair, arching and moving against his mouth as he did exactly what he'd asked me permission for – he feasted.

He wasn't quiet or delicate about it, either.

He made noise, grunting and groaning, talking to me and telling me how he loved my taste, urging me to ride his mouth, fuck his face and his hand.

Every dirty word urged me on, and I found myself doing exactly what he'd said – fucking his face, fucking his hand, begging him for more until the pleasure inside me was so intense, I couldn't talk for it. I was barely able to make weak, mewling sounds as I begged him with my body and hands.

He thrust and twisted his fingers, curling them inside and sucking on my clit. Then it was happening – I felt that tightening sensation in me, felt it squeezing me, squeezing *him*, and I was coming.

Lights exploded in front of my eyes as a raw, savage sort of fury and bliss blasted through me, rolling through my body in wave after wave.

I thought it just might kill me.

16

Kane

My heart raced, and my cock pounded like a bad tooth, but lying between Raye's thighs with my cheek on her belly, I felt better than I had in...hell. A long time. Even though I was probably going to get myself off in the shower – several times over – I felt almost stupid, I was so content.

Bringing Raye to orgasm had been one of the sweetest things I'd ever done, and I didn't even mind how goofy that sounded.

She stirred underneath me, and I shifted away immediately, not wanting her to feel trapped.

I had no idea who'd hurt her or scared her, but if I ever found him, I was going to rearrange his insides – via his throat.

As I stretched out on the bed next to her, she rolled onto her side and pushed up onto her elbow, staring at me with wide, dazed eyes.

"Still scared?" I asked, cupping her cheek.

She didn't answer, though. She swallowed, the color fading from her cheeks as she looked down at me.

I was about to ask her what was wrong when she laid a hand on my cock.

I almost came off the bed. Shit, if she'd done much more than touch me, I might have fucking come.

As it was, I was hard-pressed not to arch into her touch. Gritting my teeth, I lay there as she unzipped my jeans and freed the button, struggling with both tasks. She wouldn't look at me either.

I might have attributed it to shyness, except her entire body was trembling.

I felt her shaking like a leaf against me, and it wasn't until she went to duck her head that I understood just what it was that had her so freaked out.

As much as I wanted to feel that pretty mouth wrapped around my dick, I didn't want to do it at any cost to her.

"Hey..."

I caught her shoulders, tugging on her until she came back up to me. It didn't take much. She clearly didn't need much urging because she half-flopped against my chest, lying with her ear pressed to my pounding heart.

"I don't want you doing anything you're not ready for," I whispered against her hair even as my cock continued to pulse and jerk, ready for the attention I'd just denied it.

Stupid prick.

"I don't know how to do this." Her voice trembled and cracked.

"You don't *have* to."

"But I want..." She made a small, frustrated sound in her

throat and rose up onto her elbow, staring down at me. "I want to know how to do this."

I could tell by the way she was talking, the way she eyed me that *this* wasn't just about giving me a blow-job either.

"Give me your hand," I said softly. "Get comfortable next to me."

She wiggled around a little and tucked her head into the crook of my arm and shoulder before tucking her hand into mine. "I'm going to put your hand on my cock. Then I'll let go. If you want to touch me, you do it. You do what feels good to you. If you don't like it, then you stop."

"I...how...okay."

I could hear a hundred questions in her voice, but she let it go with that simple comment, and I squeezed my eyes shut as I guided her hand to my erect dick, grimacing in tortured pleasure as she lightly closed her fingers around me. "Like this?" she whispered. "I want it to feel good to you."

"Baby, you've got my dick in your hands. There's very little you could do that wouldn't feel good," I told her.

But still, all she did was hold me, and after a moment, I reached down and covered her hand with mine lightly. "Like this," I said, guiding her hand up, then down. "You can do this if you want." And because I'd noticed already that it turned her on when I talked to her, I added, "Because if you don't jack me off, I'll be doing it after you leave. You've got me harder than a fucking stone. Can't you tell?"

A low whimper escaped her, and she did one slow, tentative stroke down, then up, following the tutelage of my guiding hand.

"I'm going to let go. You do what you want...just, please, don't stop touching me."

To my surprise, a faint giggle escaped her. "You make it sound so dire."

"I feel like I'm going to come any damn second, so it feels pretty damn dire." I arched up into her touch, aching for more of those soft, butterfly caresses – and harder, dirtier ones. Whatever she wanted to give, I wanted it.

After a few strokes, she grew more certain and started to pump her hand faster, harder.

I grunted, and she paused. "Is that too much? Is it wrong?"

"No. You can't do this wrong...don't stop, Raye," I said. I was ready to beg, but I wasn't going to tell her that.

Not yet, at least.

"Show me more," she whispered in my ear.

Covering her hand with mine, I tightened her fist around me until it was just shy of pain. "Don't let me hurt you," I said, thrusting up until I was fucking her hand. "I like it... tight...like that. Twist your hand...there. That's it...fuck, Raye."

Her breath hitched, trembled a little and I felt the hard scrape of one nipple through her bra. I wanted to roll her onto her back and come between her thighs, driving into her.

But I held still, doing nothing more than thrusting into her fisted hand as she lay breathing next to me, her body quivering and each breath shuddering out of her.

I moaned as the heat gathered in my balls, warning me of the climax that was rushing at me.

"I'm going to come," I said, the words coming out in a pant. Lifting my head, I urged her to meet my gaze. "Stop now, or you're going to get it on you."

I didn't want her to stop. But it was her call.

She kept pumping her hand, up and down on my cock and I lowered my gaze, staring at how I filled her small palm to overflowing, the head of my prick disappearing inside her fist before rapidly reappearing, bobbing with each stroke. A small drop of pre-come appeared, and she paused.

Looking up, I saw that she was watching, too.

Taking my hand away from hers, I rubbed my thumb over that clear drop, smearing it across the head, then lifting my hand to her face. "Do you want to taste it?

She surprised the hell out of me by licking my thumb. My cock jerked in jealous reaction. "You're going to kill me," I mumbled. "You're so fucking hot."

Without thinking, I caught the back of her neck and hauled her up, so I could kiss her. She froze at first, then relaxed, opening her mouth as she began to stroke me anew, her rhythm faster and harder.

"That's it, Raye..." I muttered against her lips. "More... shit, that's good...gimme your mouth."

She whimpered, straining against me, and I felt every delicate curve, every sweet swell.

The head of my cock pulsed as she swept her thumb over it, sending sensations raining down, making my balls draw up tight against me. Hot-cold chills raced up my spine, then retraced their tracks, centering low at the base as everything in me seemed to center on my cock and the sweet pleasure of her pumping up and down.

The climax blindsided me, coming at me harder and faster than I'd expected. Semen jetted from my cock, splashing on my belly and chest, coating her fingers. She stopped, but I closed my hand over hers and guided her back into rhythm. "Don't fucking stop now," I said, pleading with her.

She hesitated a moment, then continued to move, and I showed her how to squeeze and milk every last drop from me. Each touch now was a lesson in pleasure-pain that was almost too much to handle, and I shuddered from head to toe.

When it was over, I closed my eyes, letting her hand go. My heart pounded. My breath raced in and out of my lungs, and my entire body felt numb, like I'd just ran ten miles.

My cock jerked again, and a harsh groan escaped me when she flexed her fingers once more.

Then she pulled back, wiggling away.

I laid there, not thinking much of it.

"Where's your bathroom?" she asked, her voice halting.

That was the first indicator that something was wrong.

The second came from the slamming of the bathroom door.

But the real clue was when she came out and all but dove into her clothes, pulling them on so rapidly, I heard a seam tear.

Swearing, I sat up, grabbing a t-shirt from the foot of the bed to wipe off with. Tossing it aside, I stood up and reached for Raye, but she dodged me. "I need to get going," she said, her voice tight and high.

"Are you okay?" I demanded.

"I'm fine!" She gave me a bright, too-sunny smile as she all but ran out of the bedroom and grabbed her boots from where she'd dropped them in the living room. "I just...I have to go!"

Feeling helpless, I stood there as she finished dressing.

I stood there as she fled through the door.

"What the hell?"

I WAS STILL BROODING over it all a couple hours later.

I could have handled things differently. I could have handled things a *lot* differently.

Like not making her jack you off? a sarcastic voice suggested from the back of my mind.

I didn't know if that was what had done it or what. But something had upset her, and she'd torn out of there like her ass was on fire.

"Man, if Jake finds out about this…"

No sooner had I said those words than I realized the enormity of what I was doing.

Shit.

I'd made out with his kid sister – the kid sister he'd just found out about.

He was going to fucking kick my ass over this.

"What in the hell am I doing?" I asked myself. There was no answer in the small, quiet apartment, but I hadn't expected one.

If I was smart, I'd back away now.

But I knew, as sure as I was standing there, if Raye were to knock on that door and ask me to kiss her again, I'd be all over it.

If she'd let me, if she was ready, I'd be all over *her*.

And the hell if that made any sense. I'd never done anything other than casual, but nothing about this felt casual. Nothing at all.

17

Raye

I was exhausted, the weight of the week wearing down on me like a wet cloak. As I trudged up the stairs to Michelle's apartment, I reached up to rub my eyes, taking care not to smudge the makeup. I probably shouldn't have worn any. At some point tonight, I was going to rub my eyes, and I would smear the makeup and end up looking like a panda.

Hell, if I was smart, I would have canceled because knowing my luck, I was going to end up falling asleep right in the middle of the dinner.

Jake and Michelle had invited me over earlier in the week, and if I had realized how tired I was going to be, I would have said no. But that was before...well, everything.

Before I ran into Chad.

Before I started going over to Kane's.

Definitely before Kane had introduced me to things I hadn't known about myself.

If only that had been all that happened this week, I would have considered the week a good one.

But there was the weird thing going on between me and Kane – it was going to get weirder now, wasn't it? I barely knew how to handle it as it was. Actually, that was wrong. I didn't know how to handle it. I'd run away from him, hadn't I?

Would he expect me to sleep with him if I went back?

Did I *want* to sleep with him?

That shouldn't be a confusing thing, but it was. It was even more confusing now than it had been before he touched me, too. Once he touched me and made me feel all those…wow…feelings, it'd made things worse, because suddenly, I was wondering if maybe I *could* be normal. What would happen if I slept with him? Nothing with him had been anything like it had been the other times. So, wouldn't things be different if I tried to have sex with him?

But if I failed…

These were the things that had kept me up at night, and on the rare occasion I had fallen asleep, nightmares about Chad had woken me up.

I'd known Chad back when I was still attending school at Texas A&M. To say things hadn't been pleasant was putting it mildly and I didn't like to think about that time – at all.

Who would?

Considering everything that had happened, nobody *sane* would enjoy reminiscing.

I could have gone the rest of my life without seeing Chad, or anybody else from that school.

Coming to a stop in front of Michelle and Jake's door, I tightened my hands on the salad bowl and tried to put everything out of my mind. Thinking about it now was just crazy.

If I kept this up, Michelle or Jake would notice something, and that was the last thing I needed.

After one last look at the salad I'd put together, I knocked on the door. Michelle told me I didn't need to bring anything, but I had insisted, and she had finally said a salad would go great with the steaks she had planned.

At the time, a steak had sounded divine. I hadn't had a good steak in a long time, but now I was wondering if I'd be able to eat at all.

Michelle opened the door and greeted me with a big smile and a kiss on the cheek. "Let me take this," she said, grasping the bowl and tugging it from my hands.

As I came inside, Jake appeared in the doorway of the kitchen. He grinned at me and came over, greeting me with a quick hug. Warmth unfurled in me at the casual affection.

My brother. I still didn't know what to think about that. I knew I loved it.

But beyond that? It was just so mind-boggling. I'd spent so much of my life being...*alone*. Even before this chasm had formed between my mother and me, I'd felt more like an afterthought in her life.

It wasn't that she didn't love me. I knew she did. But I also knew I was an inconvenience; she hadn't planned on having a baby. Now that I was an adult, I was just another person she could use.

Mom had called twice, leaving messages for me. I hadn't called her back.

I didn't want to listen to more requests for money, and I wasn't ready to share Jake with her yet. I was greedy about him right now.

Besides, her interest in him would only be superficial.

The main reason she even called was for the money anyway, although right now, I couldn't fault her for it. I had a brother. Sometimes it made me feel generous enough that I *almost* thought about giving her the money she wanted.

But I barely had it to spare.

"You look tired," Jake said as he pulled away.

"Oh, it's just been a busy week at work," I hedged, pasting a smile on my face. I knew how to fake my way through just about anything, and he studied me for another moment before nodding and pulling back.

"You're not working full time while you go to school, are you?" he asked.

"No." I grimaced and added, "I would if my class load would let me, but my courses are pretty intense."

He gestured for me to follow him into the kitchen, and I joined him at the island where he appeared to be slicing up potatoes. "Michelle says you're going to school for forensic accounting. What's that like?"

"Depends on the class." With a shrug, I slid my coat off and looked around, wondering where to put it. "Some of the classes are boring as hell. I'm almost done with the basic accounting classes, but those about put me to sleep. Others...? They're fascinating."

"Here, I can take your coat," Michelle said, putting the salad in the fridge. "I'm just on standby until it's time to cook the steak." She winked at me and took the coat. "We're reversed in this house. Jake can cook almost anything, but anytime he tries to make a steak, it's tougher than shoe leather."

"You can't really be a Texan." I turned my eyes to him.

He held up his hands. "Hey, I'm a New Yorker now."

"With that accent?" I teased, surprised at how natural it felt to do so.

"I wouldn't be talking about accents if I were you." He winked at me, pointing his knife at me before returning to the task of chopping up potatoes. "What can I say? I was...otherwise engaged during the formative years when I should have learned important things, like how to make steak and all that."

Whatever response I might have had died on my tongue as I recalled just how he'd been engaged. Being in prison. For something he hadn't done. I looked away hurriedly before he saw anything on my face, but it was too late.

"Hey." I glanced up at Jake to see him watching me with knowing eyes. "Don't look like that," he said, giving me a smile. "It's over and done. And even if I could go back and change things...I don't know if I would."

I stared at him. "You wouldn't?"

"Oh, if I could have my mom back..." He sighed, shaking his head. His gaze returned to the task at hand, and I watched as he scooped up the potatoes into a colander to wash them. He kept speaking as he washed. "It's a hard thing to think about. I can't bring her back, and I know that. But the road all that put me on led me to Michelle. I wouldn't give her up for anything."

Michelle moved to stand behind him, sliding her arms around his waist and dropping a kiss onto his cheek. "Same here, handsome."

It was an intimate moment, and I stared at my hands until it seemed to pass.

They had a lot of those moments, something I couldn't help but envy.

Michelle was the one to break away, and she met my eyes, smiling as she offered me some wine.

"I probably shouldn't," I said, despite the longing I felt inside. "I just might fall asleep."

"Then you fall asleep. If you need it that bad, then you must *really* need it," she said, unconcerned. She moved to the fridge and pulled a bottle out. "It will keep me from drinking alone. He won't touch a drop until the food is done anyway, and I'm dying to try this new red out."

After much coaxing from Michelle and Jake, the two of us retreated into the living room, and I sat curled across from her with the glass of wine in my hand, my feet tucked under me.

"You really do look tired. Are you sure it's just work?" Michelle asked.

"I..." Glancing past her, I eyed the doorway to the kitchen and finally confessed, "I'm having trouble sleeping."

Propping her chin on her hand, Michelle sipped at her wine before asking, "Any idea why?"

Oh, yes...

A laugh bubbled in my throat, but I swallowed it back. If I started laughing, I might just end up crying.

"Things between you and Jake...they seem so...easy," I said, instead of answering.

"They weren't always." She shrugged, looking down into her glass. "You wouldn't believe the mess I was before I found him."

"What do you mean?"

A touch of color pinkened her cheeks, and she glanced past me, her gaze lingering on the doorway to the kitchen for a long moment before she finally looked back at me. "That's a long, long story. Let's just suffice it to say that Jake just...got me."

"How?" I persisted.

"In every way a man can possibly *get* a woman," she said, lifting one shoulder in a shrug. "He's my best friend. I can tell him anything. He can tell me anything. But...it's not just that. He changed things for me. I'd been out on dates before him. Not a lot, but..." She huffed out a breath, then got up.

I frowned at her as she came and sat close to me. She wasn't so close I could say she was intruding on my space, but she was a lot closer than she had been.

"Just how personal do you want to get here?"

The question took me aback. "What do you mean?"

Michelle lifted a shoulder. "I've just got...well, some unpleasant things in my past and Jake helped me work past them. We're where we are now because of that, because he cared enough and because I trusted him."

It was an odd, awkward start to any conversation, and part of me wanted to bow out of it. But the rest of me...

"What kind of things?"

"I was assaulted when I was younger," she said in a matter-of-fact tone. "Up until Jake, I couldn't really trust a guy." She rolled her eyes. "I'm not talking sexual healing or anything..." She paused, winking at me. "I'm sure you want to hear that about your brother. But it wasn't that. Jake just... cared. That's what it takes."

A breath escaped me as I stared at her, saying words that resonated inside me in ways I couldn't explain. *He cared.*

"I can't be with guys," I blurted out, the words escaping me in a rush, squeezing out of a throat gone tight. "I'm not... I'm not normal. Not like that."

Michelle's eyes widened, then softened. I tensed as she leaned in and wrapped an arm around my shoulders. "Honey, don't say that. You damn well *are* normal."

She didn't push for details, but I felt an odd need to talk. Shooting a look toward the door where I could hear Jake moving around, I bit my lip and finally met her eyes once more. "But I'm not," I whispered. "I've gone out with guys, tried to be with them. There was this one...Michelle, I *really* liked him, and we went out, and I thought things were going to be fine, but he touched me and..."

She caught my hands before I could vault up off the couch.

She quirked up a brow. "Did it ever occur to you that maybe he was doing things wrong?" I opened my mouth, then closed it. "Is that a no?" she asked gently. When I didn't answer, she squeezed my fingers gently. "It's a two-party thing, sweetheart. If you weren't ready and he was trying to push you, then that's on him. A good guy knows when it's time and when the woman isn't quite ready."

I thought about Kane and how *he* had been able to make me feel, and without realizing it, I started to smile.

"What?" Michelle asked.

I blinked at her, confused. "What *what*?"

"That smile." She pointed at me, her eyes narrowed. "That's...what's with that smile?"

"I..." Biting my lip, I squirmed uncomfortably on the couch and glanced around, but there wasn't a polite escape route, and part of me wanted to talk about this – what if it *wasn't* me? "There *was* this one guy. He...um...well. I felt almost normal with him."

"Almost normal?" Michelle quoted. "As in...he turned you on?"

Blood rushed to my face, and I cursed my pale complexion, the bane of many a redhead. "Um..."

"He did *more*, didn't he?" Michelle's face lit with a grin, and she huddled in closer like we were sharing secrets. "See! I told you it wasn't you! Who is it? It happened here? In New York?"

"Ah...yeah." Shrugging, I said, "It's just this guy I know." I hedged away from sharing just *who* it was. I didn't know how either of them would feel if they knew there might be something between Kane and me. Were there rules to this family thing? Yet another thing I didn't know.

"Are you dating?" she asked, eyes rounding.

"No!" I blurted it out without thinking how it sounded. Trying to cover my embarrassment, I added, "We just met. I mean...oh, shit. That sounds even worse."

"Honey..." Laughing, Michelle leaned over and hugged me. "If he's helping you get over some bad experiences, then you need to go after him. He's probably good for you." She shrugged and glanced back over her shoulder. "Jake was good for me."

As if on cue, Jake called for Michelle, and she grimaced. "That's my cue." She stood up but held out a hand.

"What?" I asked warily.

"You're coming with me," she announced calmly. "I don't want you bolting when you start thinking about the fact that you opened up and suddenly get embarrassed."

"I..." Abruptly, it hit me what I'd been talking about – and with *who*. Shooting a look at the door, I thought about doing just what she mentioned.

Bolting.

But she stood there, hand outstretched and eyes patient.

She had trusted me enough to talk.

Maybe the girl-guy thing wasn't the only thing that was two-party.

Slowly, I put my hand in hers and let her help me get to my feet.

She looped our arms together. "It's nice having a girl to talk to about this," she said, leaning her head in closer to mine. "It's not something you talk about with just the casual friend, you know? But you and me...Raye, it's almost like we're sisters."

That didn't really hit me until I sat down.

And then, I felt a little dazed over what she'd just said.

Almost like we're sisters.

And...

It's nice having a girl to talk to about this.

That was something I'd never had.

And it was something I was starting to realize I desperately needed.

18

Kane

"Hand me that wrench – no. That's not a wrench...to the left. Yep." I smiled at Austen as he turned the tool over and got back to work on the car that had come in late in the afternoon.

Mom had asked if I'd mind letting him come over and help at the shop on Fridays and the weekends, trying to keep him out of trouble. I didn't *mind*, per se, but he wanted a job. One that paid. And he knew jackshit about cars.

So far, he hadn't been able to help with much except empty garbage and clean up my messes.

Of course, that was shit I hadn't had to do, so maybe it would work out, and I could always teach him.

It wasn't like I'd been born knowing one end of the engine from the other.

"Come over here and watch what I'm doing," I told him, moving over so he'd have room on the ground next to me.

"You get filthy doing this," Austen complained, but he sat down anyway.

"That's why I told you to wear old clothes."

We worked in companionable enough silence – or rather, I worked, and he watched, asking questions from time to time. I pointed things out that made sense to point out, and after a few more minutes, I turned over the wrench to him. "You do the last few, okay?"

He gave me a panicked look. "What if I mess it up?"

Rolling my eyes, I said, "That would be hard. Just do those four, right there." I pointed and made sure he saw, then rose.

As I headed over to the work table to grab my water, I heard the buzzer in the back.

Frowning, I checked the time, then went to go look. I had a hope it was Raye, but I wasn't really expecting it to be. After the way she'd run out, I didn't know if I'd ever see her again. It wasn't like I could call Jake and ask for her number, either. He'd punch my teeth out.

Running my tongue over said teeth, I peered through the small square of glass that served as a window and had to bite back a scowl at the sight of the woman on the other side.

Opening the door, I frowned down at Calie. "It's not a good time, Calie. I'm busy."

She touched her tongue to her lips. "We don't need that much time. We can be fast, baby. Or I could wait until you're free."

She slid past me before I could shut the door and I turned, glaring at her.

"I said it wasn't a good time. That doesn't mean come inside."

She shot me a flirtatious look over her shoulder as she sauntered over to one of the cars, then leaned against it.

Despite the cold, she wore a denim skirt that barely covered her butt and boots that went up a few inches over her thighs. As she adjusted her stance against the car, it was pretty obvious she wasn't wearing panties either.

Yet there was no interest for me. None at all.

"You're all work and no play anymore, Kane," she said with a heavy sigh. Shaking her head, she wagged a finger at me. "That's not good for you. How about you come over here..." She spread her legs, forcing the short excuse for a skirt up. "And play with me for a little while? Burn off some of that stress?"

"I'm not stressed." At least I hadn't been until she showed up. Thinking of my kid brother on the other side of the car, I took a step toward her and jutted my chin toward the door. "I'm busy. You need to go."

"Aw, Kane...you're no fun." She came toward me and hooked her arms around my neck.

I didn't even want to think about what *that* did to the skirt.

Through her thin sweater, I could feel the weight of her breasts, but still, nothing even remotely interested stirred in me. As a matter of fact, I found myself thinking of Raye with her nervous eyes and sweet mouth. She was a far cry from Calie.

"Let's have some fun together, you and me, Kane," Calie whispered, going to press her lips to my mouth.

I jerked my head back, fisting my hand in her hair to keep her from trying to kiss me again.

"Ooohhh... you wanna play it rough?" Her eyes sparked. She grabbed my other hand and tried to shove it between her thighs. "Play rough. Make it hurt, sweetie. I love it."

Pissed off now, I set her away from me and put a few inches between us – then made it a few feet. "I said *no*."

Then I caught sight of my brother who had come out from behind the car we'd been working on. Swearing, I passed a hand over my eyes.

Calie caught sight of where I was looking at she turned. With one hand, she tugged at the hem of her skirt as she smoothed her hair back with the other. "Oh, hi there, honey. Kane, why didn't you say you had company?" She gave Austen a blinding smile. "Oh, he must be one of your brothers. He looks like you. Aren't you a cutie."

She walked over to him, holding out a hand.

Austen took it out of courtesy, manners being something Mom had drilled into all of us.

"Hello," he said. His voice hitched on the word, and I could tell he was having a hard time keeping his eyes on her face.

But I applauded the effort. Calie had dolled herself up to look like a walking advertisement for sex.

My seventeen-year-old brother was already under the thrall of teenage hormones. A beautiful woman in a crotch length skirt with her boobs straining against the tight fit of her sweater was probably enough to feed his dreams for weeks.

"Calie," I said in a low voice.

She turned finally, and something she saw on my face must have cut through whatever fog she was in because her face sobered. "Fine," she said with a roll of her eyes. "Call me later?"

"No."

She opened her mouth, probably to argue, but I just pointed at the door.

Once she was gone, Austen looked at me with a giant grin on his face. "Is she your girlfriend?"

"No." I went over to the door and locked it. I doubted she'd come back, but I didn't want to chance it either. "She's trouble. Do me a favor, and if you see her again, go the other way."

"Aw, come on, man." He laughed. "How much trouble can a girl be if she wants to get in your pants?"

"You'd be surprised."

We got back to work on the car, and I braced myself for more questions about Calie, but none came, thankfully.

I brooded as I showed Austen more about the car, half my mind on Calie and what had just happened.

What had I ever seen in her anyway?

19

Raye

Give it a chance.

Michelle thought I should give things with Kane a chance – not that she knew it was Kane I'd been with.

It could be good for me.

I'd had a glass of wine before I went to bed last night, and that, combined with my lack of sleep during the past week, had put me out like a light. I slept so hard that when seven rolled around, I woke up clearer and feeling more refreshed than I had in days.

Because of that, I was able to do something I hadn't been able to do all week – *think*.

I pushed aside my nerves over seeing Chad. He hadn't been back, and it was possible he hadn't even recognized me, so maybe him being in the store was just a fluke. Him being in New York could have just been a fluke for all I knew.

I pushed aside my nerves over the idea of a relationship, because I didn't even want that.

I wanted to feel *normal*, and if Michelle was right, maybe Kane was the guy to help me find that.

That, to me, was more important than a relationship.

Maybe I wouldn't have to freak out the next time some good-looking guy at a bar asked me out. Maybe I wouldn't have to stammer out a reply the next time somebody asked me to dance.

Even if a dance was all it was, it was something I hadn't been able to enjoy in a while. A *long* while.

If it was an invitation to a date, something I could maybe say yes to?

Even better.

But none of that could happen until I stopped feeling like such a freak.

So that was why I found myself knocking on Kane's door Saturday night. I hadn't worn the sort of clothes he'd told me to wear for working out. No, I'd put on a pair of skinny jeans, low boots with a chunky heel and a close-fitting sweater the same color as my eyes.

It wasn't an outright sexy outfit, but it was a pretty one, and the blue did great things for my figure without being outright blatant about anything.

Under my clothes, I wore one of the prettiest sets of lingerie I'd ever bought from the boutique where I worked. The bra was midnight blue, a few shades darker than my sweater, made of real silk and the softest lace ever. The panties were the same lacy design with a tiny silk bow on the front. Just putting it on made me feel sexy, and for the first time in a long time, I had some hope that maybe the lingerie wasn't a wasted effort.

I'd also worn make-up. I knew how to put it on – it was

practically a requirement for working at a boutique store on Times Square. Looking sleek and modern and glamorous was part of the job description, something I could only attain with make-up and skyscraper heels, thanks to my petite stature.

But I rarely wore it outside of work.

And I hadn't worn makeup for a guy since college.

Tonight, though, I was going all out.

Tonight, I was going to reach for something I hadn't thought to hope was possible.

Maybe I could be normal...

Maybe.

Trying not to let my hands shake, I smoothed my hair back, then went to knock on the door.

He didn't answer at first, even though the lights in his apartment were on and the truck that was always parked out back was in its customary spot. I suspected it was his – it had a sign noted on the brick wall right in front of where it was at – *reserved*. Nobody kept a parking space in the city unless they were using it. Considering how many stores were around here and how much a parking space could go for, even tucked here back behind a garage, he had to be using that space.

I knocked again, trying not to let my nerves rise out of control again as the waiting drew out.

Just as I was about to give up hope, the door opened, and Kane appeared on the other side.

A grin curled his lips as he pushed the door open more completely and stepped aside. "Come on in. I wasn't expecting you today."

"Am I interrupting anything?" I had debated about calling, but talking to him beforehand just would have made me nervous, so I'd taken a chance that he didn't have a date.

Or a girlfriend – what if he had a girlfriend?

Oh, shit.

I hadn't even thought about that.

He opened his mouth to say something, but before he could, I blurted out, "Do you have a girlfriend?"

"No." That lopsided grin spread across his face. "Think I would have been touching you the way I did if I was in a relationship?"

The comment, so open and sincere, relaxed some of the nerves that had just flared up, but now a whole new crop took their place.

While I was trying not to fidget, he angled his head toward his apartment and said, "Why don't you come inside? It's freezing out."

I stepped inside and stood in the middle of the floor with my hands buried in the pockets of my sturdy, plain pea coat. It was a boring affair, but warm. I didn't have any sort of cold weather apparel that was pretty. I'd never needed it. But now I felt even more self-conscious as I stood there, huddled in front of him, hiding under an inch of wool.

So, stop hiding, a small voice said.

Slowly, I peeled the coat off, turning away from him so I wouldn't see his face when he took in what I was wearing.

It's not like you're here in a garter belt. It's jeans and a sweater.

But when I turned back to him, he was staring at me with speculation. Eyes hooded, they roamed over me, and I felt everywhere his gaze touched. "You look awfully pretty,

Raye," he murmured. Then he shook his head. "But I don't think those clothes are any good for practicing in."

"I'm not here to practice," I said softly. I bit my lip, then slowly took a step toward him. "I want to ask you something. If you want to say no, it's no big deal, but..."

Oh, shit. Was I actually doing this?

His gaze slid up and locked with mine.

He'd moved closer. When had he moved closer?

I didn't remember him so much as taking a step but suddenly we were only about a foot apart, and I didn't think *I* had moved that close to him.

"What do you want to ask me, Raye? I'll do it, if I can."

My breathing hitched. It seemed like all the air had been sucked out of the room. That would explain why I was having such a hard time drawing oxygen into my lungs. "I...um...well, after the other night..."

He cocked his head, his expression unreadable.

But something hot flared in his eyes.

The words trapped in my throat again.

How did I say this?

While I was struggling for words, Kane clearly didn't have any such trouble. "What about the other night?"

"I...um..." *You keep saying that!* Frustrated with myself, I forced the words out. "I have issues. With sex. You probably noticed."

"Raye..." The grin on his face took on a decidedly intimate twist. "What I noticed was that I had a hot, nearly naked woman in my bed who was letting me touch her. Then she wanted to touch me. And I enjoyed every damn second of it."

Blood rushed to my cheeks, heating my face. "That's...

um, I enjoyed it, too. That's why I wanted to ask you...will you have sex with me?" I all but threw the words at him, then backpedaled away as he lifted a hand. I didn't want him touching me right now. I was strung so tight, I felt like I might shatter.

"Raye."

My butt hit his kitchen table, and my backward retreat came to an end, but still, I flinched away when he came closer. Mild, amused exasperation appeared on his face, but I didn't get the impression he was laughing at me. More like he was just...bemused. "It's a funny thing to have a woman tell you she wants to have sex with you while she's backing away like you're on fire."

I swallowed. "I'm nervous."

"I noticed. You don't have to be."

"I don't ask guys to have sex with me on a regular basis." Feeling foolish, I jutted my chin out at him, daring him to say something else.

He did, but it wasn't what I was expecting. "Are you a virgin?"

"What?" I gaped at him. "No...I...no. Why would you ask that?"

Kane shrugged. "You're nervous as hell about sex. You were skittish the other day. I just wanted to make sure."

"I'm not a virgin," I told him. Shit, I hadn't been *this* nervous when I had been a virgin. "I had a friend in high school...Dmitri. He was my best friend. We were both still virgins and decided we'd...well, lose it together." I blushed furiously as I told him, but I didn't want him telling me no because he thought he might...I dunno, be the first to go where no man had gone before. I'd heard some men were funny about that. And I *definitely* wasn't telling him about anything else.

"Okay." He nodded at me and took a step closer.

I didn't let myself sidestep him. He was right. I'd asked him to have sex with me, so it was stupid to back away from him or act like I didn't want him to touch me. Especially when that was the furthest thing from the truth imaginable. I *did* want him to touch me. I wanted him to touch me a lot.

"What about your brother?"

Yet another question I hadn't expected. Frowning, I shook my head. "What about him?"

"He's my best friend. If he finds out about this, he might kick my ass." Kane's face twisted into a grimace. "And I'd probably let him."

"It's none of his business," I told him. "And it's not like I plan on going and telling him that I asked you to sleep with me. Besides, I'm not talking about a...a relationship." I forced the words out, then made myself continue with the explanation I'd come up with. "Sex makes me nervous. The first time I was with someone, it was with a person I trusted. Now, I freak out anytime I even get close. But I didn't freak out with you. I thought maybe..." My tongue felt thick with the lie on it, but I forced myself to continue. "Well, I need to get past it. I don't like feeling...not normal. I want to be able to be with a guy and not freak out about it."

"And you want me to help you with that?" He had that heated, hooded look in his eyes again.

It was a look that made me feel warm all over, and naked, even though I was still fully dressed. "Yes," I whispered.

His final step pretty much eliminated the distance between us, and I sucked in a desperate gulp of air as he reached up to cup my cheek. "Is this why you dressed up so pretty, Raye?" His other hand stroked up my arm, the fine knit of the sweater hardly any barrier to the heat of his hand.

"Maybe?"

He chuckled softly and dipped his head, rubbing his lips across mine.

It was a sweet, sweet kiss and it didn't scare me at all.

Maybe I could do this.

I knew I *wanted* to, and that was a thing of wonder, in and of itself.

He stood so close that his warmth reached out to me, teasing me through my clothes, and I wanted to rub up against him like a cat in heat.

"So..." Kane lifted his head to peer down at me, and I swallowed back a moan at the loss of his mouth against mine.

I could have kissed him forever, especially those light, nuzzling kisses. They turned my blood into something sweet and thick that flowed through my veins like syrup. "So, what?" I asked, staring at his mouth.

A sharp noise escaped him, and he said, "If you keep staring at me like that, Raye, we're going to have a problem."

"What kind of problem?" Confused, I looked up and met his eyes.

But he just shook his head. "Don't worry about it." He traced his finger over my mouth. "Let me see if I understand this right. You came over here to ask me if I wanted to have some no strings attached sex. Is that right?"

"Pretty much, yes."

He smiled, and that grin that lit his face was hot enough to light a thousand fires. My belly flipped over, and I swayed closer, surprising myself by lifting my mouth to his.

I think I surprised him, too, because his eyes widened fractionally before he lowered his mouth back to mine.

And this was a *real* kiss – he licked at my lips until I opened for him, and once I did, his tongue swooped inside, seeking out mine and demanding a response. I didn't know how to *not* give it.

He slid one hand up my spine, then down it, sealing our bodies together.

When he finally broke the kiss, it was to whisper against my mouth, "You sure about this, Raye?"

"Surer than I've been about anything in a very long time."

20

Kane

I felt like I'd just been given a late Christmas present, all wrapped up in shades of blue, topped off with a nervous smile.

Raye leaned against my kitchen table as I settled back on my heels to study her, half-expecting her to disappear in front of me.

Half of me wouldn't have been surprised to wake up suddenly to find that this had been a dream. After all, I'd done quite a bit of dreaming about this very woman since I ran into her that fated New Year's Eve. But even after I'd fought those guys off...even after that first kiss...I never dreamed we'd be here, together, like this.

I essentially had carte blanche with the woman who kept me awake at nights with a hard-on, and when she wasn't keeping me awake, she was giving me sweet dreams that had me waking with a smile on my face.

Not that anything would ever come of it.

Jake would kill me, that was the truth.

Besides, I wouldn't ever let anything come of it. A girl like her deserved better than a roughneck like me.

But I could do this for her – she trusted me to do this for her. She *wanted* me to do this for her, and damned if I didn't want to do it.

The sweater, soft against her warm skin, tickled my roughened palm as I stroked it up her arm, then curved it around her neck. "Come here," I whispered, tugging her in close so I could kiss her.

I kept it light and easy, something I'd have to do throughout this entire thing.

If she'd only had sex the one time, and every other time she'd attempted intimacy, things went south, it explained why she was so nervous, I guessed. Not to mention that episode on the street New Year's Eve. The way she reacted made me think it wasn't the first time some dick had tried to force the issue with her, and that would make her reservations about sex that much worse,

But she hadn't had so many reservations when I touched her.

She didn't have any now as I kissed her, sliding my tongue past her lips and delving deep into the sweet recesses of her mouth. She tasted like wine and woman, and it was enough to make me drunk on her. Deepening the kiss, I tugged her against me, turning as I did so that my hips were against the table and she was half-leaning against me. She stiffened at first, like she had several times the night I'd brought her to climax, but she relaxed almost immediately.

"I want to touch you," I whispered against her mouth.

"You don't have to ask," she said, drawing back to peer up at me.

"I just want you to know what's coming." I held her eyes as I slid my hand under her sweater and placed my palm on her side. She was built so delicately and felt almost fragile under my touch. I could feel each rib as I slid my palm higher, up until the heel of my hand grazed the curve of her breast.

Her breath stuttered in her chest.

The sound of it made my heart speed up.

Every reaction was so open, so...new.

"I love your tits," I muttered, dipping my head to nuzzle her neck. "I didn't get to play with them enough the other night. I'm going to take your sweater off now."

She whimpered in her throat but relaxed against me, letting me tug the material up, baring her flesh one slow inch at a time. I did it that slowly to tease myself as much as I did to let her adjust to it, and by the time I had the sweater off, I was almost ravenous to taste her. But I held back, leaning away so I could take in the sight of her.

It almost did me in.

She wore a bra so dark blue, it almost looked black, and her pale skin glowed like a pearl against it.

"You are so fucking beautiful," I muttered. Grasping her around the waist, I hauled her up against me and buried my face between her breasts.

A startled cry escaped her, but before I could worry if I'd moved too fast, she dipped her hands into my hair and arched against me.

She might think she was awkward or too nervous at this, but she was wrong. Raye was a natural, filled with a buried sensuality that was only now coming to the surface. I intended to enjoy every bit of it for as long as it lasted.

She moaned as I trailed a line of kisses down the fragile skin that covered her breastbone, whimpered as I kissed my way back up.

Did she know she had her legs wrapped around me?

I sure as hell did, and my cock felt like a rocket about to explode.

Grasping her hips, I began to move her up and down against me, dragging a low, hungry moan from her throat.

"I could come, just doing this to you," I whispered against her throat. "You're already wet, aren't you, baby?"

She shuddered as I spoke, and I couldn't hold back a smile. I didn't know if she planned on this being a one-time thing. I didn't know if she planned on this lasting beyond tonight. But if I had my way, sometime soon, I'd have her stretched out naked in front of me, and I'd tell her a thousand dirty things, and I'd see if I couldn't just talk her into orgasm.

"Are you wet?" I asked when she didn't answer. "Tell me."

"I...I think so."

"Let's find out." I popped the button on her jeans, turning once more and propped her on the edge of the table. She squirmed as I dragged the zipper down and her lashes fluttered shut when I slid my fingers past the top edge of her panties. But then I stopped. "I want you to see."

She jerked, startled by the words.

"I...what?"

"Check and see if you're wet. Tell me."

Her cheeks flamed, and I waited to see if she would. Her tongue slid out, wetting her lips, and I almost whimpered when she slowly lifted a hand and slid it along the lacy edge of her panties. "I'm not very good at this," she whispered, the words shy and nervous.

"I think you're wrong. Show me that you're wet, Raye." I challenged her with my eyes.

And I was gratified a moment later when she slid her hands inside her panties. Her lashes fluttered, a husky breath escaping her.

"Are you?" I pressed my mouth to hers, waiting for the answer, even though I already knew.

"Yes."

"Good." I closed my fingers over her wrist and nudged her hand closer. "Touch yourself. I want to kiss you while you're doing that."

She gasped as I pushed my tongue into her mouth and that faint inhalation made it seem like she was drawing me inside her.

Between us, I felt the slow, almost shy movements of her wrist as she massaged herself. I kept my hand on her wrist, and when her movements slowed, I whispered, "More."

Soon, she was moaning and rocking against her hand, all but riding it as her excitement rose.

"Can you make yourself come for me, Raye? That would be so fucking hot."

Her head fell back, and she stared at me with bleary, uncomprehending eyes. I let go of her wrist but reached down to press at her crotch through her jeans. I felt her hand, lodged in that tight space and it made me go a little crazy. "Fuck your fingers, Raye. Make yourself come and let me watch."

Her eyes started to clear so I kissed her, and soon, she was writhing against her own touch again.

She came with a choked, startled gasp and a weak shudder, and when it was over, she pulled away to gape up at me. Even before she said it, I knew. "I've never been able to do that before."

"You just don't think," I told her. Watching her, I took her wrist and tugged.

Still watching her, I guided her fingers to my mouth and licked them clean. "I love the taste of you."

Another one of those pretty blushes scalded her cheeks, and I laughed, dipping my head to rub my cheek against hers. "You just made yourself come in front of me, and that's what makes you blush."

"Quit teasing me," she said, shoving at my chest.

"I can't help it." Covering her mouth with mine, I kissed her to let her know I was just playing. "Everything about you is just so fun. Kiss me, Raye. I love it when you kiss me back."

And she did, sighing into my mouth. She stiffened when I caught her wrist and brought her fingers up, though, replacing my mouth with them. "Taste...see how sweet?"

She hesitated, but slowly, as I watched her, she slid her tongue out. "It's salty."

"Sweet," I corrected her, taking her hand back and closing her mouth over her middle finger. There was only the faintest taste now, mostly gone and I was greedy for more. Tugging her off the table, I eased the jeans down over her hips, then nudged her back down before I slowly knelt in front of her, dragging the material the rest of the way off.

I left her panties alone, although the sight of her encased in the same midnight blue that matched her bra was almost enough to stop my heart.

Once I had her jeans off, I leaned back over her and

pressed my mouth to her cunt. Through the silk of her panties, I could taste her, feel how wet she was, and it was enough to make the threads of my control tremble.

But I ignored the pulse of want burning inside me as I focused on her.

Pulling her panties aside, I told her, "I'm going to eat you up now, Raye."

Her cheeks went red, and before she could decide whether or not to panic, I pressed my mouth to her. She jolted against me, one hand raising, then falling to smack against the table. She cried out and made a low, hungry sound in her throat.

It made my cock throb and pulse, aching like a bad tooth.

Pulling back, I blew a puff of air against her, then caught her clit between my teeth and tugged.

She whimpered.

"Tell me what you like," I demanded.

She just moaned.

"Do you like this?" I asked, sucking on her clit.

Another moan.

I circled her clit with my thumb and used my tongue to fuck her. "This?"

She whimpered.

"Tell me, Raye."

"All of it, Kane. I like it all."

I caught her hand and brought it to my hair. "Show me."

I pressed my face back to her and slowly, she caught on, her fingers slipping through my hair, then tangling in it. A series of hitching, high-pitched breaths started to burn out of her as I slid two fingers into her pussy and I began to pump them, twisting my wrist so they screwed in and out of her cunt.

"Yes, please!"

She jerked against me, and I felt the start of her climax just as I was ready to pull away. Startled at how easy it was to bring her pleasure, I pressed my mouth to her clit and licked, sucked, worked her through it.

She was whimpering when I finished her off, and I stood up, catching her face in my hands to kiss her. "Taste yourself on me."

She blushed but didn't pull away as I kissed her.

As I slid my tongue past her lips, she curled her arms around my torso and arched against me, letting me feel her tight nipples through her bra and the curvy, soft lines of her body. Cupping her breasts in my hands, I plumped them together, groaning in delight at the softness.

"You're so fucking sexy," I muttered against her lips. "I can't wait to feel you wrapped around my dick."

A sharp noise broke free from her throat, and I lifted my head to smile down at her. "That's how this is going to end, Raye. I'm going to pick you up, carry you to bed, and you're going to straddle me and take my dick inside you. You're going to ride me and make us both go a little crazy."

Her eyes were glassy now, and I asked her, "You ready to do that?"

"I..." She bit her lower lip but nodded. "I think so."

I wasn't sure if she was, but at least she hadn't freaked out at the idea of going to my room.

Boosting her up, I said, "Wrap your legs around me."

She did so and gasped at the feel of me rubbing against her cunt. "Feels good, doesn't it?"

"Yes..." She moaned, her head falling back.

Unable to resist, I leaned forward and bit her neck, right on the curve where her neck and shoulder joined. She shivered and pressed in closer, her fingers dipping into my hair.

Fuck, I had so many things I wanted to do to her.

Slow, Kane...I had to remember that. We had to go slow.

In my bedroom, I put her on the bed and stood by the side, reaching for the hem of my shirt. "I'm going to take off my clothes. That okay?"

Her eyes cleared momentarily, and something that might have been panic lit her gaze.

"We can wait," I offered.

But she shook her head. "No." She touched her tongue to her lips and whispered, "I want to see you."

How could such a simple statement make me so hot?

I didn't know, but my hands ended up fumbling a little as I peeled my t-shirt upward, then went to deal with the zipper of my jeans. I'd already kicked my boots off, and I was able to slide the rest of my clothes off in a few economical motions. When I was done, I stood by the side of the bed, waiting.

Her eyes centered on my cock, and it jerked in response as if she'd reached out and cupped me in her hand.

"Nothing happens until you're ready," I told her.

She licked her lips once more, and my cock bobbed again, greedy to feel that mouth on it.

But that was a pleasure that would have to wait for another day, and I knew it.

I braced a knee on the mattress next to her and held out my hand. She hesitantly offered hers, and I guided it to my chest. She stiffened at first, then slowly, slid her hand up. "You've got scars," she said, her voice tight, almost rusty.

"Yeah." I grimaced and glanced down as her fingers played over one on my ribs. I'd gotten that one in prison, trying to avoid a shiv. I hadn't managed to avoid it entirely, but it hadn't punctured anything – just scraped the surface. "A few."

Something that might have been amusement danced in her eyes. "If this is what you call a few, what's a lot?"

"Let's not talk about my sorry, scarred hide now. You'll make me self-conscious," I teased her, moving to slide down next to her so I was laying while she sat over me.

"I didn't say anything about you being sorry." The words seemed to surprise her, and she shot me a look, her lips parted. "I just...I meant...it's not that you aren't attractive. You...um..."

I caught her around the neck and pulled her down. "Come here."

I kissed her, holding her naked body close to mine, but not pulling her on top of me the way I wanted. Once I did that, it was going to be close to all over. Or at least, I'd be pushing for that. The second I felt her weight on me, I was going to want it all, but for now, she still needed time.

And she was letting her hand roam over my chest, and I didn't mind that at all.

When she reached my shoulder, she pulled away, panting a little as she peered down at me. "You're not doing anything."

"I am, too. I'm enjoying things." Watching her from under hooded eyes, I fought to stay relaxed, keeping my hands loose at my sides. "I want you to do what you want."

She bit her lower lip. "What I want. Whatever I want?"

I nodded.

She looked me over from head to toe, then dipped her head, pressing a kiss to my mouth. Then she moved lower, her lips cruising down my jaw bone, my neck. She echoed the path I'd taken on her earlier, and when she reached my breastbone, she paused and looked up. "Am I doing this right?"

"I'm naked, and you got your mouth on me," I told her. "There is no wrong to it."

Her lids dropped low, and she bent over me once more, her mouth pressing to the midline of my torso. She went lower, and my cock jerked as her breast brushed up against it. I felt her chest move as her breathing hitched, and I wanted to reach down, cup my hand over the back of her scalp and urge her on, but I didn't dare.

She kept to her own pace and finally, *finally*, her lips brushed the head of my cock.

A drop of pre-come leaked out, and she pulled up, staring down at it.

"It's your fault," I told her. She blinked up at me owlishly. "You've got me so fucking turned on, I could come right now."

"Really?" She cocked her head, and then, as I fought to find words to tell her what she was doing to me, she reached down and closed her hand around my dick, stroking up, then down. I grunted and arched up into her touch before I could stop myself.

Another drop of pre-come leaked out.

She bent over me and licked it away.

I fisted my hands in the sheets and swore a blue streak.

She gave me another owlish look.

"You keep putting your mouth on me, I'm going to lose

it," I warned her.

To my surprise, a slow smile curled her lips. "I think I might like that."

"I think I've created a monster," I muttered. Reaching out, I fumbled in the drawer of the small table by the side of the bed, feeling around for the box of condoms I'd put inside.

I found it and pulled it out.

"Unless you want this to end the way it did last time, I'm going to need one of these shortly."

I pulled it off and dropped it down next to me. Raye rose to her knees, her hands tucked between her thighs. "Put it on now."

I eyed her, then reached for the foil packet and tore it open. "You ready for this?" I asked after dropping the empty packet on the nightstand.

A breath huffed out of her, and her eyes slid away as I rolled it on. "I don't know."

I tugged her toward me. "You let me know if you decide you aren't."

She fell against my chest, her breasts a soft, warm weight. "What do I do?" She stared down at me.

Catching one of her legs, I drew it over my hip. "Ride me." Her face went pink again, and I chuckled. "You've had my dick in your hand, and you've touched me all over, let me touch you all over, and that embarrasses you?"

"Stop it," she huffed out, smacking my chest and squirming against me. Then her eyes went wide.

I knew why, too.

She had wiggled until her wet, waiting cunt tucked snug against my hard, waiting cock and I was so ready to fill her, I hurt with it.

Gritting my teeth against the urge to do just that, I gripped her hips and tugged until she lifted. "You're killing me, Raye," I told her, heart racing in my chest.

"I...what do I do?" she demanded, hunger a razor-sharp edge in her voice. She braced her hands against my chest, her hips wiggling and rocking in my hands.

"Take my cock. Hold it up. You're going to slide down on me. Take as much as you want, or as little. Go as fast or slow as you want. It's all up to you."

Her spine arched as she lifted higher, her movements awkward as she followed my instructions. Her eyes widened as the head of my cock pressed against her and the folds of her pussy yielded slowly, opening for me as she let her weight bear down.

A faint whimper escaped her lips, and I steadied her. "Take..." I grunted, sweat beading on my brow. "Take your time, Raye."

She was so tight...

Another whimper escaped her as she slid down another inch, then she swayed forward, bracing her hands on my chest. Eyes over bright, she stared down at me.

Still cupping her hips, I had to clench my teeth not to thrust up and fill her completely. "You okay?"

She nodded, mouth parted as she rocked back, taking more of me.

Just...not enough.

Fuck, this really might just kill me.

She tightened around me as she started to slip away, and involuntarily, my hands tightened.

She stilled. "What is it?"

"Just..." I shuddered underneath her. "It's nothing."

"*What?*" she persisted, panic starting to edge into her voice.

"You feel too fucking good, and I want more," I said, arching up the slightest.

Her spine curved and her eyes widened. "Oh..." Lashes fluttering down, she whispered, "Do that again."

Slowly, I did, and she whimpered, her body opening to take me more deeply. A short cry escaped her.

"More?"

She nodded, her nails kneading my chest. Slowly, I started to rock up against her, thrusting into the cradle of her thighs, pleasure spilling through me with every hot, aching second.

My balls were so tight, I thought they might explode, and I wasn't even completely buried inside her yet.

She twisted on top of me, her spine arching as she fought to take more of me, then I *was* buried inside her. She wailed, her mouth parting on the sharp sound. Her nails dug even deeper into my chest, and I stilled. "Are you hurting?"

"A...a little?" She didn't sound certain. "I don't know."

"Do we need to stop?"

"No!" The sound tore out of her, and she went to move against me.

"Okay...okay..." I smoothed my hand down her hip, then rocked upward. "Just...can I?"

I moved against her again, and she nodded. "Please."

Hungry little mewling sounds escaped her as I thrust up in slow, shallow motions, and she started to move, finding the right rhythm as she began to ride me. I caught her ass in my hands, tugging her down just the slightest every time she went to pull up. Her eyes locked on mine, dazed delight making them cloudy.

"Kane..."

My name came out on a broken sigh as her pussy went even tighter around me, and I knew she was close.

Sliding a hand between us, I sought out her clitoris. "Come for me, Raye. I want to watch you."

She moaned, her body racking and trembling as the sound escaped her. Fine tremors shook her, and her pussy clutched at me, a tight, snug fist.

Just as the orgasm hit, I caught her behind the neck and pulled her face to mine. "Kiss me."

She did, and the two of us came together.

RAYE SLEPT NEXT TO ME, and I lay against her back, one hand on her hip.

She'd told me, right before she fell asleep, that it hadn't been like that for her before.

I'd never tell her, but it hadn't been like that for me either. Not ever. As many women as I'd been with, it had never felt...new, like that. I always made sure the woman I was with was happy, but it hadn't ever mattered as much as it had with Raye, and it hadn't ever been so...tender before.

I couldn't let myself get caught up in it though.

It wasn't just that Jake would have my ass.

I wasn't good enough for somebody as sweet as Raye.

She deserved somebody, *some thing*, better in her life. Somebody more than an ex-con with a tiny old garage in Brooklyn and a future that was uncertain at best.

21

Raye

Michelle had invited me out for coffee the other night, and I'd taken her up on it, although a part of me wished I was still back in the garage in Brooklyn, wrapped around Kane.

Or maybe wrapped around his dick, as he told me I'd be at some point last night.

And I had been. Not just last night, but this morning.

This morning, he'd woken me up by going down on me. A little bit of time with him, and I understood, finally, the allure of oral sex. Something that had seemed maybe a little gross and way too intimate had turned into a drug in his hands.

"You seem a little distracted today," Michelle said as we sat down in a small booth near the back.

"I...ah...I didn't sleep a whole lot," I hedged, forcing a smile.

Something must have shown on my face, though, because she leaned back and studied me. Before long, a grin lit her face. "Did you take my advice?"

"Your advice?" My voice cracked. So much for playing dumb.

"You *did*, didn't you?" She curled her hands around her mocha and leaned forward conspiratorially. "How did it go?"

"I...um..." I knew women talked about this kind of thing, but what was I supposed to say? He melted my brain?

"That good?" Michelle fanned herself.

"I didn't say anything," I protested.

"Your face said it *all*." She sipped at her coffee, then braced an elbow on the table. "So...I guess you went over there...when? Last night? Friday?"

"Last night." Blushing, I squirmed on the seat, which made me aware of the fact that I was a little sore. It was a good kind of sore, though, an ache that reminded me of everything Kane and I had done.

"You must have been on the fence about him already then," Michelle mused, her eyes narrowed.

"Ah...maybe?" I took a sip of my chai, studying the swirls in it instead of looking at her. "I...I like him. He makes me feel...safe. That's crazy, isn't it?"

"Why's it crazy?"

"I slept with a guy because he made me feel safe?" I laughed, but Michelle just shook her head.

"I don't think that's crazy. I felt safe with Jake after...well, you know." She shrugged and picked up her spoon, swirling it through her mocha for a few seconds, clearly thinking something through. "It's not like you decided to get with him because he was a teddy bear or something. No teddy bear makes a woman look like...*that*."

She finally looked back at me and grinned, and I had to

smile back because I understood. I had no idea what I *looked* like, but I knew how I felt when I was thinking about Kane, and no...he didn't inspire teddy bear like feelings.

"Still, it is kind of crazy. He's this big, rough-looking guy... all these tattoos and these scars..." Without thinking, I reached up and brushed my fingertip down my left eyebrow, echoing the path that the scar on Kane's face took. "He's scary looking, and he makes me feel safer than I have in a long time."

I glanced at Michelle, a wry grin on my face.

But the expression on hers had my grin fading. "What is it?"

She bit her lip. "I'm about to get really personal. I'm sorry...but...hell. Did you sleep with Kane?"

My mouth fell open.

She winced. "I'm sorry! I just...you described him exactly the way I would. I mean, I even get what you mean by feeling safe around him. Jake's like that, although Jake isn't as rough as Kane. But...I'm right, aren't I?"

"Yes." I grabbed my chai and lifted it to my lips, taking a sip. "Is that so bad?"

"Honey..." She reached out as I put the cup down, covering my hand with hers. "It's just that...well, Jake would flip out. He's missed having a family, and he wouldn't want to see anybody taking advantage of you."

"Kane isn't taking advantage of me," I retorted. "*I* went to him. *I* asked him. Maybe *I* am taking advantage of *him*?"

Michelle's brows rose at that.

"Well, maybe I am!"

"Okay, okay..." She held up her hands. "Look, I get it. It's just…I don't want to see you get hurt. Kane doesn't do relationships, okay?"

"I'm not looking for one," I insisted and took a deep breath. "I'm just…I want to feel normal. He…I feel good with him."

Michelle's face softened. "Okay. I just…I just wanted you to know." She reached for her cup again, taking another sip. As she put it down, she said, "It's not that he's not a good guy. He is. I mean, Jake wouldn't hang around him if he wasn't. The two of them are tight, have been for years."

"How did they meet?" I was greedy, not just for information about my brother, I realized, but to find out what I could about Kane.

He would only tell me so much.

This was dangerous territory to be wading into.

I'm just curious, I told myself.

But it was more than that, and I already knew it.

Michelle did too, judging by the assessing look she sent my way. But she answered anyway, her tone guarded as she replied, "They met while they were in prison together."

Prison!

I cut off the immediate knee-jerk response, reaching for my coffee so I had something to do with my hands.

"He was in prison?"

Michelle inclined her head. "Yes. He got out about a year after Jake did. I don't know what he did, in case you were wondering. Jake never told me, and I never saw any reason to ask." She lifted a shoulder. "But Jake says he's one of the best guys he knows…and that's good enough for me."

"Then it's enough for me, too."

Michelle's gaze was skeptical, but I shook my head. "You seem like a good judge of character, and I've already decided I want to trust my brother. I want to have a family, Michelle. So, if you two trust him, that's enough for me."

22

Kane

I was alone in the garage, save for a couple of unfinished cars and a sweet 1965 cherry-red Mustang that was waiting for the owner to pick it up tomorrow. I was entertaining the fantasy of laying Raye out on the hood of that sleek car and having my way with her – not that it was going to happen, but a guy could dream.

I'd already pictured her straddling me in the beat-up old chair in the tiny little closet that served as my office and just about everywhere else that one might be able to have sex in my small garage – and the apartment. There were a lot more options than I'd realized.

The sound of a knock at the back door had anticipation lighting inside me, and I didn't think about it until it was too late that it wasn't likely to be Raye. She'd already told me she wouldn't be over until close to six. It wasn't even five-thirty now.

Still, I went over to check the window.

Irritation kicked up inside me the second I laid eyes on the man on the other side of the door, and I thought about sending him away. Tank Jones was the last man I wanted in here when Raye was due to arrive, but he always paid well, and it wasn't like I couldn't use the money.

Despite the foreboding I felt, I unlocked the door.

He gestured to the car parked out behind him.

"I had an accident." A sly grin curled his lips, and he added, "Insurance isn't going to help me out. Was kind of hoping you would."

That probably meant there was damage to the car he wanted fixed on the sly.

It could also mean that whatever damage had probably happened had been done while doing something illegal. I didn't know and wasn't going to ask. I figured it was safer that way.

"Let's take a look at it." I joined him outside, and we spent a few minutes out in the cold while I circled the car, taking in what I could under the piss-yellow security light behind the garage. My truck took up one of the two parking spaces, and I gestured to the other, telling him to pull into the spot. "I'll have to work on it after hours. Don't figure you want my crew knowing about the...damage."

"Appreciate that, Kane." The smile didn't soften his scarred face at all, neither did the look he cast around the alley. "I was thinking...hey, you got a beer? Got a question I want to toss at you."

I should have told him no.

But old habits died hard. Tank and I used to run together, back in the old gang. It had fallen apart in the years since I'd been in prison and whether Tank was affiliated with a new one now, I didn't know, nor did I want to. He still came around the garage, like a few others did and I didn't turn them away. They'd meant a lot to me at one point, and they still brought money with them. I didn't turn away money.

But sometimes, maybe saying no was the wiser course.

I never was a quick learner, though.

I brought him a beer out from my apartment, reluctant to invite him back into my personal living space. This was business, and despite the fact that I might still take jobs from some of the old crew, there were certain lines I'd never cross with them again.

Letting them cross the lines that bled over into my personal life was one thing that wouldn't happen.

"So...I got this thing lined up," Tank said, twisting the top off his bottle of beer.

I lifted mine to my lips, an uneasy feeling already curling through my gut. Yeah, I should have bypassed the chance to chat over a couple of beers.

He paused, clearly waiting for me to ask what kind of thing, but I stayed quiet. I wasn't going to take any lines he offered or anything.

When I didn't take the bait, Tank shrugged. "It's not a big deal or anything, but there could be some sweet money in it."

Yep.

This was going to be trouble, a shitload of it. Lowering my gaze, I focused on the bottle of beer and started thinking of the various ways to tell him to get the hell out of my place.

I had come up with about five by the time he explained what he wanted – he needed a place to keep a delivery he was going to be receiving in a few days. I wouldn't be involved in any way, blah, blah, blah, but of course, he'd be happy to pay me for my trouble, blah, blah, blah.

He finished and lifted his beer to his lips, taking a long pull from it as he waited for my answer.

I opened my mouth, ready to issue a polite *thank you, but no, fuck off* when a knock at the back door cut me off. The door swung open a second later, and I mentally started to swear a blue streak.

Tank reacted in pretty much the same way, only he didn't keep anything on a mental level.

"Who the fuck are you?" he demanded, coming off the counter he'd been leaning against, aggression leaking from him as if it seeped from his pores.

I spun around, moving across the garage, already knowing who it was. I shielded Raye with my body, shooting a look at Tank. "It doesn't matter who she is. She's of no concern to you, Tank."

"I thought you didn't have anybody coming around after hours, Kane," Tank bit off. "Who the fuck is the skirt?"

Raye's dark blue gaze flitted to mine, nerves dancing there. She didn't look at Tank, and whether it was experience or just instinct, I had to appreciate that. "Hey," she said in a low voice. "Is this a bad time?"

"No. You're fine." Angling my chin toward the door that opened into my apartment, I said, "Why don't you wait in there?"

She turned on her heel, and as she beat a fast retreat, I turned back to find Tank edging closer, his eyes dark and angry, his mouth in a tight set line.

"What the fuck, Kane? You always said it was safe to come by after the shop's closed and now you got women running in and out of here? You trying to fuck me over?" he demanded.

His eyes shot toward the door where Raye had disappeared and every protective instinct I had welled up inside me.

"I don't know where the fuck you got the idea that I'd never had anybody over at my place, *ever*, just in case one of you guys decided to show up," I said, sarcasm thick in my words. "If I decide I want to have a female friend over, I think that's my fucking concern and not yours. You want privacy, pick up the phone and make a fucking appointment."

Tank opened his mouth, fury dancing in his eyes.

I took a step toward him.

"What the fuck am I supposed to do?" Tank asked, flinging a hand out. "I don't need some chick seeing me here. I come here because it's supposed to be a clean place, you're supposed to be a safe zone where I can get my ride fixed, and nobody will connect me to you. And you fuck me over having a bitch here."

"Call her a bitch again," I invited. "See where it gets you."

He opened his mouth, then shut it. After a few more seconds, he lifted a hand, pointing at me. "If this comes back to bite me on the ass, I'll be back to kick yours, Kane."

"Don't you threaten me, Tank." Clenching a hand into a fist, I stared him down.

"Just make sure your bitch doesn't cause any problems for me."

Closing the distance between us, I stared down at him over the few inches that separated us. "That's your last chance. Say it again and pick up your teeth on the way out."

He sneered at me, and on the way out the door, he flipped me off.

"Hey!"

He glanced back.

I threw his keys at him. "Take your ride elsewhere."

He gaped at me.

I gave him a sardonic smile and pointed at the sign hanging near the entrance.

We reserve the right to refuse service to anyone.

"I'm invoking my right, asshole."

"HEY."

Raye was sitting on my couch, hands clasped together between her knees. She jumped at the sound of my voice, and I winced. "It's just me," I said.

"I know. Sorry. Jumpy. I interrupted something," she said, her voice hesitant.

"Not really." I moved across the room and sat down on the worn-out, old oak coffee table. "He's just somebody I used to know. He didn't have to be an asshole to you. I'm sorry."

I was half-prepared for her to bolt off the table and take off into the night, and the idea bothered me more than I liked.

Caring about people outside of my family was something I tried hard not to do, and here I was, worrying about what was going to happen in the next few minutes. It wasn't because I didn't care about Raye.

I did care.

I cared too much.

And I wasn't too happy about it either.

Caring about somebody who was probably going to disappear from my life in a few short weeks – or less – was a complication I didn't need.

It was even worse that it was somebody like Raye...somebody I didn't deserve to have in my life.

23

Raye

"Who was he?" I asked, not certain if he'd tell me any more than he'd already said.

I was right. Kane glanced away, clearly uncomfortable.

I'd already pieced together enough and wondered how to approach this without making it seem like I'd been nosing around in his past. Then I realized, no matter what, he'd know I'd asked about him. Might as well come clean.

Softly, I said, "Michelle told me you'd done time in prison – that's where you met Jake."

His entire body went taut, his gaze flying to meet mine.

"I wasn't asking about you...not exactly. She just..." Huffing out an awkward breath, I said, "She sort of figured out that you and I kind of...hooked up. She was a little worried – she told me you don't do relationships. I told her I wasn't looking for one and we got to talking. I asked her how you and Jake met, and she told me." I met his eyes levelly. "I'm not worried about your past. It doesn't have to define you any more than mine has to define me."

I wanted to believe that, too.

Kane leaned back, his weight falling onto the hands propped up behind him. His dark eyes held mine as he studied me, his long hair falling into his eyes. "You're not concerned that I did time."

"I know Michelle trusts you." Lifting a shoulder, I said, "She seems like a good judge of character and..." Uncertain how to continue, I looked away for a long moment. How did I explain to him that I felt safer with him than I'd ever felt with anybody? All those *good* guys that a girl should want in her life...they hadn't made me feel safe. I had good reason to *not* feel safe around some of them, too. But Kane...he'd rushed out of a crowd on New Year's Eve to chase off a couple of guys who'd been hassling me.

He'd been there for me that day when I ran into Chad, and more, he hadn't just *been* there – he'd recognized my fear and offered to help me overcome it.

"You make me feel safe," I said finally. "I don't think you realize how rare that is for me."

His eyes held mine, but the uncertainty I'd glimpsed there still hadn't gone away.

"I don't know how you can feel safe around me," he finally said. "That guy that just left...I knew him back when he and I used to run together in the same gang. That's part of why I went to prison, Raye. I got caught up with the wrong guys. And I'm not going to blame being with the wrong kind of people when I was a kid. I knew what I was doing, and I knew it was wrong, and I did it anyway. I got caught running drugs in Texas and had to do time in prison. That's how I met Jake. You still so certain you feel safe around me?"

"Are you involved in any of that now?" I watched him, my heart racing.

"I...no." He shook his head. "I smartened up. I've got people who count on me, and I'm not going to fuck up like that again. But sometimes the guys come around, needing work on their cars or shit like that. I don't tell them no."

"They're part of your past." Lifting a shoulder in a shrug, I said, "It's probably hard to do that. But none of that changes how I feel around you."

"And what the hell would Jake think?"

"Jake's my brother. He's not my parent," I said calmly. Cocking a brow at him, I added, "And I don't plan on telling him. Do you?"

With a nonplussed look on his face, Kane blew out a breath and tore his gaze from mine. He still looked uncertain, unsure how to process any of this.

I bit my lip as I shifted around on the couch, rising so that I could move forward. At my movement, his gaze returned to mine, and he held still as I pressed my lips to his. He'd prodded me into making moves the other night, but now I was doing it on my own, and I was insanely nervous.

Lifting my hand, I placed it on his cheek.

Rough stubble scraped against my palm as I edged closer. His mouth opened under mine, but he didn't do anything else to deepen the kiss.

I took the initiative and slid my tongue across his lower lip, echoing the way he often kissed me.

He tasted like beer, and under it was the familiar taste I'd come to associate with him. Kane. He tasted like Kane, and I loved it.

His head craned back as I moved to stand in front of him,

my head bent low as I continued to kiss him. I shivered as he moved his hands to my hips, his big palms restlessly kneading my waist.

Dipping my tongue past his lips, I sought out more of his taste and was rewarded when he closed his mouth around my tongue, sucking with a deep, sensual rhythm that weakened my knees. The sensation sent a thrill rushing through me, and the shivers in my body increased, arrowing down to center in my core. I wanted to wrap myself around him and rock against the heat that always emanated from him.

He'd be hard and ready, I thought, and the slick wet tissues between my thighs grew slicker, wetter in preparation. Drawing back, I stared down at him as I struggled to catch my breath.

Kane's eyes glittered as he stared up at me from under his lashes.

I rested my hands on his shoulders, slowly stroking down, letting myself enjoy the feel of hard, roped muscle under my hands. "Can we take this off?"

Kane pushed up from the table, sitting straighter in front of me. "You do it."

It was the first time I'd ever undressed a man and my hands tangled in the fabric as I drew it up, then away from him.

Dropping the shirt down on the table next to him, I stared at him, my hands returning to his shoulders. Despite the fact that it was winter, his skin was a mellow gold, and the scrolling ink of tattoos marked almost every inch of his upper body. A phoenix, mouth open in a defiant scream, spread across his right shoulder, the wings sweeping down from over his chest and back. There was a dragon on his left shoulder. I traced my fingers over the feathers of the eagle's wings, studied the dragon's scales.

Under my hands, his flesh was warm, and his chest hitched as I stroked my hands down.

He cupped my ass in his hands and tugged me closer. "Come here."

I ended up sprawled on his lap, one hand curled over the back of my neck, the other gripping my hip and holding me steady as he rocked up against me.

Heat spilled through me with every movement of his hips, and I was whimpering by the time he brought his mouth to mine. "I can make you come just like this, Raye," he told me. "Want me to do it?"

Dazed, I met his eyes.

I didn't doubt his words, but I wanted to have him inside me when I climaxed.

I lacked the breath to speak, though, and he took my silence for acquiescence. He rose from the coffee table and moved to the couch, stretching out on the cushions with his legs sprawled out before pulling me down on top of him. He arched up against me and every roll of his hips, he used his grasp on my butt to rub me over him.

I was whimpering and shaking by the third or fourth, writhing against him by the sixth.

And by the time he hit his ninth or tenth stroke, I was coming, chanting his name and grasping his wrists as if I feared he'd pull away.

He didn't. He pulled me even closer and moved faster, each movement more furious, more demanding. It was almost enough to trip that lever of fear that was never very far away. Almost.

But not quite.

As the climax shivered and rolled through me, he rocked forward and spilled me onto the couch.

I barely noticed much of anything, including him stripping my jeans and panties away. I did notice the heat of his hands as he pushed my thighs wide and bent over me, pressing his mouth to the slick wet flesh between my thighs. "You're so delicious," he whispered against me.

I lay half sprawled against the couch, my hips hanging over the edge. Staring up at him as he rose to kneel over me, I sucked in desperate gulps of air.

He covered my sex with his hand. "I want to fuck you like this. Can I?"

I blushed to the roots of my hair. Panic fluttered inside me. But I nervously nodded.

He reached down, and I heard foil ripping.

I didn't look away from his face as he rolled the condom on, nor did I look away as he bent back over me.

The head of his cock probed me. He had one hand under my ass, lifting me just the slightest. As he started to enter me, I gasped at the sensation, the weight on my lower body forcing me to accept him, forcing me to yield to him. He took me slowly, making me excruciatingly aware of who was filling me with his cock.

The intimacy of it hit me in the core, and I closed my eyes, my face turning away. But Kane cupped my cheek, guided my face back to his. "Look at me, Raye." His palm slid down to my neck, his thumb aligning to my jawbone as he angled my head back. "Look at me," he said again.

Then he rolled his hips, filling me completely before

withdrawing, pulling out until only the head of his cock held me open.

I moaned, shivering around him, aching to feel more, but he was already withdrawing.

The next thrust took him deeper, faster.

The one after that was harder, all but knocking my breath from my lungs.

"Raye..." Kane's lids drifted shut, my name a harsh grunt on his lips. His cock jerked inside me, the head of it passing over me in a way that sent shivers of pleasure slamming through me, and I couldn't keep from twisting against him, seeking to deepen the sensation.

More...

I wanted to beg him for it, but a fist had clamped itself around my throat, and I couldn't breathe.

More...

He did it again, and a harsh whimper of pleasure ripped out of me as he butted the head of his cock right up against me one more time.

I reached down and caught his wrists, my eyes seeking his out, desperate for more but unsure how to tell him. He swiveled his hips in the cradle of mine this time, and the sensations that lit inside me stole the breath from me, and I cried out, my nails biting into his skin as I rocked against him, seeking to deepen the contact.

More...more...more...

Kane reared forward and bent over me until his face filled my vision. His hands came up, cupping my breasts. I moaned, arching up against him as he circled my nipples with his hands.

"I fucking love your tits, Raye," he muttered. "They're so damned pretty."

He bent low then, catching one nipple in his mouth. He sucked it deep, almost to the edge of pain before letting go and switching sides.

When he lifted, he stared down at me with glittering eyes, his face harsh with hunger. With need.

He drove into me, harder than before, deeper.

Panic flared.

The pleasure flared.

They mingled and became one, and I shoved my hands against his chest, uncertain if I wanted to push him away or pull him closer.

The climax slammed into me, hard and fast, stealing breath, thought, and reason.

When it ended, my mind was spinning itself in dizzying circles, and I couldn't keep up any of the thoughts racing through my brain.

Kane hefted us up onto the couch and laid down, my body sprawled out atop his.

His heart slammed into mine.

Mine raced like a caged rabbit's, and I laid there with my hands fisted against this chest.

What the hell...

My mind ran in circles, over and over, that one thought the only clear one.

What the hell?

"What do you think about ordering some pizza?" Kane murmured, nuzzling my ear.

I jerked at the sound of his voice, then sat up. My eyes landed on the clothes that had gone flying, and the sight of my pretty, green silk blouse served to calm my brain, surprisingly.

It was one of the shirts I wore to work.

Work.

I had to work tonight.

"I can't," I said, my voice weak. "I've got to be at work in a few hours."

A soft groan escaped him, and his arms came around me. It took me a moment to realize he was hugging me.

I lay there, tense and uncertain. He was *hugging* me.

"How about a rain check?"

Making a noncommittal sound in my throat, I eased away from him and sat up, staring off into the dim corners of the room.

I needed to get out of there.

I didn't know what was going on, but my mind was racing.

I *needed* to get out of there...*now*.

Get out of there, away from him...so I could think.

24

Kane

My apartment felt surprisingly empty after Raye left.

I'd pulled my jeans back on, so I could walk her outside, but once I came back in, I dropped back down on the couch and just laid there, smelling her on my skin and reliving the last thirty minutes...including the conversation we'd had.

She told me I made her feel safe.

I didn't get that.

I wasn't entirely certain *I* felt safe around *her*. She undid things when she was around. I liked the status quo, and it got shaky when she was in the equation. Like now. Sitting there thinking about how the apartment seemed dimmer and quieter and just a little too big without her there.

It wasn't like I had a big apartment, so how could the absence of a woman I barely knew make such a big difference? I didn't understand it, and I wasn't sure I liked it.

"Stop thinking about it," I told myself.

It wasn't like I had a lot of time to kill tonight anyway. We didn't even have time for the pizza I'd ask her about.

My nephew Connor had a basketball game, and I tried to make it to all the games. I'd missed out on enough things with the family when I'd been behind bars. Now that I was out, I made it a rule to do what I could to make it to the events.

You could have always asked her to go with you.

Not that it would have worked. She had a job.

But even the thought that I'd consider asking her was...weird.

My family was mine. Any woman I ever slept with...well, it was just sex. Sex and my personal life didn't mix. That was another rule.

And yet there I was thinking about asking her to go to one of the family events with me.

"Shit, son." Rising to my feet, I collected my clothes. "You've gone and lost your mind."

―――

I WAS no longer in the mood for pizza, but on my way to Connor's school in Brooklyn, I grabbed a slice and a soft drink, so I wouldn't sit through the game hungry. The family might decide to go out to eat after the game, but I rarely joined them when they ate out. Mom always offered to buy, but I never took her up on it, and I was pinching pennies and saving as much money as I could, so I could pay down the loan.

Besides, I had to get up at the crack of dawn to open the garage. Staying out until ten or so, then getting up at four-thirty was something that just did not mix in my books.

I found my mother sitting with Connor's parents in the

bleachers, a few seats held for the rest of the family who trickled in not long after I did.

The kids had yet to take to the court, and I glanced over at Nathaniel as he wrestled Rose out of her coat. Zoe was fighting with her own, insisting to her mother that she could do it. Madison lifted her hands and gestured for her to do just that. While Zoe stubbornly fought with the zipper, Rose snuck her way over and climbed into my lap.

I breathed in the scent of sweet baby girl and smiled as she wrapped pudgy arms around my neck. "Unca Kane."

"Hey, baby doll," I murmured, nuzzling her hair and squeezing her into a hug.

She giggled. "I baby doll."

"You're my baby doll."

"Me, too!" Zoe insisted, shoving her way into the hug. "I'm baby doll."

My mother snapped a picture of me with two little girls on my lap, and I felt my damn cheeks grow hot as she spun her phone around, brandishing the picture like a weapon. "Look at how sweet you look," she said, smiling proudly.

Sweet was not a word I associated with myself, and the sight of me with my arms around two little girls didn't change that.

The arrival of Eddie and Dinah caused a ripple effect among the little kids, each one needing to go to the various adults they hadn't seen in several days. It wasn't until the buzzer rang signifying it was time for the game to start that everybody in the family was finally seated.

Connor's team came out onto the court, and everybody in our section broke out in hoots and cheers, clapping as if it was the Harlem Globetrotters that had just taken the court.

Connor had his very own cheering section with the family being there.

The game started.

Eddie sat next to me, and we chatted about our weeks. He shot me a look. "I heard Austen had been helping out over at the garage. How is *that* going?"

I shrugged. "It's...going. We'll let it go at that." I glanced around, noting my baby brother's absence. "He's not here tonight."

"Yeah." Eddie's mouth went tight. "I noticed. Connor will, too. Connor adores that kid."

"We'll figure out something to tell him," I said.

Connor scored two points and shouts went out among the crowd, all of us cheering.

As relative quiet settled back in the gym and the game progressed, my mind started to wander...right to Raye.

Would she enjoy something like this? An elementary school basketball game?

I could think of any number of women I knew who'd be bored senseless by it.

But Raye...?

I realized I was smiling when Eddie nudged me and leaned over. "What in the hell are you grinning about?"

I was grinning because I had the weird idea that Raye would like the game...and my family, too.

What in the hell did *that* matter? It wasn't like I was planning on introducing her to them.

What we had was purely a physical relationship.

It wouldn't last more than a couple of weeks, probably.

At Eddie's questioning look, I shook my head. "Just remembering something."

"With a smile like *that*, you got me wondering just what in the hell you're remembering...or who." A sly glint lit my brother's eyes.

Giving him a dark look, I shook my head. "Don't go getting any ideas. I've told you. I don't do relationships."

"Yeah. And tell me, straight on...were you or were you *not* thinking about a woman?" Eddie asked, his dark brows shooting up into his hairline.

"Are you a firefighter or a lawyer?" I reached for the drink I'd put between my feet and lifted it to my lips, still stalling as I tried to figure out a way around answering him. He wouldn't go running to tell the family or anything, but he'd nag me endlessly, and I didn't need that shit.

I didn't even understand why I'd been thinking about Raye so much anyway.

Sure, she was a beautiful woman, and I loved having sex with her, but I'd been with a lot of beautiful women who were fun to have sex with. Sex was fun. It was something I missed while in prison, and I was determined to make up for lost time now that I was out. I'd been free for several years, and I was *still* making up for lost time.

But Raye...

Things felt different with her.

Next to me, Eddie laughed.

I shot him a look.

He met my gaze as he picked up the nachos he'd bought. "You go ahead and tell yourself that you don't do relationships, brother. But you're doing something right now, and that look right there? The only time I've ever seen a look like that on my brothers' faces is when they're thinking about a woman."

25

Raye

Work didn't prove to be the distraction it normally was.

Every customer seemed to grate on my nerves, and my co-workers did the same thing.

The chai tea I bought from the coffee shop across the square that normally settled my nerves tasted off. When I went to go eat my dinner, I discovered I'd forgotten it – probably at Kane's, because I remembered packing it earlier.

I had to make do with a bag of chips from the vending machine because I was even tighter on funds than normal, thanks to the holidays and the new semester expenses.

I was going to be starving *and* exhausted when I got home because I'd agreed to close the store tonight. Those extra expenses meant I needed extra hours, which meant I'd get less sleep.

As it edged closer to closing time, I hauled out my school books and put them on the counter behind the cash register. We'd made it past New Year's week which was one of the craziest weeks, but now we were slowing down, and I hoped to have a few minutes here and there to study.

But even though the odd lull did come here and there, I couldn't get my mind to focus on anything.

Except Kane.

It kept going back to those intense minutes on his couch earlier in the evening.

You make me feel safe.

He did.

He'd made me feel safe enough that I'd been able to start things, that I'd been able to kiss him and touch him. And when he'd put his hands on me, I felt things inside me I hadn't thought I'd ever feel. He'd come inside me and brought me pleasure that was...wow...earth-shaking.

And yet there'd been that odd instance of panic as he crouched over me. What was that?

A memory so fragmented it could barely be called one washed up from the recesses of my mind – another man, another face, somebody crouched over me, hands gripping me, a hand tangled in my hair.

"No," I muttered, shoving the thought aside.

The bell of the door jangled, and I looked up, eager for the distraction. But Toni, the girl who was closing with me had already moved in on the two young women coming into the boutique.

Sighing, I closed my books and moved out from behind the counter, going over to the clearance racks to start straightening them.

Another half hour and we could start closing the store, then I could go home.

I'd have a glass of wine – or maybe I'd go straight to the

cheap rum I'd picked up and mix it with some soda. One drink and I'd be out like a light and this weird-ass day would be *over*.

AN HOUR LATER, I was finally home, and I did decide to go for the rum and soda. It hit me hard, considering I hadn't had much to eat since lunchtime, but I didn't bother rummaging around looking for anything to eat.

Most of what I had in the apartment was stuff like canned pasta or ramen noodles, and none of that sounded appetizing.

Part of me wished I'd taken Kane up on his offer of pizza. Not that I'd had the time, but I'd loved our casual meals together, followed by quiet chatter about everything and nothing.

And he wondered why I felt safe with him.

Brooding into my cocktail, I lay propped up in bed in my pajamas while the news played in the background. My mind was wandering, and I waited for the drink to catch up and hit me, so I could sleep. I had to be up in six hours, so I could catch the subway in time to make my first class.

My mind was comfortably hazed, finally, and I thought maybe I'd get some sleep, some real sleep.

"...local football star indicted for rape..."

I blinked and focused on the TV as a local newscaster continued to talk, reporting a story that had been dominating the area media for the past few days. Cringing mentally, I reached for the remote, but in the end, I sat there, clutching the remote and watching the TV.

"...witnesses reported seeing the victim lying unresponsive when they came across the two. The accused, according to witness reports, was on top..."

I closed my eyes, blocking out the mental image the reporter's words painted. As she continued to drone on, I grabbed the remote and turned the TV off. Straightening up in bed, I tossed back the rest of the drink and got up to mix another. I was probably going to end up with a headache in the morning.

But now I needed the alcohol to sleep.

Returning to bed, I hit the lights and sat there, drinking in the dark.

"...STOP SCREAMING..."

His voice rasped in my ear, and when I opened my mouth to scream again, he kissed me, his tongue thick and intrusive in my mouth. It gagged me, and I gasped for air when he finally stopped.

Hard hands ripped at my clothes, shoving my shirt up, jerking at my skirt.

"Look at your pretty titties, Raye!"

His voice echoed in my ears, and I tried to focus on his face. Darkness obscured much of him, but I caught sight of his eyes. Dark brown and they stared down at me.

His hands, so big and hard and cruel, closed over my breasts and I cried out in pain as he squeezed.

"Be quiet!"

He smashed his lips down on mine again, jerking up only when light flared.

A door opened! I turned my head, calling out.

"Shut the fucking door!"

Light spilled across his face, and I shrank away as I recognized him. My head spun, and my belly roiled.

No. This wasn't happening.

But the spinning in my head got worse, and when he bent back over me, there wasn't just one of him but two.

He fisted a hand in my hair, jerked my head back. This time when he kissed me, I didn't have the strength to pull away or even try to turn my head. I didn't have the strength to shove at him when he pulled my panties off.

"That's better. You know you want this...why are you trying to fight?"

I choked out something. Did I tell him to stop? Did I say no?

I couldn't tell.

But I slapped at his hands until he grabbed them and jerked them overhead, pinning me down.

When he drove into me, it hurt.

He grunted and muttered, "Fuck, you're dry, bitch. Don't you know how to do this?"

I whimpered, trying to curl up in a ball, but all that did was get me a punch in the stomach.

Dazed, I laid there, trying to breathe, but I couldn't.

My head spun.

He moved over me.

Somebody laughed.

He said something.

A door opened again, and light spilled across his face as he panted down into my face.

And I saw his.

Brown eyes.
A scar bisecting his eyebrow.

I JERKED AWAKE.

Sweating and shivering, I lay huddled in a ball on the bed as the nightmare faded, already almost out of reach.

I'd never been able to remember my dreams very well, and the nightmares like this were the worst.

Some might think it was a blessing, but some didn't know what I knew.

The *not knowing* was a curse.

The uncertainty, the fear, the doubt, all of that was a nightmare of its own, one that I'd been living with for years.

This time, I dreamed it was Kane.

For a minute, I thought I'd get sick.

I sat there on the side of the bed, swallowing the spit in my mouth and breathing shallowly until the urge past. Then, slowly, feeling like I'd aged a decade, I climbed out of bed and grabbed my robe. Shivering, I pulled it on. The heavyweight material did nothing to penetrate the chill that gripped me, and I knew it would be hours before I felt warm. It would take days for me to feel clean again.

Half stumbling into the bathroom, I turned on the lights, refusing to look at myself in the mirror.

I knew what I'd see, and it wouldn't help anything.

My pallor, my over-dark eyes, the trembling lips and the shadows that would linger in my gaze for the next few days, it was all familiar territory. What I needed now was a hot shower and a hot cup of tea. I'd curl up in my chair, and if I was lucky, I'd drowse for a few more hours.

I stood under the minuscule showerhead, scrubbing at my skin until it was pink.

It did nothing to alleviate the fact that I felt dirty, but the attempt mattered. There was a pattern I had to follow after the dreams, and the shower was part of it. Once I was done, I slathered myself in a lotion I saved for certain occasions – not special, per se, but the scent of it comforted me, and this was a time when I needed comfort. The scent of vanilla and lavender rose around me as I tugged my pajamas and robe back on.

Heading back into the main room of my apartment, I went to the stove and started a pot of water to boil.

As the water heated, I got down my box of teas and took my time looking for the lavender-chamomile mix.

Throughout the entire process, I didn't let my mind wander past anything except what I was doing.

I couldn't afford it.

I already felt just this side of shattering.

I was going to have to think, and soon.

But I wasn't ready to do it yet.

Thinking could wait.

It could wait until I was a little more focused. A little more centered. A little less wracked by cold and chills.

A few minutes later, I curled up in my chair, a heavy fleece blanket wrapped around me. I stared outside at the Christmas tree that filled the window of the apartment of my neighbor across the street. She hadn't taken it down yet. Part of me hoped she wouldn't. I found the lights calming.

I took a sip of tea.

The dregs of the dream were all but gone when I finally let myself think about it.

Only one thing remained clear.

But that one thing was enough.

I'd dreamt it was Kane.

I'd thought I'd been doing better.

I'd thought I'd come so far.

And something had set me back.

Was it just because I'd been with Kane?

Was it because I'd seen Chad?

Was it because I'd fallen asleep right after that one newscast?

Or was it simply because I was just that fucked up?

I really didn't know.

But I'd thought I was doing better. I'd thought maybe I could have a relationship with somebody. But even casual sex with a guy who made me feel as safe as Kane did had somehow wound up with me dreaming about him raping me.

I couldn't handle these dreams again.

It had taken forever for them to fade.

I wasn't going down this road again.

Not for anything.

"I'm going to have to end things with Kane."

To my horror, tears pricked my eyes.

But I wasn't going to change my mind, either.

26

Kane

I'd just cut my hand, and I stood there swearing a blue streak.

I was alone in the garage, which was a good thing. My temper was foul, and my mood was toxic.

It had nothing to do with the cut on my hand and everything to do with a phone call I'd gotten two days earlier.

Hey, Kane...it's Michelle...we need to talk.

Anytime anybody said those words, it led to trouble.

But I hadn't been expecting the conversation that followed.

Raye didn't want to see me anymore. And she didn't even have the balls to tell me herself. She'd had Michelle call me up and tell me.

I didn't even get a reason, although Michelle insisted there was something else going on. She couldn't tell me what it was, of course.

I don't know what it is...I just know Raye's holding something back.

Michelle could be right.

Maybe Raye was hiding something. Maybe she wasn't. But it wasn't like I'd be able to ask her. She didn't want to see me anymore, and I wasn't about to chase after her.

It wasn't in my makeup.

Besides, we weren't having a relationship. We'd just been having sex. Now, we weren't having anything. And she couldn't even tell me face to face.

Shit.

I had to get over this.

I hated the idea of never seeing her again, but I'd known it wouldn't last.

Still, I felt uneasy about the whole thing, especially Michelle's insistence that she thought there was more going on than what we knew. I kept thinking about the way she'd rushed out of the apartment after the last time we'd been together. We'd had a good time, right?

I'd ask her for pizza, and she'd been lying limp and lax against me, then...just like that, things had changed.

I was missing something.

Thinking about the nerves and fear I'd seen in her eyes so many times, thinking about the way she'd rushed out of here, then what Michelle had said, I pulled my phone out, half a mind to call Raye. I had her number, although I hadn't once called her. She'd texted me a few times, but why couldn't I call her? Just...we could do coffee, and I could ask her what changed, right?

My phone rang as I stood there staring at it and the sight of my mother's face on the screen made me groan. I wasn't in the mood to talk to her – or anybody. Except maybe Raye, but she wasn't going to be coming around, now was she?

It wasn't in my makeup to ignore a call from my mother, though, so I answered with a curt, "Hello."

"Kane, honey, I'm sorry to bother you, but...it's Austen."

What the fuck else is new? I managed, barely, not to snap the words, keeping them behind my teeth through sheer will. "What's going on?"

"He hasn't been to school all week." The words came rushing out of her, worry edging her voice. "The school called, and if this keeps up, he's going to either be expelled or have to repeat, and you know Austen...he won't do another year at school. I called him to see what's going on, but he won't answer his phone. He never talks to me anymore, and I'm scared, Kane. I'm just plain scared."

Frustration bubbled inside me, but I shoved it down.

"Okay, Mom. What do you want me to do?"

"He's not even answering his phone. Can you try to find him? Maybe he'll talk to you."

It wasn't very likely, but I didn't tell her that. "I'll do what I can, Mom."

As I disconnected the call, I shoved the phone into my pocket. So much for trying to reach out to Raye.

I was more than a little disgusted with the fact that I was going to have to hunt down my baby brother – *again*.

I swear, if I found him at another underground fight, I was going to nail his ass.

Maybe that was what I needed to do anyway. I'd been taking it too easy on him.

If that kid kept going on the road he was on, he was going to end up like I had...or worse. He had absolutely no sense of self-preservation these days.

27

Raye

My nerves were no better now than they had been before I ended things with Kane.

The nightmare had come again, although this time, it hadn't featured Kane front and center. It was more like a vague blur of fogged memories, stuck on repeat in my dreams.

It had been several days since Michelle had called me to let me know she'd delivered the message to Kane, then offered a shoulder if I needed one. I'd almost took her up on that and I might yet, but I wasn't sure I wanted to go down that rabbit hole, and all that might be exposed if I finally let myself open up.

Near the display in front of the store, I checked the time, eager to be out of there so I could go home and just...be away from people.

The bell over the door chimed, and I turned, a smile in place to greet the customer.

It froze as I saw who the customer was.

Chad.

Son of a bitch.

It was Chad.

"Raye..." He stepped toward me, an expansive smile on his face.

When he went to touch me, I backed away in a hurry, barely escaping his hands before he could put them on me.

He chuckled. "Sorry. Probably shouldn't be going and hugging on you while you're at work, huh?" He gave me a quick wink and looked around, rocking back on his heels as he did so. "I knew that was you I saw in here when I came by the other day. You disappeared so fast, I didn't have time to talk to you. I guess you were going on break or something."

"Or something," I said stiffly.

My breathing hitched in my lungs, and my throat shrank down to the size of a pinhole, making it almost impossible to draw in air. Heart hammering against my ribs, I felt the tips of my fingers going numb.

Panic attack. I recognized the symptoms. I'd had them before but not recently. I had to get control of myself.

If I didn't, I'd end up crouched in a corner and the thought of Chad seeing me like that was more than I could bear.

Breathe, I told myself. *You can breathe.*

Flaring my nostrils wide, I drew in a slow breath of air and forced my lungs to accept it. *It's mind over matter, Raye. Remember that.*

Chad was still talking. I had no idea what he was saying.

I managed another breath.

Some of the white noise in my head retreated.

Swallowing, I darted a look around, hoping I could find one of my co-workers to dump him on, but the only one nearby was already talking to a young woman roughly my age.

Chad's mouth finally stopped moving, and he stared at me expectantly.

"Is there something I can help you with?" I managed to say.

"Well, I'll be honest..." He stepped in closer, but not so close that it would appear inappropriate to anybody standing nearby. "I came by to see you. It's been a long time. I had no idea you'd moved to New York. Honestly, I haven't seen much of you since..." His eyes narrowed as he cocked his head. "Man, I guess it's been a couple years. Didn't see you around much after that frat party. Hell, that was some party, wasn't it? Remember?"

His tone dropped lower, almost intimate.

Did I *remember*? I felt like I was going to hurl. My hand clenched, and some part of me wanted to *hit* him.

"I'm afraid I don't think a whole lot about that time, Chad," I said, my voice rigid. "I left Texas A&M a while back, and honestly, that time doesn't cross my mind much."

Something flashed in his pale, watery blue eyes, and I braced myself for his reaction. But all he did was laugh. "Shit, maybe that's the way to handle those wild times in college. We all have them, don't we?" Another quick wink and he added, "You had some *wild* times, didn't you, Raye?"

Wild times.

Son of a bitch.

That son of a bitch.

He sidled another step closer to me, and I backed away a bit, circling around the table to keep it as a barrier of sorts between us. From the corner of my eye, I saw that my coworker had finished with the girl she'd been waiting on. "Chad, my shift's nearly over so I need to go wrap some things up. I'll turn you over to Emery, and she can help you with anything you might need here in the store."

He opened his mouth to say something, but I flagged Emery down.

She was at my side, a bright smile in place before he could say a word, and I made quick my escape.

Darting into the back of the shop, I locked myself in the bathroom and braced my hands on the sink, staring at my pale face and struggling to keep the air going in and out of my lungs.

I had to breathe.

I had to keep breathing.

If I didn't, I'd pass out, and even though he was in the front of the shop and I was back here, I refused to be in that sort of vulnerable position with him anywhere near me.

Turning on the cold water, I bent over the sink and cupped my hands under the flow, catching some and splashing it on my face. The encroaching fog washed back some. I breathed in deep. Splashed more water on my face. Breathed more.

Turning off the water, I stood there and focused on breathing.

After a couple of minutes, the rest of the panic edged back.

I needed to get out of there.

But the idea of going home no longer sounded at all appealing. Being at home where my memories swam in and engulfed me?

No, thanks.

But where in the hell was I going to go?

It wasn't a surprise when a particular face flashed through my mind.

Kane.

I wanted to see Kane.

I thought about the nightmare but shrugged it off far easier than I had any other time.

Fuck that nightmare and fuck my nerves. I wanted to see Kane. He made me feel safe, and right now, I felt so far from that, it was almost laughable.

I peeked out the front and saw that Chad was still out there, talking to Emery. Grabbing my coat and purse, I slid out the back and hurried up W. 35th. I was getting out of there and going to see Kane.

Hopefully, he'd understand that I just freaked out a little bit.

Maybe I'd explain why.

Michelle had offered a shoulder to cry on, but the shoulder I really wanted was covered in intricate tattoos.

28

Raye

I got off the subway just a block away from Kane's garage, and my breath came easier with every step I took toward his place.

By the time I rounded the building to head toward the back door, I was almost breathing normally and knew I'd made the right decision.

Turning the corner, I felt the muscles in my neck loosen, as I had made a decision. I was going to talk to him, explain why I'd wanted to call things off. He'd understand. We'd talk, and he'd do or say something that would make me feel better, just as he always did.

He'd–

"Who are you?"

A woman's voice cut me short, and I stopped dead in my tracks, staring at the tall, slim woman standing near Kane's back door. She stared at me with wariness in her expression and aggression in her stance.

"I...what?"

She looked around, her expression furtive.

I glanced toward Kane's back door, my uneasiness returning in leaps and bounds. The small square of glass that acted as a window revealed that it was dark inside the garage, only a few lights on to relieve that blackness. Kane wasn't here. I could tell that right away.

"Are you here to see Kane?" she asked, taking a step toward me.

I backed away immediately, the instinct second nature. "Why?" I asked warily.

"Just..." She licked her lips, her expression altering subtly. "Are you?"

Please don't be a girlfriend. Immediately after, I felt foolish. Not so much because of how well I knew Kane – I didn't know him *that* well, but because of how much I trusted Michelle. And yeah, I trusted Kane, too. They'd both told me he didn't do relationships.

This couldn't be his girlfriend.

"Are you here to see Kane?" she persisted, her sharp-featured face taking on a pinched look.

"Yes." I lifted my chin as I stared at her and she looked away, passing a hand in front of her eyes, a disbelieving look on her face. "Why? What does it matter to you?"

She whipped her head back around to glare at me. A harsh laugh escaped her, and she demanded, "What does it *matter* to me?"

She stormed closer to me, although when I jerked back, she stilled. "That son of a bitch and his sick little brother *raped* me. *That* is why it matters. I came over here to..."

She trailed off, but nothing else she'd said would have penetrated the veil of shock that had dropped down on me.

They raped me.

Ugly, awful memories swam up, trying to drag me down. I fought them back.

"What are you talking about?" I demanded, although the words sounded hollow to my ears.

"You heard me." The woman wrapped her arms around her middle, looking around with over bright eyes. "He raped me. Him, and his brother."

I shook my head, backing away.

I was almost to the corner of the building when I crashed into somebody. Reacting on instinct, I spun around and drove the heel of my hand upward, just the way Kane had shown me.

And Kane jerked back.

I caught sight of his startled face in the piss-yellow security light.

"Hey, Raye...calm down. It's me," he said.

But that didn't help.

The woman's voice echoed in the back of my mind. *He raped me...*

"Do you know her?" I demanded, half turning and gesturing to the woman standing near the stoop of his back door.

Kane's mouth tightened, but he glanced from me to the woman standing over near his garage. His mouth got even tighter as he stared at her, then he met my eyes. "Yeah, I know her. We used to...hang out."

"Hang out?" I laughed, almost hysterical.

The stress of the day, hell, the past *few* days crashed into me, and I slammed my hands against his chest.

"Is that what you call it?" I demanded. "*Hanging out?*"

I thought of some of the things they'd called it when I'd been in this kind of situation, and anger, shame, all of it exploded through me. Slamming my hands against his chest again, I repeated myself, "Is that what you call it?"

"Shit, Raye!" He caught my wrists, but I twisted away from him. He didn't make any attempt to hold me, but I was too angry to notice. "Look, we used to sleep together, is that what you want to know?"

"She says you raped her! You and your brother!"

A dumbstruck look came over Kane's face.

It niggled at the doubt that had already taken root in me, but I shoved it aside. People had doubted *me*, too.

"What in the hell are you talking about?" he demanded. Then his gaze slammed into the woman standing behind me. "Calie...what have you been telling her?"

"Nothing but the truth," the woman said, her voice shaking.

Calie, I thought. Her name was Calie.

"Look," Kane said, looking away from her to meet my eyes. His were dark and intense. "I used to sleep with her. I broke it off a week or so ago. But I *never* forced her, okay? My brother doesn't even know her."

"That's not true!" Calie shouted, crossing the distance that separated us to come to a stop next to me. "He's still in my bed, for fuck's sake. I had to wait until he was *asleep* to get the hell out of there."

I felt sick.

Head spinning, I turned away from them both. Rubbing my face, I tried not to let the trembling in my hands show.

Behind me, Kane said, "You are so full of shit, Calie."

"No, I'm not!" She sniffed. "He's sleeping, and if you

know what's good for you, you'll get him the hell out of my place before I call the cops."

"You're lying," Kane said, and his voice was remote. Cool. Calm.

"Is *this* lying?" she demanded.

I spun around just as she shoved a phone into Kane's face.

Something flickered in his eyes. He snatched the phone out of her hand, shock flickering across his expression as he stared at the phone.

And I knew.

Calie wasn't lying about Kane's brother being in her bed.

Fuck. She was telling the truth. I didn't have to see the picture to know.

I was going to be sick.

I'd let him put his hands on me.

Nausea roiled in my belly, and I turned away, pressing my hand to my mouth. Behind me, I heard Calie speaking, her voice loud and plaintive. The words made no sense, but they didn't need to. I heard somebody hurting, somebody in pain.

Without thinking, I turned to her and held out a hand. "It's going to be okay," I told her. She accepted my hand, her fingers closing around mine, squeezing tight. "I know that sounds hard to believe, but it's going to be okay."

From the corner of my eye, I saw Kane drawing near. "Shit...Raye, don't tell me you believe her."

I shot him a look, eyes narrowed.

He turned away, looking disgusted.

29

Kane

Of all the bullshit things Calie had done, of all the bullshit things I thought her capable of, this was the last thing I could imagine her doing. I felt half sick, but I wasn't sure if it was because she'd accused me of raping her, because it looked like she'd put her hands on my baby brother, or because Raye had *believed* her.

I didn't know which one was worse, but all three made my stomach turn.

One thing was certain, though – there was only one thing I could fix, and that was keeping Calie away from my brother.

He was seventeen, even if he didn't look it. That made him a minor, and I'd move heaven and earth to keep a leech like Calie from putting her hands on him again.

I had no doubt that she'd touched him, either.

The poor, stupid idiot probably had no idea that she'd been using him to get to me.

Idiot. I was frustrated beyond all belief at this insane turn of events.

The target of two turbulent female gazes, I debated on what to do. I couldn't believe that Raye had chosen to believe Calie over me, but there was nothing I could do about that.

And I needed to find my brother, get him the hell away from Calie, out of her reach and beyond that? I needed to find out just what they'd done, and then, as much as it turned my stomach to think about it, I might have to drag him to the police.

He'd never want to go, but the two of us had shit on our hands now, thanks to this stunt Calie was pulling. I'd risk talking to cops, something I personally tried to avoid, if it would protect my brother.

Under the intensity of Raye's gaze, I had to fight not to wilt.

I shot Calie a look, and she flinched, but Raye didn't even notice.

"Be gone when I get back," I advised her.

Raye opened her mouth to snap at me, but I turned on my heel and strode off.

Now that I had a destination of where to look for my brother, I wasn't going to waste any more time.

I FOUND him just a block from Calie's, heading in the direction of the subway I'd just left.

He caught sight of me and went still.

"What are you doing here?" he demanded.

"Looking for you." I braced myself in case he decided to try and go around me. He didn't, though.

Rocking back on his heels, Austen eyed me up and down. "Why are you looking for me? I'm doing just fine."

"The hell you are," I snapped. "School's calling Mom, hassling her and threatening to take her to court because of your truancy issues. You're on the verge of flunking out of school, and that's not exactly the ideal way to start off your adult life, you idiot kid." Leaning in closer, I added, "And let's not talk about the way Calie Smalls has accused the two of us of *raping* her."

For a few seconds, he just stared at me, no reaction.

Then he blinked and shook his head. "What?"

"You heard me."

"That's a bunch of bullshit," Austen fired back at me. "You're just fucking jealous because she wants *me* now."

"She doesn't want *you*," I snapped. "She came after you after I told her I didn't want her anymore. She's using you to get to me, and guess what? It worked."

He opened his mouth, then closed it. "You're so fucking full of it."

"How in the hell do you think I knew where to come looking for you?" Lowering my voice, I added, "Girls don't typically run around bragging to one guy that they went and shacked up with their baby brother. Not unless they're up to something."

THE TWO OF us trudged back to the garage, not speaking much.

He'd asked several questions, and I'd answered him the best I could.

I'd asked him a few questions myself, and I was still debating on how to go forward.

He and Calie had most definitely slept together.

He wasn't too keen on the idea that what happened between them was anything other than a hot chick being into him. But he was slowly coming around to accept the idea that Calie had accused both of us of raping her. I didn't know what changed his mind, but maybe he knew I wasn't the type to jerk him around about much of anything.

I had no idea.

When we finally got to the alleyway that opened up to the back of my garage, I said, "I'm going to call Mom and let her know you're going to crash with me for the night. We need to figure out what we're going to do." I pulled my keys from my pocket, thinking about nothing more than getting warm and getting a beer.

Both thoughts left my mind the second we turned the corner because the miserable excuse of a security light was shining down on a familiar head of flame-red hair.

Raye.

She was still here.

She huddled against the back door of the garage, arms wrapped around her midsection, head tucked low.

Something must have alerted her to our presence, because no sooner had I realized she was there than she was raising her head.

Her gaze met mine, and she shoved off the door, her chin coming up as she looked from me to the teenaged boy standing next to me.

"Is this Austen?" she demanded.

I didn't answer her.

"Calie left." She moved a few steps away from the door but didn't leave the stoop, eying me warily. "She told me she doesn't want to press charges because she's afraid nobody will believe her. But I think the two of you should do the right thing and turn yourselves in."

I snorted. "I just bet she doesn't want to press charges."

"Nobody ever wants to believe the victim," Raye said, her voice tight. "But I believe her."

"It's kind of funny how you'll believe a total stranger, somebody you've never even met, over *me*," I said, fuming and at the same time...*hurt*. How could she believe that lying bitch over me? I didn't understand it. And I didn't understand why I was so damn *hurt* by the idea.

Raye stared at me with haunted eyes. "Nobody ever wants to believe the victim."

"Yeah, I can believe that, but the problem is, you don't know who the fucking victim is," I told her. Cupping a hand over my brother's shoulder, I nudged him toward the door. "You need to go on inside, kid. I'll deal with this."

"You'll *deal* with it? This concerns both of you–"

I clamped my hand tighter on Austen's shoulder, squeezing until it had to be hurting him. "Go inside," I said again. "You got me?"

He nodded, and I caught sight of his pale face, realized he'd finally figured out, once and for all, that I hadn't been jerking him around.

I turned on Raye. "No," I said in a cool voice. "This *doesn't* concern both of us. At least not in the way you're talking." I almost told her off, so sick with anger I couldn't see straight. Instead, I focused on the hurt. "I *can't* believe you're choosing to believe her. This is a fucking joke."

"I guess it was a fucking joke when nobody decided to believe me when *I* was raped!" Her voice cracked as she shouted at me, the words left to linger between us.

I gaped at her, shock jolting through me. "Raye?"

She flinched at the sound of her name and whispered, "Nobody believed me."

30

Raye

Humiliation slammed into me.

I couldn't believe I'd just told him.

I'd promised myself I'd never tell another living soul, not after the way things had gone after the last time.

Nobody had ever believed me. My own mother hadn't even believed me.

Shaking, I stared at Kane.

"Um..."

I flinched at the sound of a young voice coming from just a few feet away.

Jerking my head around, I stared at a face that was a version of what Kane must have looked like when he'd been a kid.

"Hey..." The kid licked his lips, then looked over at Kane before looking back at me. "I don't know what all is going on, but I swear, Kane and I didn't hurt Calie. Shit, *she* came on to me. She was hanging out here one day when I got here after school – Kane had to run a car somewhere, and we got to talking..." His cheeks flushed, and he shot a look at Kane. "Man, I'm sorry. I really fucked things up, didn't I?"

Something about the way he said it cut through the fog in my head. Maybe it was because I could remember being young and scared – victimized.

As if he sensed my attention, the boy looked back at me, and I saw him, really saw him. Just a scared kid. "Lady," he said, voice shaking a little. "Kane and me didn't hurt her. I mean, me and her...we might have..." He blushed bright red then, and I knew exactly what they *might* have done, and I held up a hand to keep him from going on.

My blood continued to roar in my ears, and I turned away from them both trying to reconcile what Calie had insisted happened to what had happened to me, to everything Kane was saying and to what my gut was saying. Shoving all the noise aside, I focused on my gut.

I wasn't scared to be here.

That had to mean something.

I couldn't even stand to be in the same room with Chad, years later. Whether we were alone or not, I didn't want to be around him. And I hadn't *liked* him before...well. Before. Some part of me had recognized that something about him was off even before the night my life went straight to hell.

"Kane?"

Behind me, I heard them talking, and the kid asked, "Should I maybe go home? Do you two need to..."

"I'm going home," I announced, turning around to face them.

I had to get out of here, had to think, and I sure as hell couldn't do that with this kid's young, frightened eyes watching me, nor could I do it while I kept worrying about

Kane and Calie, while Kane kept standing there, watching me.

"I have to go," the kid said. "My mom...she's worried." He tried to smile at me. "She made Kane come find me because I kept ignoring her phone calls. Right, Kane?"

Kane offered the kid a tired smile. "Yeah. You should head on home, Austen. Go straight there. Take the subway and text me when you get there, okay?"

Austen nodded, but before he turned to go, he looked back at me. "You believe me, right? We didn't do nothing to that woman. Really."

I didn't know what I believed, but I didn't think the boy would leave unless I offered something, so I gave him a strained smile.

He looked relieved and turned to go.

Once he disappeared down the alley, I said, "I've got to go."

But I didn't even make it two steps before Kane caught up to me. "We should talk."

"No," I said softly. "We shouldn't."

"I don't want you leaving here thinking I could hurt a woman, Raye. I'd never do anything like that," he said, and there was a soft urging in his voice that compelled me to believe him.

I *wanted* to.

I thought about Calie's persistent pleas, and I thought about everything I knew about Kane, and my need to believe him still won out.

But...

"I was raped at a frat party my freshman year of college."

Kane's head jerked back as if I'd slapped him.

I sucked in a breath of air and blew it out, looking away from him as heat swept up to scald my cheeks. I felt sick, a nauseous greasy sensation in the pit of my belly spreading through me.

I already knew how this would go. I'd been through this before. He wouldn't believe me. Nobody ever had. But I wasn't going to hide anymore either.

After what felt like unending moments of silence, I finally forced myself to look back at him.

I didn't see the scathing look of disbelief on his face that I had come to expect from so many. He was just...waiting.

"I'd had a couple of drinks," I said defensively. "I think somebody spiked the last one. I don't remember a lot of what happened. All the memories are hazy. But I remember this one guy..."

Chad's face loomed large in my mind, and *those* memories sharpened, clarified. I thought I might get sick. Spinning away from Kane, I took a few steps forward and ran my hands over my face, fighting back the surge of nausea.

"You should sit down," Kane said gently.

I shot him a look over my shoulder.

He gestured toward his garage. "Do you...you can come in if you want. It's cold out here."

I didn't know what I wanted. But I was cold.

I followed him inside, and when he headed into the little apartment off the back, I trudged along after him. He stood by the couch after I sat, one hand absently tapping his thigh as he asked, "You want a beer?"

"Got anything stronger?"

In response, he turned away and moved to the stove. He pulled down a bottle of whiskey and a minute later, I had a glass in my hand. The aroma alone was strong enough to make my head spin, and one sip of it had warmth running down my throat to heat my belly.

"I didn't go to parties," I told him softly, staring at the floor. "I wouldn't have gone to that one, but my roommate asked me and…" Shrugging, I glanced over at him. Thoughts of May Wynn on top of everything else weren't going to help me settle, but May Wynn was part of it. A *huge* part of it. The way she'd laughed in the days that followed…I suppressed a shudder and focused on the glass I held. "We hadn't gotten along all year. I hadn't made many friends, and when she asked me to go with her, I was so excited. It was the end of the year, and I thought maybe, just maybe, I was finally figuring out how to fit in."

Pretty, popular, and as vicious as a tiger shark, May was the reason I'd gone to the party to begin with. She was also behind so many of the rumors that had been started afterward.

If it was in me to hate, I would have hated her with a passion.

"She told me the party was going to be fun. I get there, and there are all these upperclassmen, and everybody is drinking…I'd never had more than a glass of wine before, and May keeps pushing drinks on me. By the third one, I was already feeling a little tipsy. And that one…it tasted funny. I told her, but she just laughed it off." I licked my lips, looked down at the glass of whiskey I held.

"Don't drink it if you don't want it," Kane said.

"I want it," I told him, lifting it to my lips in the hopes it would steady my nerves. "I only drank about half of it. I put it down, and I think maybe I was going to get some water or something. But this guy...his name was Chad...he...um...he came up to me and asked me if I wanted to dance. I told him no, but he insisted, and I was feeling too bad to fight with him. We were dancing, and that wasn't too bad – I didn't like the guy. He'd been bothering me all year. But the dancing wasn't too bad," I said it again, staring into the whiskey. "I don't remember when we left the room. I just remember we were in the crowd with everybody else. Then it was someplace dark, and Chad was pulling at my clothes...and he...um..."

Kane's hands closed over mine. He was gentle as he took the whiskey away, just as gentle as he held my hands. "You don't have to keep talking, Raye. It's okay."

"His friend videotaped it. It got uploaded to the internet. Everybody *saw* it. People laughed," I whispered. "And they didn't believe me when I said I'd been drugged, that he hurt me."

Fury ripped across Kane's face. He bowed his head so that all I could see was the crown and his dark, thick hair. He tugged my hands to his lips, and I shuddered when he kissed them.

Finally, he looked back at me and whispered, "I believe you."

I jolted in surprise.

Nobody had ever told me that.

I believe you.

"You...you do?" Dazed, I fought to keep the strength in my body, fought not to go lax and collapse back on the couch. It was as if the strength it had taken just to go through life with everybody who knew me thinking I'd *lied* had drained me. And now that somebody had said those three words, it was more than I could handle.

I believe you.

Tears burned my eyes. Dropping my head down, I pressed my lips to his head, felt his hair against my mouth as I whispered again, "You do?"

Kane just nodded.

"May told everybody she'd seen me hanging all over him, that I'd been teasing and flirting with him all year. She told everybody I was just a tease and that I'd told her I'd was going to fuck him that night – that was why I wanted to go to the frat party all along. Everything was just horrible. Going to class, seeing people..." I shuddered, remembering the humiliation of those final days. "Then I went home, and I thought things would get better. But my mom didn't believe me either."

Kane's body went tense. "Okay. Okay."

He lifted his head, and I let him cup my chin, lifted my gaze to his.

"I can't imagine what you went through, Raye," he said, his voice gruff. "It makes me sick just to hear it, so I can't imagine what it did to you. But I *never* forced myself on Calie. She was pissed I broke things off with her. I guess that's why she went and did this."

He brushed his thumb over my lower lip. "If I came across a man hurting a woman, I'd rip him apart. I can't stand the idea of it. And if I ever meet the guy who hurt you..."

I thought about Chad, how he'd all but cornered me in the boutique, and I looked away.

He took a shuttering breath. In. Out. "Do you believe me?"

31

Kane

Her eyes met mine, so big and dark and uncertain, and it was enough to break my heart.

I didn't think she *would* believe me. Maybe with her history, it would just be too hard.

But to my surprise, after a few more seconds, she offered a tentative nod. "Yes…I think I do." A nervous smile quirked her lips, and she added, "Some part of me didn't accept her accusations from the very start, anyway."

One of the nervous knots in my gut uncurled at her words, and I wanted to cup her face, bring her mouth to mine.

I didn't let myself.

"I'm sorry I didn't believe in you," she whispered.

"I think I get it." Reaching up, I brushed her hair back from her face, relieved when she didn't tense or pull away. "After what you went through, it's a miracle you can trust anybody."

She bit her lip, her eyes darting away before returning to mine. "Up until you, I don't think I really did."

Those words melted something inside me.

"Still," she continued, reaching up to grip my wrist. "Whether you understand or not, it doesn't change what I did, doesn't make it right. If anybody knows what it's like to have people not believe them, it's me. I should know better."

"You were trying to stand up for somebody you saw as a victim," I reminded her. "That's...well, I understand why you did it. Nobody did it for you." I cupped her cheek in my hand, her skin soft and delicate against my work-roughened palms. "I'm sorry you didn't have anybody decent to stand up for you. Maybe...hell, maybe if I wasn't such a roughneck, it would have been easier for you to believe in me. That's the kind of person you deserve anyway."

She frowned at me.

I started to pull my hand away.

She caught it.

Without thinking about it, I closed my fingers around hers, forcing myself to keep going. "There are plenty of decent guys out there, Raye, guys who aren't like the asswipe who hurt you. You need somebody like that, somebody who will be there for you and take care of you."

And it was a bitch for me to understand now that I wanted to be that guy.

Not just for a little while, but for real. For good.

I wasn't supposed to want that kind of thing, but here I was wanting it with Raye, of all people.

"What are you saying?" she asked. "You...I mean, I guess you don't want to be that guy, huh?"

She gave me a wobbly smile and nodded, pulling her hand away from mine. "I understand. I mean, it's not like this was supposed to be a relationship or anything, right?"

As she slid off the couch, I stared at her.

You don't want to be that guy...

What was she, blind?

"Raye..."

She got to her feet and started for the door. "Look, like I said, I'm sorry about not believing you. And...thanks. You know, for listening. For everything." She shot a look at me over her shoulder.

I caught up with her just as she went to pull the door open.

"Hold up."

She didn't listen, tugging on the handle.

I closed my hand over hers, keeping her from opening the door. "Turn around and look at me, Raye," I whispered into her ear.

She hitched up her shoulder, but slowly, she did turn, still gripping the doorknob in one hand, her back pressed to the door, her eyes not quite meeting mine. "I should get going," she whispered.

"In a minute." I dipped my head and pressed my lips to the corner of her mouth. "I'm really not all that good with words. I think things and I know what I mean, but getting others to understand...that's a different story entirely. But maybe...maybe this will help."

I rubbed my lips against hers, using my tongue to tease the entrance of her lips until she opened for me with a moan.

Just before taking her up on that sweet offer, I paused to

whisper, "If you think I don't *want* to be that man, you're mistaken. I just...maybe you deserve better, Raye."

Her arms curled around my neck and she tugged me down close.

"Maybe you should let me decide."

32

Raye

Kane's eyes widened slightly, then his mouth was on mine. He cupped the back of my head, and there weren't any nightmares as he pulled me up against him. I felt the hard, heavy weight of his chest, felt the muscled length of him and just...*wanted*.

Curling my arms around his neck, I strained to be closer, although there was no way I could be close enough.

His hands carefully peeled away every piece of clothing I wore and when he had me naked, I pushed him back and reached for the waist of his t-shirt, tugging at the tight material. He started to pull it off, but I smacked at his hands, surprising both of us. "I want to do it," I said, meeting his gaze.

His hands fell limp to his sides, and he offered a crooked grin. "By all means."

He stood there, utterly still as I began to strip him naked, starting with his shirt and working my way down to his booted feet before returning to tug at his belt and jeans.

Once I had him naked, I stood in front of him again and laid my hands on his chest.

Still nervous, I flicked a look up at him. "I'm really curious about all your tattoos...can I?"

"You can do whatever you want."

The blunt answer, spoken in his rough voice, made my toes curl into the worn carpet. The phoenix rising from the ashes had been the first to catch my attention, but there were others. A dragon on the other shoulder, the two creatures facing like they were at war. Flames curled and twisted between them, a tiger peering through them to snarl at me.

Leaning in, I pressed my mouth to the tiger's snarling face.

Kane cupped the back of my head, urging me on.

I kissed my way over to one flat male nipple and licked him.

His broad chest shuddered.

I made my way over to the other and did the same, then kissed a path up to his neck and bit him.

His body jerked.

Pulling back, I stared up at him. "No?"

He shook his head and tugged me close again. "Yes. Like I said, you can do whatever you want."

We ended up on the couch, me sprawled on top of him, our naked bodies perfectly aligned, but he made no move to take control from me as I kissed and explored his scarred, beautiful body. When I reached his cock, I slid off the couch to kneel next to him, darting a look up at him. Nerves anew flared in me as he reached down, closing a hand around his length.

"You do only what you want, Raye," he said, voice gruff.

"I want to do this," I told him. Then I leaned forward and pressed my mouth to the head of his cock, startled at how hot and smooth he felt against me.

A harsh noise escaped his throat, and I shot a look up at him.

His eyes were closed, head arched back, the veins in his neck standing out in furious, stark relief. Turning back to the task at hand, I opened my mouth more and licked him.

A breath stuttered out of him.

I felt his hand feather down my spine, then back up, but he made no other attempt to touch me.

"Raye..."

I glanced at him, but his eyes were still closed. He held his cock so that it pointed straight up, and I closed my mouth around the top, sucking a little.

Kane's body arched up off the couch in a long, lean line, the muscles in his thighs and belly flexing.

"Fuck, Raye."

His voice was grittier, rougher.

"I don't know how to do this," I said, telling myself not to feel embarrassed by it.

His lids lifted, and he met my eyes. "You're doing it just fine. There's not a right or wrong way."

"But I..." I hesitated, then asked, "Show me how you like it?"

His chest expanded with a hard breath, then he nodded, gesturing for me to come closer. As I did, he cupped the back of my head.

I tensed at first, the echo of a memory washing up, but I shoved it back.

"We good?"

I nodded and rubbed my cheek against his length.

"You really don't need my help with this," he muttered. Then he cleared his throat. "Just...take me in."

I opened my mouth and took him inside, moved up, then down, following the guidance of his hand. After a few strokes, his hand fell away, and he went back to gripping his cock. I felt his hand shift and pulled back, watched as he cupped and squeezed his balls.

"You keep looking at me like that, and I'm going to come from that alone."

"You like me watching you?"

"I don't know if like is the word," he said ruefully. "But my dick sure as hell likes the attention." His gaze dropped to my mouth, and he added, "But it likes your mouth more."

I leaned back in and kissed the head, opening to take him back in, moving slower as I learned the taste and feel of him. When he hit the back of my throat, I slid back up. Each time I went down, I discovered I could take him deeper, and soon, I had him rocking up to meet me, muttering and swearing under his breath.

I didn't need any more encouragement after that. I knew he was loving everything I did, and more, I was enjoying it, too.

I was wet, growing wetter, and found myself clutching at his thighs, my nails biting in as I squirmed and clenched my knees together to still the ache inside me.

"Stop!" he demanded abruptly, his voice ragged.

I pulled back, staring at him in confusion. "What?"

"I'm going to come in about five seconds if you keep it up."

"Oh." I blinked, understanding dawning. "Um..."

He sat up, then rose, holding out a hand to me. I let him pull me to my feet, leaning against him and just enjoying the feel of him.

He swept me up into his arms, and I gasped, startled.

"Bed," he said, dipping his head to kiss me.

He carried me through the small apartment, and we ended up in the bed, but when he went to roll over and pull me on top of him, I shook my head. I wanted to bury the demons once and for all. "Come here," I said, pulling him on top of me.

I gasped at the feel of his weight pushing me into the mattress, at the feel of his cock burning my belly like a brand.

"Raye..." He caught my face in his hands, dipping his head to kiss me, and at the touch of his mouth on mine, I forgot everything but his kiss.

Lost in that, I didn't even notice him reaching for a condom until he pulled back to roll it on. I sat up and tugged it away from him. "Let me."

It was awkward, yet another new thing for me, but he was patient. Or at least he pretended to be. I could see the fine tremors of his muscles as I smoothed it down into place. Once I was done, I shot him a look. "That right?"

He made a few adjustments as I laid back down.

I felt naked, overly exposed but not for long. He covered me, his weight a warm, heavy blanket covering every inch of me in his security. He cupped the back of my head and said, "Open for me, Raye."

I did, and he slid his tongue into my mouth. The taste of him filled me, and I closed my mouth around him the way he did when I kissed him. He growled against my mouth, the sound rumbling all the way down to vibrate against my breasts. I shivered and arched against him, drawing him closer to me.

He rocked his hips against me, and I felt the press of his cock.

I widened my thighs.

"You ready?"

I nodded, surprised he even had to ask.

I gasped as he entered me, feeling him stretch me. Grasping his biceps, I arched up against him, desperate for more. I looked in his eyes, struggling for the words to tell him. That was when I saw the shuttered expression in his gaze and realized that he was holding back.

He'd *always* been holding back with me. Always been so careful.

I rose up and pressed my lips to his chin. "Make love to me, Kane," I whispered, using my knees to squeeze his hips.

He shuddered inside me, and I felt his cock jerk.

Instinctively, my muscles clenched around him, and a groan stuttered out of his throat.

His cock jerked again, and it tore a moan out of me. I clamped around him again, tighter this time and another low noise escaped him. "Stop doing that," he said, voice ragged.

"I can't help it. You feel so good."

He tensed inside me, then abruptly surged back and drove into me harder. A startled shriek escaped me, and he froze. "Raye?"

"Do it again…"

He did, each thrust strong and full and deep.

By the third one, I was shaking.

By the fifth, chills wracked my entire body.

And he had me coming by the seventh, wiggling and

pumping against him as he drove into me. I clung to him and still, he moved.

The pleasure built inside me again, and I reached up, burying my hands in his hair. He came to me when I pulled him down, his mouth meeting mine.

The kiss was wet, wild, and deep, a little bit crazed, and I thought maybe I could die right there and go happy.

Kane rolled onto his back and pulled my hand until I straddled him. "Ride me," he said, gripping my hips and guiding me into the right rhythm. I found it easier this time, bracing my hands on his chest and staring down at him.

His head fell back, and he watched me with hooded eyes, his lips parted, harsh flags of color dotting his cheeks. I raked my nails down his chest, and he hissed out a breath, arching under me in pleasure.

His cock swelled inside me, the head passing over that spot deep inside.

Pleasure exploded, and I cried out, sinking my nails into his skin as the orgasm sank into me.

Dimly, I was aware of Kane rocking up and grabbing me, plastering me against him, his mouth covering mine in a deep, rough kiss.

When it was over, I collapsed against him, mindless, breathless...feeling more complete than I had in my entire life.

33

Kane

I came awake with a warm, soft body tucked up against mine.

The familiar scent wrapped around me and a smile lit my face before I was even fully aware.

Raye.

She'd spent the night.

More, I got the feeling she'd be spending a lot of nights from here on out.

It was an idea I found *very* appealing.

Against my side, she mumbled under her breath, then stretched and shifted against me, reminding me that we'd fallen asleep naked. Not that I needed much of a reminder. Her breasts pressed into my side, and with every breath she took, they rose and fell against me.

Rolling onto my side, I stroked a hand down her hip.

Her eyes stayed closed.

I eased her onto her back, studying her in the faint light filtering in through the one small window in my room. That faint light gilded her skin with gold as I settled between her thighs, pressing my mouth to the crease where her leg and hip joined.

She stirred underneath me. Easing my mouth closer to the curls shielding her cunt, I murmured her name.

She stirred again.

But she didn't wake up.

Not even when I flicked my tongue against her clit.

Okay, then.

I nuzzled the folds between her thighs and found her wet. Licking deeper into her center, I returned to her clit, sucking it into my mouth, taking it with my teeth.

A low moan escaped her, and a hand curled around my neck.

Darting a look up her sweet body, our eyes met, hers still hooded with sleep and now...passion.

"You finally going to wake up and join the party?"

A drowsy smile curled her lips. "Depends...you going to keep that up?"

Instead of answering out loud, I flicked her clit again.

She shivered and thrust herself against me. I loved it when she did that. Guiding both of her hands to my hair, I urged her on until she was rocking up, all but fucking my face with each thrust of her hips, each wiggle of her pelvis.

She came with a low whimpering sound that I felt all the way down to my balls.

Just as I started to crawl up from my place between her thighs, though, there was a knock at my apartment door. My *apartment* door...meaning somebody from the garage was knocking.

"Shit."

She laughed against my mouth as I froze, all ready to bury myself inside her and get lost for a little while.

"Make whoever it is go away," she suggested, her eyes sparkling as she stared at me. She looked happier than I'd ever seen her, and the sweetness of her expression made my heart flip over in my chest.

"I'll do that." I dropped a quick hard kiss on her mouth and got up, grabbing a pair of jogging pants from the foot of the bed, hauling them up over my hips before leaving to deal with the person at the door.

But one look through the peephole told me I wouldn't be returning to bed with Raye. "Hold on," I called through the door. Then I went back to the bedroom and peered inside. "Raye...it's my kid brother, Austen. I'm going to need to talk to him."

She sat up, staring at me. "Oh. Of course." Her cheeks flushed as she looked around. "I...I think my clothes are out there."

"I'll get them." I fetched the various pieces of clothing and brought them to her.

"I'll wait in here until–"

I caught her face and craned it up to mine. "No. You're not waiting in here. Get dressed. Come out."

Raye's cheeks blushed that delectable, delicate pink and I kissed her once more, gentle and slow. "My brother knows what sex is, Raye. I'm not worried about him knowing about us."

"Oh." She nodded, a tentative smile curling her lips.

As I turned to go greet him, I wondered if she had any idea how different a thing this was for me. Because I *didn't* let women spend the night. I didn't introduce women to my family.

But I wanted Raye to get to know mine.

She'd gone and changed everything.

AUSTEN and I were at the kitchen table when she emerged a few minutes later, wearing the same clothes from last night, a nervous smile on her pretty face.

I'd told Austen she was there, and he'd grinned at me. "That's great."

Now, as she drew closer to the table, my brother got up and held out his hand. "Hi, I'm Austen. We didn't really have a chance to meet last night."

"Raye," she said, her voice soft.

I'd risen the moment she came out of the bedroom, and now I nudged a chair out from under the table with my foot. "Want a seat?" I asked.

"I...well, you two are talking. Maybe I could make some breakfast?"

Austen darted a look at me. "I didn't eat before I left. I could eat."

"I can make cereal," I said shortly. "Raye, you don't need to wait on us."

"I'm kind of hungry," she hedged. "And there's no *making* cereal. You pour milk on it."

"It's one of my number one kitchen skills," I told her.

"I'm highly adept at it myself, but I've got a few other talents." She back-stepped, then cut around me.

I groaned at the mental image of my mostly bare fridge.

"Well...you've got...cheese. And eggs. Omelets?"

My belly rumbled. "Fine. If you're going to insist on cooking."

I dropped back down into the chair across from Austen and met his eyes. We'd only been talking a few minutes, and I was almost certain he'd freeze back up again on me now that Raye was out, but to my surprise, he said, "I think we should probably go to the cops. Now that I'm not being all stupid, I can look back, and I think she's pretty pissed at you, Kane. I don't want her trying to cause trouble for you."

"Don't you worry about me," I told him, watching Raye from the corner of my eye.

She was pretty at home in the kitchen, even my small, mostly useless one. I could fry an egg and burn bacon with the best of them, and heating up canned soups and making a grilled cheese ranked right up there with my ability to make cereal, but that was about the end of my kitchen skills.

Clearly, Raye outreached me in that area.

She was whipping eggs in a bowl. Whipping or beating, whatever it was, and she did it with an ease that told me she was no stranger to the task.

"I can't help but worry. If she causes trouble, then I'm partly to blame," Austen said, his young voice sharp.

"We're going to take care of that," I told him, turning my gaze to meet his. "I was going to call you about that later today, but since you're here..." Blowing out a breath, I shrugged off my unease about talking to the police and told him, "I think you're right about going to the cops. Not so much about her so-called rape story, but because the two of you were intimate. She's twenty-five, Austen. You're seventeen."

"So?" He blinked at me, looking confused.

"You're a minor." Bracing my elbows on the table, I leaned forward and met his eyes. "Did she ever ask you how old you were? Did you ever tell her?"

"I...hell. No." He scoffed, clearly embarrassed but trying to hide it. "What's that matter?"

"It's called statutory rape. The law is meant to keep adults from preying on minors...kind of like Calie preyed on you."

"Look, man..." He shifted around, looking uncomfortable. "I mean, she came on to me, but it wasn't like I didn't want it or anything."

"She took advantage of a kid for her own selfish purposes." I held his eyes. "If she thinks she can use you to get to me, she's going to have to think again."

"KANE AND AUSTEN JONSON?"

A tired looking detective in a rumpled suit stood in the doorway, eying us.

Raye stood when we did, her hand coming out to take mine. "You want me to come with you?"

I nodded, surprised at how much easier it had been to walk into the police station with her at my side.

She gave Austen an encouraging smile as we started toward the cop. I knew enough about cops after my dealing with them to know the guy in front of us had to be at least a detective.

He looked too young to be much higher ranked than that,

although there was age in his eyes, a look that said he'd seen some shit.

Once we were at his desk, he gestured for us to sit, then he frowned, taking note of Raye and added, "I'll dig up another seat."

I let Raye take the second one, opting to stand for as long as I could.

Once the cop brought a chair over, though, I accepted it out of courtesy and told him thanks. Maybe being nice would win me some brownie points. Still, I wasn't sure if this trip to the police station was going to do us much good. I'd even warned Austen that we might be wasting our time.

With my history, they might just write us off, which meant I needed to start thinking about the next alternative in case Calie did come in and try to press charges.

My gut churned just thinking about it.

I hadn't put hands on her in a couple of weeks, but it would come down to her word against mine. Her word against mine and my brother's. And my brother *had* been with her.

Fuck, this was a mess.

"I'm Detective Gus Winters, and I'll be handling your complaint today, Mr. Jonson." He nodded at me, then glanced at Austen. He clicked on the mouse on his computer, then asked, "Curious...are you related to a firefighter by the name of Eddie?"

"Yeah." I summoned up the polite smile my mother had drilled into me. "He's my brother."

"That a fact?" A smile lit the tired detective's face. "You're the mechanic, then? Eddie's mentioned you. He's good people, Eddie is." The cop's eyes slid to Austen, and he nodded at him. "He's mentioned you, too. You're the youngest one, right? I'm also the youngest in my family. Five brothers, pains in the ass, all of them."

Austen squirmed, looking a little uncomfortable. "They ain't so bad. At least not all the time."

Winters barked out a laugh. "They ain't so bad when you need them. That's the truth. Family's family, right?"

He cracked his neck, turning his head to the left, then to the right. "Alright, folks. Why don't you tell me what brings ya down here today?"

After a quick look at Austen, I started to talk.

WINTERS TOOK IT ALL DOWN, his face a blank mask that revealed absolutely nothing, but when he was done taking the information, he leaned back in the seat.

"You can press charges. Is that what you want to do?"

"I..." Austen looked at me, then at the cop. "I can press charges?"

But the cop was staring at me. "He's a minor."

"I know. But this will boil down to he said, she said." I frowned, glancing over at Raye.

"There's a picture," she said softly, reminding me.

I leaned in close, shaking my head. "Just of him in her bed. It's something, but not everything."

The cop was clearly listening.

"I don't want to press charges," Austen said, speaking in a firm voice. "I mean...shit. I knew what was going down. I was stupid, and I feel stupider knowing she did it all to get to my brother, but I knew what was going down. I'd rather the whole world not know how stupid I was."

The cop tapped a pen on his desk, eyes thoughtful.

"Maybe what we can do is this. Take the complaint. Hold off doing anything. If she comes in to file charges...then we decide." Winters slid a look from Austen to me. "Of course, it really is up to the guardian..."

Austen paled. "Mom..."

"I'll handle talking to Mom," I told him. She was going to be pissed. Nobody fucked around with her boys. I'd be lucky if she didn't hit the streets looking for Calie herself. "I think that sounds like the best way to handle it," I finally said.

"Okay." Winters leaned back over his desk, punching at the keyboard in a staccato fashion. "I'm making a note in the system. If she does come in, I get flagged. As long as it happens during the day, I'll get notified, and I'll handle it. Regardless of when it does happen, *if* it happens, I'll get word of it, and I'll be in contact. Okay?"

It was, I decided, the best outcome we could hope for.

34

Raye

It was amazing the difference a day could make.

I could have skipped my way to work, I felt so light. It sounded silly, and I couldn't really put a finger on what had changed. Unless it was true, and I'd really, deeply, honestly opened myself up to another human being. To a man. To Kane.

It had made all the difference in the world, though.

In truth, I felt a little odd, feeling so light inside while knowing that Calie could still cause trouble for Austen and Kane. The thing was, my gut doubted it would come to much, and for my part, I knew the brothers hadn't hurt her.

If I was honest, I'd known that truth deep down from the first moment the accusation had been made.

It had never made sense. It hadn't fit.

No man with the ability to make me feel as safe as Kane could be the sort of man who'd force himself on another woman.

But getting one part of me to accept that truth while I

was still struggling to trust Kane after everything I'd gone through was a different story.

I'd let those walls down, though.

I trusted him, and it had changed everything.

"What are you smiling about?"

I glanced up to see Emery waiting at the computer in the back, probably for me to clock in so she could do the same. "Am I smiling?" I asked.

"Only a little." She winked at me. "He must be amazing."

"Ah...yeah. Yeah, he is." I wasn't sure if *amazing* touched Kane, but at least it gave an idea. Hurriedly, I clocked in so Emery could do the same.

"Well, good for you. I'm going to go out on a limb here and assume it wasn't that asswipe from the other day." Emery clocked in and turned to face me, her long brown hair swept up in a half ponytail that put her beautiful features on display. Her bright green eyes met mine, and she rolled them emphatically. "I can see why you didn't want to wait on him. Talk about a *douche*."

The reminder of Chad was one I could have done without, but I refused to let it dull my mood.

I gave her a smile and nodded. "We went to the same college my freshman year." Hesitating a moment, I finally said, "He...ah...he hassled me a lot, you know?"

"He seems like the type. Thinks he's God's gift, and when he finds out he's not, he turns into the biggest dick." Emery shook her head. "I've met the kind, honey. Believe me. Best to just steer clear of that shit."

It felt good to have somebody validate my feelings about him, but I didn't elaborate as we headed out to the sales floor. The morning shift was happy to be relieved, and once we'd traded out, I offered to handle bringing in the new stock from the back of the store.

The first few hours passed easily enough, but that dreaded lull in the afternoon came as expected, and Emery left for her lunch hour right as I was debating whether to take mine or not.

The store manager was in the back, and I was alone in the front when the bell tone signified a customer. The sight of the man filling the doorway caused bile to churn in my stomach. It was the absolute last person I wanted to see.

Don't panic.

Kane's voice from the lessons he'd given me rose up to murmur from the back of my mind, and I tucked them deep inside. *Don't panic.*

It was harder than I liked because, as he stood there, Chad took a long, slow look around the sales floor, and I couldn't help but notice the way he smiled when he saw it was just him and me.

Think that's going to be your advantage, dickhead?

I couldn't help the spurt of anger that rose inside me. The asshole had come back here, looking for me. I knew he had. To harass? To hurt? How far was he willing to go? How far was I?

As he took a step in my direction, I edged away, careful to keep something in between us the entire time.

When you can, you want to keep him from getting close. That's always the best tactic. Got it?

Like we were back together in his garage, Kane's voice guided me.

"Raye..." Chad smiled at me, his lips peeling back from his teeth in a broad, easy grin.

"Did you need something, Chad?" I asked, keeping my voice calm and level.

He hitched up a shoulder. I noticed that at some point in the past two years all that muscle had started to go a little soft. He was still big and solid, but there was a layer of fat that hadn't been there before.

"We just never had much of a chance to finish talking." He edged closer, eying me over the table I kept between us. "I thought maybe I'd drop by again. See if you wanted to go out...grab a bite to eat." His lashes drooped low, and he added, "We could catch up on old times."

"There's nothing I want to catch up on, thanks." I held his eyes levelly, surprised I had the guts to do it.

A grin spread across his face, and I could see the laughter in his eyes.

Laughter...and *knowledge*.

He knew what he was doing to me.

The piece of shit.

"Aw, come on, Raye." He moved a little faster and tried to come around the table to corner me.

I dodged in the other direction, feeling a little foolish at the Ring Around the Rosie game we were playing, but I wasn't letting him get close to me either.

"What's the matter, Raye?" He gave me the same wide, charming grin he'd flashed a hundred co-eds. "You look a little spooked. You got ants in your pants or something? Stop dancing around and talk to me."

"I don't want to talk to you. If you're not going to buy something, maybe you should just leave."

His mouth tightened then, and he moved toward me once more, quicker this time. My high heel caught on the display, causing me to slip a little. That tiny hesitation was just enough for him to pounce, and he caught me up against the table.

Instinct took over, and I reacted, striking up with my hand the way Kane had told me to.

Of course, he hadn't told me it would *hurt*.

I jabbed Chad straight in the neck, and he stumbled back, his face red as he choked for air. The red slowly turned to rage, though, and he swiped out with a hand.

I wasn't where I had been, and he came up empty.

When he swung out again, he swung wild, and I stepped outside his reach, slapping both my hands against his arm before shoving him off balance. "I'm not the easy target I used to be, Chad. Leave me the hell alone."

He spun around to face me, his eyes huge and furious.

But when he took a step toward me, I jutted my chin up. "Leave me *alone*," I warned him. "Come near me again, and I'll call the cops."

He sneered at me. "Yeah, like that worked out for you so well last time."

"I'm not some scared little freshman, desperate for people to like her anymore," I said, curling my lip at him. "And this isn't *your* town. If I call the cops, people are going to listen to me."

He scoffed and opened his mouth to speak, but I didn't give him the chance.

"And what's more...if you keep fucking with me, I'm going to go online and ruin you." I took a step closer to him and glared at him in challenge. "What do you think your boss and clients will think when you're accused of being a rapist, Chad?"

"You little cunt..." He lifted a hand, his face florid with rage.

Fear bloomed inside me, but I didn't take back what I said. "What's the matter? You scared?" I challenged.

The creaking of the door was the only indicator that something had changed.

I heard it.

Chad didn't.

He advanced on me, and I stood my ground. I had a witness. If he touched me, I was taking him down.

But before his hands came down on my shoulders, my manager said, "Raye, is there a problem here?"

The sound of her voice had never been so welcome, yet at the same time, I was disappointed that she stopped him before a physical threat had been witnessed. Turning my head, I looked at Pauline and met her gaze. "No, ma'am. Everything's fine. This gentleman was just leaving."

The look Chad gave me on his way out the door was a familiar one. I'd seen it a dozen times – no, more – during my freshman year in college. *I'm not done with you*, that look said.

I managed to suppress a shudder as I turned to focus on my manager. Pauline gave me a concerned look, her dark eyes softening as she studied me. "Raye, is everything alright?"

"I'll be fine," I told her.

I just hoped I wasn't lying.

35

Kane

Let me decide...

Her words kept circling around in my head, and I wished I would have thought to ask her what she needed to decide on.

I mean, I knew what I thought she'd meant, but I wanted to be certain.

I still thought she deserved somebody better to take care of her, but she knew I wanted her. No. I more than wanted her, I wanted to *be* that guy.

And if she wanted me like I wanted her, there was no chance in hell of me walking away from her. From us.

But I needed to be sure that was what she'd meant.

How you going to be sure of that, genius?

There was only one way, logically, and that was for us to have one of those relationship talks.

The idea scared the shit out of me and for good reason. I'd never been in a relationship, so the idea of a *relationship* talk was new to me. New and unfathomable.

I was approaching a lot of unfathomable territory with her, though.

Like...do I go and see her today?

Should I give her space?

I had no idea what the right thing to do was, or if there *was* a right thing.

What I did know was that I couldn't quit thinking about her and I most definitely did want to see her, so when the time came for me to close up shop, I did so in double time, moving through the routine quicker than normal so I could get the hell out of there.

Once I was done, I headed uptown, eager to see her. I hoped she was still at work because I had no idea where she lived.

That was another thing I hoped to change.

I wanted to know where she lived, what she did when she wasn't working and what sort of things she liked, what she hated.

I also found myself brooding about what she'd told me.

It made sense.

As much as I'd hated to hear her story, none of it had surprised me. I'd known there was something at the core of the fear I'd often seen in her, but to hear the whole thing...

The urge to protect her, to keep anything else in life from hurting her again was almost overwhelming.

Maybe I'd ask her if we could go out to dinner and we could have that...talk.

If not, I'd ask if I could at least see her home. I didn't like to think about her going home alone late at night. Not by herself. She'd already been through enough, and nobody knew better than me what kind of low-lives loitered in the New York City streets.

I'd been one of them and I sure as hell hadn't been the worst.

As the subway came to a stop, I gripped the pole a little tighter and tried to pretend I wasn't nervous about seeing her. Getting nervous about a girl, brooding about a girl. Things that were so unfamiliar to me, I couldn't even process them.

The doors to the train car slid open, and I moved with the flow, exiting out and heading up the stairs into the chilly night air. It was a block to get to Raye's work from where I was, and I shoved my hands into my coat pockets, walking fast.

Outside the store, I paused, staring inside for a brief moment as I took everything in.

It was the kind of store I didn't normally frequent and not just because all it sold was women's underwear.

It had *classy* all but written across the plate glass window.

Classy. One thing I was not.

I could see my reflection in that window, just barely, but I didn't need the reminder to know what I looked like. At least I'd changed clothes and wasn't covered in car grease, although I doubted it would make much of a difference to the ladies inside the shop. I could see one of them now, dressed in sleek black, her hair pulled away from her face, moving around the pretty store as she did whatever it was shop clerks did when they weren't waiting on people.

I had no doubt none of them would want to wait on me.

This might have been a mistake, I realized.

Don't be a chickenshit, I told myself. *Go on inside.*

In the end, my desire to see Raye won out, and I pulled

the door open, slipping inside and hoping that maybe I could go unnoticed by the staff.

Fat chance of that.

It wasn't busy in the store, just a few customers here and there, and the moment I pulled on the door, a bell-like tone sounded in the air.

A woman's voice called out, almost songlike, "Good evening, sir! We'll be with you momentarily!"

I fought the urge to hunch my shoulders and retreat inside the heavy work coat I'd pulled on against the chill of the day.

I tried to get lost among the racks of silk and lace, but a guy as big as me, a guy as rough looking as me tended to stand out when surrounded by pretty pastels and rich red silk. Finally, I stopped trying and ended up standing by a table with a display of silvery blue lingerie. I found myself thinking how Raye would look in some of the pieces on the table and was about to check the price when I sensed a pair of eyes on me.

Glancing up, I saw one of the store clerks watching me with a disdainful look scrawled across her expression.

Blood rushed to my face. The look was a reminder that I was out of place here.

Screw the bitch, I told myself.

Part of me wanted to leave, but the other part was determined to find Raye.

Would she be embarrassed to find me here?

That idea pissed me off, and I snatched the pair of panties off the table to distract myself. The price tag on them sure as hell proved to be a distraction. That much for a scrap of silk?

What the hell?

"Sir. Can I help you?"

Please don't be the snooty bitch, I thought.

I looked up and found a woman who was *beyond* pregnant standing in front of me. She gave me a polite smile, then glanced at the panties I was clutching in my hand.

I must have looked like an idiot.

"I...um..."

She waited patiently, like guys came in here and stuttered in front of her all the time.

A door opened, and a familiar voice called out, saving me. "I'll see you later..." There was a little gasp. "Kane?"

"Raye," I said, tearing my gaze away from the sales clerk.

Raye was already halfway across the store to me by the time I'd made my way around two of the delicate looking tables, and we met in the middle, me catching her up in a hug.

Somebody whistled.

I pulled back, not letting myself kiss her because that probably wasn't the thing to do in the middle of her place of employment. I wanted to, though, and the sight of her eyes shining up at me made the impulse that much stronger.

"I was going to see if I could take you out to dinner."

She rose up on her toes and tugged my head down to meet hers.

Well, okay. If she was going to kiss me while she was here at work, who was I to argue with her?

WE ENDED up at a chain restaurant on the square, one I'd

only eaten at once or twice. Raye had commented that she loved the food there and that was all it had taken.

She'd grinned at me when I took her hand and pulled her inside, but now that we were sitting down at a table, she looked...pale. Strained, really.

"Everything okay?" I asked.

"I'm just stressed about school." She hitched up a shoulder. "I've got a heavy class load this semester, and between that and work, I've probably taken on more than I can handle."

"Should we have skipped coming here?" I asked.

"No!" She shot me a smile. It was faint, but real. "I need some food. I never eat much more than a salad or canned soup when I'm working, and I'm *starving*. Besides, I love eating here. I can't do it too often because I'm always strapped for cash, but I love this place."

Her answer made me relax a little, and when the server appeared, she ordered a cocktail while I stuck with beer.

After we'd finished studying the menus, we placed our orders, and once more, an odd, strained sort of silence fell.

"You sure everything is okay?" I asked again when I noticed she was folding the napkin up into a small triangle.

She gave me a wan smile. "I'm fine."

"You don't look fine. You look stressed out. If me showing up at your work was a problem—"

"No!" She shook her head. "It wasn't that."

"So, there *is* something."

Raye bit her lip, then slowly nodded. "Yes. There was something." She huffed out a breath, and I realized how tense she was, as if one wrong move might make her shatter.

"Want to talk about it?" I prodded.

She slumped back against the seat and closed her eyes. When she finally opened them, the expression I saw there filled me with conflicting urges – I wanted to hug her up close to me. I wanted to pummel something.

She looked scared and upset.

Leaning forward, I took her hand. "What's wrong, Raye?"

She looked uncertain for a moment, then a heavy sigh escaped her, and she started to talk.

The bastard who'd hurt her was named Chad.

Apparently, he'd shown up at her work that day and had gotten in her face. Plus, it wasn't the only time he'd been around. It was the first time he'd gotten confrontational, though.

As she told me about how she'd handled it, I wanted to hug her tight. One, because she'd handled the piece of shit like a pro. But for another reason, she shouldn't have *had* to handle the asshole.

"Want me to dig him up and tear him apart?" I offered once she finished talking. "The two of us can...have a chat. He won't ever touch you again by the time our conversation is finished."

Raye laughed, the sound light, almost easy. "No. I'm good." She turned her hand over in mind and squeezed my fingers. "Thank you. Talking about it helped."

Me beating the piece of shit up so he never bothered her again would help more.

It was an idea that held way too much appeal for me.

"Stop," Raye said, her voice gentle but firm.

Flicking my eyes at her, I cocked my head.

She gave me a knowing look, her hand tightening on

mine. "I know what that look on your face means. But I don't need you to tear him apart for me. I just...hell. I want to just forget about it."

"I can help you with that." I lifted her hand to my lips.

Heat softened her dark blue eyes.

"I like the sound of that."

"I LIKE THE SOUND OF THAT," Raye said, her voice breathy as I kissed my way down her torso, straight on a path down.

I'd just told her I had a goal in mind to kiss every last inch of her.

It was just one of the fantasies I had involving her.

She keened out my name as I thrust my tongue into her cunt, loving the way she rocked up, both her knees and her hands coming up to urge me on. Her knees squeezed at the sides of my head, her heels digging into my back while her fingers tangled and twisted in my hair, pulling me closer. Not that I could get much closer.

I had my mouth sealed to the heart of her, and I didn't ever want to stop.

My cock pulsed, and I amended that. Eventually, my dick would get its way and be seated inside her, but for now, I was happy to just eat her sweet pussy and listen to her moan.

Moans that turned more frantic and urgent as I lingered here, tugged there, sucked and nuzzled. She became demanding, something that hadn't happened before, and the sound of her begging me, "Right there...just...*there*, Kane...don't you dare stop..." was about the hottest damn thing I'd ever heard.

She came hard and fast, but even as the climax worked through her, she didn't let go of my hair, demanding I give her more.

I climbed my way up her body and slanted my mouth over hers, feeding her the taste I'd stolen from her.

"Open for me," I muttered against her lips, using my knee to spread her legs wider.

She wrapped them around me, and I felt the hot, wet kiss of her pussy. Without thinking, I arched my hips and pushed inside her.

That was when I realized the error – no condom.

She felt it, too, arching under me and bracing her hands against my chest. "Kane?"

"I need a condom," I said, panting against her lips. "Tell me you have one."

She shook her head, eyes wide.

"*Fuck!*"

But when I went to pull out, she locked her ankles just under my ass. "Do we have to stop? I'm on the pill. I started after..." Her eyes clouded, and I bent my head, kissing her hard and fast.

"Don't think about that. Don't think about him," I ordered her. "Not here with me. Not ever, if I can help it."

"No. Not here," she agreed. "But..." She arched against me once more, her nipples stabbing against my chest, another wicked temptation in a sea of them. "But...do we have to stop?"

I stared down at her beautiful face. Common sense warred with want. "We should. It's the smart thing to do."

"I've tried to be smart my entire life," she said, a smile playing on her lips. "It's overrated."

When she undulated under me, I was lost. "Fuck smart," I said hoarsely.

With a groan, I sank all the way inside her, experiencing the bliss of being skin to skin for the first time. She was hot, wet silk around my dick, and it was the sweetest ecstasy I'd ever known.

"You feel so good," I muttered against her ear.

"You, too." She shivered under me.

I withdrew and thrust back inside, keeping it slow, wanting to savor every moment.

But nothing that good ever lasted.

She tightened around me, the muscles in her pussy milking my cock until I squeezed my eyes shut against the sensation. I almost saw stars the next time she did it, and I slammed into her harder than before.

She cried out.

"Raye?"

"Do it again," she pleaded.

Who was I to reject a lady's request.

I did as she asked, and what had been slow, almost sweet turned dirty and frantic, bordering on rough. Her nails dug into my shoulders, her mouth biting into mine as she sank her teeth into my lower lip. I thrust my tongue into her mouth, and she responded by sucking on my tongue the same way I'd like to have her sucking on my prick.

It drove me crazy, and I had to fight not to let go of my baser instincts.

Warning tingles raced up and down my spine, and I clenched a hand in the sheets beneath her, trying to ride it out.

But she came around me, her silken tissues starting to spasm and grip me tighter than a fist.

Her climax triggered my own, and those chills racing down my spine turned into something with all the force of a neutron bomb. It hit low and fast, and I exploded.

I groaned into her mouth as the orgasm slammed into me. She spasmed around me, milking...squeezing...draining me dry.

36

Raye

It seemed impossible that only a week had passed.

It seemed impossible that a week *really* had passed.

I hadn't seen or heard from Chad.

Kane had told me he hadn't seen or heard from Calie... and neither had Austen.

Maybe things were going to actually settle down, and I could enjoy this new time with my...*boyfriend*.

Wow.

I was still having a hard time believing it. Kane and I had what we considered was a *talk*. A big one. Neither of us had ever been in a serious relationship before, a fact that baffled me when it came to Kane, but he'd told me that he'd never really considered himself relationship material.

You changed all of that, Raye, he'd said.

I still found myself grinning whenever I thought about it.

But Kane had gone and changed everything for me, too.

That was the amazing thing. We'd gone and changed

things for each other. And today, he wanted me to meet his family.

He'd already told me that his dad died when he was a kid, but he wanted me to meet his mom, brothers, and sisters – well, one of his sisters. The other was back at school at M.I.T., a fact I found a little intimidating, although I wasn't going to tell him. Not yet anyway.

But his other sister and the rest of his brothers, their families, he wanted me to meet them and his mother.

Which explained why I was standing in front of the mirror at ten a.m. on a Sunday morning, fussing with my hair and getting ready. I normally didn't even crawl out of bed before ten on a Sunday, and here I was with my makeup already on and debating between a gray sweater that made my eyes look bluer and a blue sweater that made my eyes look lighter.

I went with the blue sweater. It featured a V-neck that I thought would appeal to Kane, although it wasn't at all revealing.

I decided I'd picked right not even five minutes later when I answered the door, and he looked at me with a gleam in his eyes and a smile on his face.

"You look gorgeous," Kane said, a low growl in his voice as he stepped inside. He pulled me up against him, and I giggled as he rubbed his face against my exposed neck. "Way too good for me to waste on taking over to meet my family. Let's get naked instead."

"That means I'm wasting it on you too, goofy," I said, pulling away before he messed up my lipstick.

His lids drooped low as he stared at me. "It's not a waste. I'd appreciate it more than they would."

"Stay," I said, holding a hand up as he advanced on me.

He did, but not without a surly look...and a sexy one that ended up sending pangs right square to the core of me.

Huffing, I turned on my heel. "You wait here," I told him over my shoulder as I headed to grab my boots.

If he ended up following me, we'd be late getting over to his mother's, something I didn't want to do the first time I met her.

I'M NOT GOING to have a panic attack.

I'm not going to have a panic attack.

"Will you relax?" Kane murmured, leaning in to whisper the words in my ear as we trudged up the final flight of stairs. "You're so nervous, you're making *me* nervous."

"I'm sorry," I squeaked out. "I just...what if they don't like me?"

"The only person you need to worry about is Dinah, and half the time she doesn't like *me*," he said, as brutally honest as he always was. He pulled me to a stop once we reached the top of the stairs, tugging me over to the wall.

I leaned up against it, and he partially caged me in, leaning over me with one arm barring me in.

I didn't feel trapped with him doing this. I felt...protected.

He cupped my face with his free hand and rubbed his thumb over my lower lip.

"Why doesn't Dinah like you?" I asked, irritated by that idea. I knew who Dinah was – the oldest girl, just a little younger than him. She'd made far different choices than he had, and he'd never made any attempt to hide how proud he was of her – or any of his siblings.

He'd made mistakes. I'd never deny that. But he'd overcome them and was trying to do better. That should count for *something*.

"Because I fucked up. She won't ever forget that."

I huffed out a breath, already deciding that maybe I wouldn't like Dinah.

I wasn't very good at hiding how I felt because Kane's face lit with a grin. "You'll like her just fine," he told me.

I raised my chin. "Not if she doesn't like you."

"It's not that she doesn't *like* me," he said, hedging. "She just...I think she worries about the kind of example I might set for the younger kids in the family. I mean, hell. Look at Austen."

"Austen is old enough to make his own choices," I said tartly.

Kane opened his mouth, maybe to argue, but in the end, he just closed it and shook his head. "It's going to be fine," he muttered. But I don't know if he was saying it to me...or to himself.

I FELL IN LOVE.

Several times over.

The first time was with his brother, Eddie, who kissed my hand and told me I better be careful and not break his brother's heart.

The second time was with Kane's brother-in-law, Justin – Dinah's husband. "I knew somebody would get him, sooner or later," he said with a huge grin. "It was just a matter of time."

The third time was with two twin little girls, Rose and Zoe, who took one look at me and instantly held up their arms, demanding to be hugged.

But the fourth and most important time happened when Kane led me to the kitchen and said, "Mom?"

A slim woman with graying brown hair turned away from the stove.

She looked at him, then her gaze fell on me.

Her eyes widened slightly, then to my horror, they filled with tears.

I wanted to hide, but even as I was considering the option, she rushed toward me and caught me up in a hug. "You're Raye," she said simply. "Kane's told me so much about you."

It was the first time I'd ever felt such simple, non-demanding warmth.

Without thinking, I curled my arms around her and hugged her back.

"Hi," I said through the emotion clogging my throat.

She laughed and pulled back, staring up at me. "You want to help me with lunch?"

I MET Dinah maybe halfway through lunch.

She'd been there all along, but according to a comment I'd heard from Eddie's boyfriend, Rick, she'd gone to lay down and didn't get up to join us until seconds were being passed.

The moment she appeared in the doorway, Eva Jonson got up to fetch the plate she'd set aside for her oldest daughter, and when she brought it back, Dinah frowned down at it.

"No meatloaf?"

"You wouldn't eat it anyway," Eva said, waving a dismissive hand.

I didn't think much of the comment until later, when Eva leaned forward, elbows on the table. "Are you going to tell us, Dinah?"

Dinah looked at her mother, a perplexed expression on her face. "Tell you what?"

Eva laughed as she sat back. "You took an hour-long nap in the middle of the day, and you've bolted from the table twice. I think you know what I'm talking about."

"Oh, fine..." Dinah rolled her eyes while her husband leaned over and covered her hand with his. Her announcement of *"I'm pregnant,"* was almost drowned out by hoots and hollers as everybody else in the room figured out what Eva was getting at, and Dinah was soon enveloped by people wanting to hug her and ask questions.

I stayed where I was.

Surprisingly, so did Kane.

"Aren't you going to rush over and hug her?"

He shrugged, a faint smile playing on his lips. "She's getting plenty of hugs right now. I'll catch her later." He slanted a look at me. "You don't seem too ready to bolt for the door. My family not scared you off yet?"

"Nah," I said lightly. I wasn't about to tell him that I was about as enamored with his family as I was with him. That might scare *him* off. "This isn't so bad."

The grin on his face told me that he'd seen some of what I was trying to hide.

It was okay, though. I realized it as his gaze softened, and he leaned over to press a kiss to my temple, hugging me tight. I was surrounded by the scent of him, the feel and strength of him, and I let myself sink into his embrace.

"None of that now," a playful voice said.

I looked up to see Eddie wagging a finger at us. His gaze locked with mine and he winked at me. "Leading my brother astray, I see how it is," he said.

I blushed while Kane swatted out with a hand, connecting with the back of his brother's head.

Eddie took it with good-natured humor, settling back in his seat next to Kane while eying the rest of the family, most of whom were across the table. "Looks like just about all of us are settling down, huh?"

Kane's arm came around my shoulders, and he tugged me in tight. "Looks like."

I leaned into him and let myself think about what Eddie had said.

Settling down.

That kind of meant...*home*, right?

I realized I was smiling.

Home.

Here. Not this place, exactly. But here in New York. With Kane, even. Maybe we were moving fast, and maybe I was the only one who was thinking like this, but I didn't think so.

For the first time in forever, maybe the first time *ever*, I felt like I had a home, like I had a place where I belonged.

37

Kane

My brothers and I took over the clean-up for the day.

Mom wanted to fuss over Dinah, and I think she also wanted to hover over Raye, although she was too...gentle, too good at it to make Raye feel smothered.

The look in Raye's eyes when my mother had hugged her was one that was going to stay with me for a long, long time, probably the rest of my life.

"Your girl's a sweetheart," Eddie said in a low voice as we washed dishes, both of us attuned to the voices out in the other room.

"I know."

"You serious about her?" He shot me a look as he passed me a pot to rinse off. Once I was done, I turned it over to Justin to dry, and Austen took care of putting it up. We had the system nailed down.

"Yeah, Eddie." I met his eyes. "I'm serious about her."

"Been going out long?"

I shrugged, not wanting to tell him we'd actually only

been out on one or two dates in the past week, and before that...what did I call what we'd been doing before that? Not like I was going to tell him, but no. We hadn't been going out long.

The timing didn't matter though.

She felt right to me.

And when she looked at me, I could see it in her eyes that she felt it, too.

I wasn't going to question that.

"Well, good for you," Eddie said, bumping my shoulder with his. "She makes you smile a lot. Shit, I didn't know you could smile that much. So...yeah, good for you."

"She's a good cook," Austen piped up from his spot at the end of the line. He was moving to the beat of the music pulsing out of the headphones he had draped around his neck. The music was loud enough that all of us could hear it, but he was the only one who seemed to appreciate the loud, discordant tones.

"When did you get to try her cooking?" Eddie asked, looking put out.

I met Austen's eyes.

I didn't have to do anything else.

I'd had a talk with Mom – and yes, she had wanted to go after Calie, but other than her, nobody knew about the mess with Calie and Austen.

And Austen seemed to have settled himself down in the days since it had happened. It was early yet, but maybe he'd gotten himself scared enough to get his act together. Not exactly the ideal way to do it, but it was better than not having it happen at all.

Under Eddie's sharp eyes, Austen shrugged and grinned.

"Don't worry, man. I'm sure she won't mind cooking for you at some point. She just likes me more."

The good-natured ribbing kept up even once we were finished.

Meeting Raye out in the living room, I looped my arms around her waist and asked if she was ready to go. Eddie could be as nosy as an old mother hen when the mood got on him, so I figured it was best to head out.

She nodded, tipping her head back to meet my eyes. "We can go if you're ready."

Once we were out on the street, I took her hand, trying to think up a subtle way to ask her if she wanted to spend the night, but Raye stepped in front of me, bringing me to a stop.

She cocked her head, eying me nervously, then she blurted out, "You want to come over to my place?"

I kissed her. "Sounds good to me."

The subway ride was becoming familiar, and I spent the time with my arm around her shoulders while she held my hand and traced her index finger over and around some of the scars on the back of my knuckles and my palm.

Once we got to her place, she started up the steps.

My phone rang, and I pulled it out, checked the number. It was one of the guys from work, so I let it go to voicemail and put the phone on vibrate. I could take a few hours away from the world, right?

I went to put the phone in my pocket just as Raye rounded the corner, disappearing out of sight.

I missed my pocket, dropping the phone in the process, my hands still numb from the cold. Swearing, I knelt to grab it. Once I had it in hand, I rotated it to check and make sure I hadn't broken the screen. I'd lost more than a few phones that way.

Luckily, the expensive case I'd invested in this time had protected it. As I went to shove it in my pocket, I heard a rush of footsteps and Raye's startled voice.

Adrenaline kicked in.

I rushed around the corner just in time to see her driving her fist into the temple of a man nearly twice her size.

He jerked back, but not in time to entirely avoid the blow. He looked slightly dazed, but he managed to catch her by the arm, jerking her up against him.

That was as far as he got before I reached him, coming up behind him and wrapping my forearm around his neck. "Let me guess..." I said, anger pulsing inside. "You must be Chad."

He jerked against my hold, and I loosened my grip enough for him to slip away, but then I caught him again and slammed him into the wall, glaring into watery blue eyes that now held more than a little fear.

"You like going around and terrorizing women?" I asked, shoving my forearm against his windpipe. His pale face started to go red.

He opened his mouth, trying to choke out something. I doubted it was an answer to my question.

"I'm going to put this to you plainly. You're going to stay away from Raye. Permanently. For like...the rest of your life," I said, speaking in a slow, measured voice. "If you come around her again, I'm going to round up some friends of mine. And let me tell you, these friends make me look like Santa Claus. Do I look like Santa right now?"

The sleazy bastard frantically shook his head.

"So, you can imagine what kind of friends I can round up, right?"

He nodded, face now almost purple.

I eased up on the windpipe and let him suck in air. Couldn't have him passing out before I issued my big threat.

"Now that you seem to get the picture, let me tell you what we'll do to you if you ever come near her again." I dipped my head and murmured close to his ear, feeling his body twitch and jerk with fear. "And if you touch her? There won't be enough left of you to bury."

I drew back, letting him go.

He sagged against the wall, reaching up to rub at his throat.

"What do you think, Chad?" I made a sneer out of his name. "Think maybe you should stay away from Raye now?"

He nodded and practically tripped over his feet as he ran away.

38

Raye

The sight of Chad running away was one of the more satisfying things I'd seen in a long, long time.

But even as I mused over that, my gaze was drawn back to Kane, and the look in his eyes caught me off-guard.

He looked...uneasy.

His eyes met mine, then slid away.

It only took a few seconds to figure out what the problem was. Slowly, I went to him and held out a hand.

He took it, and I walked backward, leading him to my apartment.

"Come inside," I said softly.

He opened his mouth, but I pressed my index finger to his lips, overcome with a massive need for him, and oddly enough, tenderness. He'd protected me, this big, brooding, intimidating man, and he was now worried that...what? That I'd reject him? That I might be afraid of him?

I felt safer with him than I'd ever felt with anybody.

The idea of being afraid was almost laughable.

Still holding his hand, I turned away and undid the series of locks on the door. Once I was done, I tugged him inside and redid each lock, still holding his hand in one of mine.

Once the locks were set, I turned and nudged him back up against the door, pressing my mouth to his.

He tensed in reaction.

I traced my fingers along his cheek, felt a muscle pulse under my fingers.

"Thank you," I said, murmuring the words against his lips. I had no idea exactly what he'd said that had made Chad freak out, but I'd seen pure terror in the man's eyes, and I doubted Chad would be back.

It was knowledge that lightened my heart far more than I'd ever dared to imagine.

Moving my lips from his, I kissed a line down his jaw to his neck.

One of his hands came up, cupping the back of my head.

It tightened as I drew a line down, down, down, stopping when I hit the V-neck of the sweater he wore under a heavy work coat. Pulling away, I shoved the coat from his shoulders, then caught the hem of the sweater. He had to help me drag it the rest of the way off, leaning back up against the door once we let it fall to the floor.

I pressed my mouth to his chest and the muscles jerked under my lips. His breathing sped up, and against my lips, I could feel the rapid beat of his heart.

"Raye..."

The sound of my name on his lips was incredibly erotic, so guttural and rough, and I shivered against him.

He closed a hand over my hip and dragged me closer.

Against my belly, I felt the hard press of his cock, and I

whimpered, wiggling against him, but when he went to pull at my clothes, I caught his hands and urged them back to his sides.

"My turn," I said stubbornly.

He closed his hands into fists, but closed his eyes and nodded, his fisted hands pressed against the door at his back. I kissed a path down his torso, lingering over each tattoo I came across. As I went lower, I bent my knees, kneeling in front of him. When I tugged his jeans open, his entire body went rigid, and his hands moved to my shoulders, squeezing tight. "Raye..."

"Shhh..."

Leaning in, I kissed him through the heather-gray material of his boxers. His cock jumped, pulsing against my touch. I grabbed the waist of his jeans and dragged the thick denim down to mid-thigh, then tugged his boxers lower, freeing his cock. After a quick glance upward, I swayed closer and took him in my mouth.

A muttered curse escaped him.

One hand cupped the back of my neck.

He was thick, stretching my mouth as I took him inside, but I kept going until the head butted against the back of my throat. Then I stopped and slowly withdrew, running my tongue over the heavy vein, sucking on him as I pulled back.

A low noise escaped him as I started the process all over again.

By the third stroke, he was moving against my mouth, one hand cupping my face, strangely gentle, while the other held the back of my neck. He no longer leaned against the door. Instead, he hovered over me and rocked into me with each forward movement I made.

He spoke, but the words were low, almost nonsensical, a series of syllables and grunts and disjointed words that still somehow managed to turn me on even more.

"Yeah...with your...right...*fuck, Raye...*"

I took him as deep as I could when he swelled in my mouth, gripping his hips and holding him in place. Lodged against the back of my throat now, his cock pulsed and jerked, and I swallowed, eager for more.

"I'm going to come," he said, trying to pull me off.

I sucked on him and began to move faster.

Between my thighs, liquid heat gathered, and I squirmed, desperate to relieve the ache building inside me, but there was no way in hell I was going to stop what I was doing.

Something salty filled my mouth, and Kane grunted.

"Last chance, Raye," he warned me.

I slowed down and slid him a look, staring up at him over the length of his body before drawing him back into my mouth once more. Slow, teasingly.

He groaned and slid a hand between us, fisting his cock. His hand bumped up against my mouth, but as he began to pump himself, I decided I didn't mind. He held me in place with his hand at the base of my neck, and I knew this was the most erotic thing I'd ever experienced, him fisting himself while I held the head of his cock in my mouth, kneeling still fully clothed in front of him.

A wash of fluid hit the back of my tongue. Reflexively, I swallowed, then swallowed again as another rush of it followed. Kane kept pumping. I swallowed again, and he let go of his cock to grab my head in both hands, pumping his dick in and out of my mouth.

The sheer eroticism of it was enough to stun away any

wariness I might have felt at being held so tightly, and when his hands fell away, I felt off-balance, cut adrift from the things that had held me centered.

But I wasn't adrift for long.

Kane pulled me up and spun me around, crowding me up against the door as he busily pulled at my clothes.

It seemed like it took him mere seconds to get me naked and then he was on his knees in front of me, my ass in his hands as he tilted my hips forward and pressed his mouth to me.

I gasped, then cried out, startled as he buried his tongue inside me.

His hands tightened on my ass, and he tugged me closer, groaning against me.

I was closer to the edge than it should have been possible and just a few jabs of his tongue against my clit had me hurtling dangerously closer to that precipice. Shuddering, I buried my hands in his hair.

He bit my clit.

With a cry, I bucked against him and came.

He rose up and buried himself inside me, lifting me in his arms in seemingly one smooth motion. My back to the door, he rode me hard. Seeking his mouth with mine, I fisted my hands in his hair and urged him on.

Mine...it was a thought that struck me with near giddiness, as he thrust deep inside, as if seeking the heart of me.

I clung to him with legs and arms as the thought reverberated through me. *Mine*.

The orgasm hit us, nearly at the same time. One second, I was straining toward it, then I was falling over. Then, with a shudder, Kane drove into me one last time and groaned, his cock pulsing as he emptied himself.

He dropped his head onto my shoulder, the two of us both trembling and panting for air.

I didn't mean to say it. Not out loud. But as I clung to his wide shoulders with one arm, the fingers of my free hand playing through his hair, I heard myself whisper, "Mine."

Kane heard it, too.

He lifted his head and looked down at me, eyes glittering. "Yours, huh?"

I blushed. I could feel how bright red I must have gone, simply by the rush of heat that stung my cheeks. But I didn't look away or try to take it back. I lifted my chin and stared into his eyes. "That a problem?"

He chuckled and lowered his head to rub his lips against mine. "If I'm yours, that makes you mine, doesn't it?"

"Yes." *His*. The thought was almost dazzling, and I sighed in satisfaction as he pulled me closer.

"Then...no. No problem."

39

Kane

A few hours later, we lay in bed, half entwined.

Raye had her head on my chest, and my fingers were curled around the back of her neck.

She kept tracing her fingers over the tattoos on my chest and belly. Occasionally, it veered toward the ticklish zone, and she laugh when I flinched. "I never thought a big, tough guy like you would be ticklish."

I finally retaliated by finding every last ticklish spot she had.

And there were a lot.

But even though I tickled her until she was begging for mercy, that didn't keep her from tracing the tail feathers of the phoenix where they spread down low over my rib cage, or the flames that licked around my navel. I wasn't going to stop her either. If she wanted to be touching me, I wanted her to be touching me.

Mine. The covetous way she'd whispered it kept circling around in my head.

There was something else floating around in my thoughts, too. Something that had hit me when I'd seen her slam her fist into Chad's head.

I loved her.

As her hand wandered down near my lower abdomen once more, I caught her wrist. Rolling her onto her back, I threw my leg over hers and stared down into her face.

She made a face at me. "I'm not trying to tickle you," she said. "I just like touching you."

"I didn't say anything," I said mildly.

"You've got a look in your eyes." She cocked her head, studying me. "What's that look for?"

"You and I ...we can't even say we've been dating. We've only been out on a real date twice, and that's this past week. I know this is going to sound kind of crazy..." I took a deep breath. I hadn't ever been a coward, not in my whole life. I wasn't going to start now. "But I don't care if it's crazy. And I'm not expecting anything from you, either. I just...Raye, I'm in love with you."

Her dark blue eyes went wide. Her lashes fluttered. She opened her mouth, then closed it. I could see her throat working as she swallowed.

"You don't have to say anything," I told her. "I just...I wanted you to know."

She lifted a hand and pressed it to my cheek. "Kane."

As Raye tugged me down so she could kiss me, my heart flipped over. I'd told her, and here she was, kissing me and clinging tight.

I'd told her and...

"I love you, too," she whispered against my lips. "Yeah, it's fast, but it feels right."

Her words knocked me sideways.

Jerking my head up, I stared down at her. "You...say that again."

"I love you, too." She shrugged as she smiled up at me. "I've never had anything in my life feel this right, so fast or not...I'm not going to fight it."

I hooked my forearm around her neck and pulled her in close, burying my face against her neck.

She smoothed a hand up and down my spine. I didn't even care when her hands reached that spot low on my back that was just the slightest bit ticklish.

"FINISH SCHOOL," Raye said.

We had four boxes of Chinese in front of us and sat eating them naked on her bed. All those dates we hadn't had and the time we were just now starting to spend together had made me aware of something – we had a lot ahead of us in the *getting to know you* department.

I wasn't much on relationships, but I did know that it helped to know the person you were with.

One of her top five goals in life was to finish school.

I'd already told her I planned on owning the garage outright before another ten years passed.

"It won't leave me with a lot of free spending money. I'm not real big on going on and partying or eating out a lot."

Raye waved a hand. "My mother wasn't much of a cook. I hardly ever got home-cooked food at home. That was one of the reasons I learned how to cook – and do it well – as young as I did. I prefer eating at home anyway. It costs too much.

Except for Chinese from time to time." She winked at me over a bite of crab Rangoon.

"Next goal?" I snatched the last piece of crab Rangoon from the box. She'd eaten three of the five.

She stuck her tongue out at me, but a grin flirted with her lips. It faded though, and she looked pensive, clearly thinking. "I want to get to know my brother better. Both him and Michelle. Family wasn't something I had much of as a kid. I'd like to change that."

I couldn't imagine not having mine. Laying a hand on her knee, I squeezed lightly. She smiled at me and covered my hand with hers.

"What about your father? Do you want to meet him?"

Raye started to shake her head, then she stopped. "I don't know. Jake mentioned it, said he'd probably love to meet me. Mom always told me he didn't care about me, but...maybe she lied?"

"Would she do that?" Raye hadn't told me much about her mom, but what little she had shared hadn't exactly painted a pretty picture.

Raye made a face, tapping her chopsticks on the box in front of her. "I want to say no." She shot a look at me. "I want to...but I can't." With a shrug, she looked away.

"What's stopping you from meeting him?" I asked.

She opened her mouth, then closed it. After a few seconds, she said, "I just..." But she ended up shaking her head, one hand lifted as if she could pull the words she needed from thin air.

"You don't want to be rejected, do you?"

"No," she whispered, looking vulnerable.

Turning my hand over, I laced our fingers together. "Take

your time and think it through. You'll figure out what's right for you." Letting go of her hand, I took my fork – chopsticks were yet another skill I hadn't mastered. Stabbing a piece of sweet and sour chicken, I shot Raye a look. "I'd like to mend fences with Dinah. We're better now than we were, but we're not close the way we were as kids. I'd like to fix that. But the only way to do it is to show her I'm not going to mess up again."

"You've been doing that since you got out of prison." Raye swayed close and kissed me. "You can't keep trying to prove yourself. She can either accept you or not. If she doesn't, that's her loss."

When she would have pulled back, I cupped her cheek and held her close for another soft, slow kiss.

She tried to turn her head away, laughing. "I taste like kung pao chicken," she said.

"You taste like Raye." It was a taste I'd never get enough of.

She broke away first and the two of us, without saying a word, started to clear the food from the bed. She rose up onto her knees, leaning over to put everything on her dresser, just barely in arms reach. As she leaned forward to add the last box, I caught her hips and bent my head, pressing my lips to her butt.

She hissed out a breath and looked over her shoulder at me.

"I've got so many ways I want to take you," I murmured against her skin, kissing a path upward and moving in closer.

"Is that a fact?"

"Hmmmm..." I reached her shoulder, using my grip on her hips to pull her back flush against me. "Look."

I felt her head move, felt her body tense and knew she'd seen.

There was a mirror on the wall across the room, and she could see us, see me as I slid a hand around and cupped one full, lush breast. "Do you see me touching you?" I asked, even though I knew the answer.

"Yes..." The breath stuttered out of her and she arched her spine, thrusting her hips back against me.

I rolled mine forward, and she jerked as my cock cuddled up against her ass.

Adjusting us on the bed, I nudged her forward until her hands were braced on the mattress. "Keep watching," I told her. Then I tucked the head of my cock against her entrance and slowly fed it into her wet, waiting depths.

She whimpered, tightening around me, so slick and hot already.

Her head bowed forward. I caught her jaw and nudged upward. "Keep watching, Raye."

Her eyes met mine in the mirror, and she shuddered, her spine arching in a long, elegant curve. But she watched.

As I withdrew, then drove back in.

As I slid a hand around and toyed with her clit.

As I began to shaft her with hard, deep digs of my cock.

Even as her body began to quake in reaction, the orgasm bearing down on her.

She kept watching.

I curved my hand over her throat and felt the mad flutter of her pulse. She clamped down tight around me, then abruptly shoved back against me, sitting on my cock. I groaned as her silken wet pussy clamped around me like a fist and she wiggled and bounced, trying to take me deeper and faster.

"More?" I asked.

"Please!"

I grabbed her hips and lifted her, then brought her down. Up, down, feeling the drag and glide of her cunt. It was erotic, sweet as hell.

She wailed out my name and came, hard and fast.

I buried my face against her back and started to grind against her, gritting my teeth as the sensations spread through me.

She milked and squeezed me, still in the grips of her climax and the final milking sensation sent me over.

We fell back into the bed, me clutching her to me, Raye curling up into the curve of my body.

"I love you," I whispered against her neck.

She shivered, a soft sigh escaping her. "I love you, too."

40

Raye

My apartment looked like Christmas had exploded all over it.

I didn't know how long it would take to clean everything up, but I didn't care. I'd just spent my first Christmas with Kane – and with Jake, Michelle, and Kane's family. It had been the best Christmas of my life, and it wasn't even over.

Kane stood up amid all the boxes and bags, striding over to sit next to me on the couch. "There's barely room for me here with all this stuff," he said, a rueful grin on his lips. "I think Jake tried to make up for more than twenty Christmases in one year."

"I'll make room for it all." I smiled at him. Silently, I agreed with him. My brother had gone above and beyond, but I wasn't going to complain. I'd been a little spoiled this past year between Kane and Jake, and I kind of loved it.

Having somebody fuss over me was something I'd never had, and now I had two guys doing it, my lover and my brother.

"I can't decide who got more spoiled by my family this

year...you, or the little kids." Kane cupped the back of my neck, rubbing his thumb up and down my skin, sending shivers through me.

"Oh, that's easy. It was Dinah's little girl." I stuck my tongue out at him. "There was no question. Did you see all the clothes Eddie and Rick bought for her? She's going to be the best-dressed baby in New York City."

"Dinah won't have to go shopping for clothes for months," he agreed.

Snuggling up against him, I closed my eyes, tired and drained, but in the best possible way. "I can't believe Rick and Eddie are engaged now. They look stupid-happy."

"Stupid-happy." Kane rubbed his lips over the top of my head. "Is that a good thing?"

"Absolutely." I yawned and stretched against him, craning my head back so I could meet his eyes. "And Nathaniel's going to be a daddy again. He better start making bank if he's going to feed all those mouths under his roof."

Kane laughed. "He'll handle it. That's what he does."

"Your mother looked over the moon. You'd think all the grandbabies she's got would be enough, but hearing she's going to have another was all the Christmas present she needed."

"She loves being a grandma." He cupped my cheek and dipped his head to mine. "Sometimes, I think she loves it more than she loves being a mom."

He kissed me softly, but just as I started to respond, he lifted his head, looking down at me with an odd look in his eyes.

"What is it?" I asked.

"Just thinking about you...the past year."

"Good thoughts?"

He pressed his brow to mine. "Nothing but."

My heart flipped over at the look I saw in his eyes, and I curled my arms around his neck. "Why don't you take me to bed and I'll give you another Christmas present?" I told him.

I actually had one more for him, but now he had me thinking thoughts about naked skin and smooth sheets.

The other present could wait.

But instead of responding, he kissed me, then straightened.

He started to pace, and there seemed to be something oddly nervous about his movements. He paused here and there, picking up stray boxes or pieces of wrapping paper. "It's a good thing we decided to have our Christmas at your place," he said absently. "My apartment never would have held all of this."

"That's why we did it," I reminded him. I barely had room for the big tree I'd wanted. It never would have fit into his place, although I did insist he get a tabletop sized version and we'd decorated it one night while eating pizza and watching *How the Grinch Stole Christmas*.

He nodded, still with that nervous, restless look on his face.

He hadn't looked that nervous the night I'd graduated from college, just a few short weeks ago and he'd surprised me with a pearl necklace. I reached up and touched the strand now, wondering what had gotten into him. "What's going on, Kane?"

"Nothing." He turned and faced me, straightening his shoulders and taking a deep breath. He looked like he was bracing himself.

I eyed him warily as he came striding back toward me.

Then he sank down on one knee.

I sucked in a breath as he pulled a small black box out of his front pocket. "There's one last present," he said, his voice rough. Then he flipped it open and turned it to face me. "Will you marry me, Raye?"

For a few seconds, I couldn't even think, much less answer.

Then, as the question finally sank in, I launched myself off the couch toward him, laughing and kissing him at the same time. "Yes." Kiss. "Yes, yes." Kiss. "Yes, absolutely yes."

He grinned up at me from where he laid beneath me on the floor. "I take it that's a yes." He slid the ring onto my finger without even looking.

"Let me think..." I pursed my lips and cocked my head, lifting my hand so I could study it. "Hmmm...yes."

He stood up, holding me effortlessly, but when he went to carry me over to the bed, I wiggled and pushed at him until he put me down.

"Hold on," I insisted. Since he'd gone and given me one last present, it was time I give him *his* last present. "I've got something for you, too."

I turned around and had to circumnavigate the piles of boxes and gift bags on my way over to my purse. Sliding him a sly look, I said, "You do know this means we should start looking for a new place to live."

He opened, then closed his mouth. "Ah...maybe? Yeah. I guess."

"No." I shook my head, a thoughtful look on my face. "I'm pretty sure we'll need to find a place...a bigger place."

I tugged the card out of my purse and walked over to him, placing it in his hands.

"What's this?"

"A Christmas card." I grinned at him, wondering if he'd get it right away.

I had no idea, but I'd be more than happy to explain it to him. It had killed me to keep this a secret the past week.

He glanced at the card, then at me. "I didn't know I was supposed to get you a card."

I laughed at the panicked look in his eyes. "Oh, you weren't!" I cupped his face in my hands. My new engagement ring sparkled back at me. Rising on my toes, I tugged him down for a kiss. "I just wanted to get you one. Now...open it."

He looked a little self-conscious as he ripped it open.

Some of the confetti I'd stuffed inside spilled out, and he glanced down, frowning at the sparkle of pink and blue that hit the toes of his boots. He eyed it, then glanced back at the red and green card. When he opened the card, the rest of it fell out in a shower, raining all over the floor.

I grinned at him as he read it. I remembered exactly what I'd written.

There's another present on the way. Should be here in just under eight months.

HE READ IT, then closed his eyes, shaking his head a little. Then he read it a second time.

"What the...?"

His eyes slid to the confetti on the floor, all the pink and blue pacifiers that covered the toes of his boots and my threadbare carpet.

"Are you pregnant?" he whispered, his voice hoarse.

I nodded, suddenly nervous. What if he wasn't happy? What if he blamed me for not realizing the antibiotics I'd taken for strep throat would KO my birth control pills?

He reached for me and hauled me up against him.

As his lips came down over mine, I sank into him, and he whispered against my mouth, "Merry Christmas."

I smiled against his lips. "Merry Christmas to us both.

His hand splayed across my belly. "Merry Christmas to us all."

THE END

Thank you so much for reading Big O's. Don't miss the final Sex Coach book, *Pleasure Island*, coming in the spring.

Also by M. S. Parker

Rescued by the Woodsman

Sex Coach

The Billionaire's Muse

Bound

One Night Only

Damage Control

Take Me, Sir

Make Me Yours

The Billionaire's Sub

The Billionaire's Mistress

Con Man Box Set

HERO Box Set

A Legal Affair Box Set

The Client

Indecent Encounter

Dom X Box Set

Unlawful Attraction Box Set

Chasing Perfection Box Set

Blindfold Box Set

Club Prive Box Set

The Pleasure Series Box Set

Exotic Desires Box Set

Pure Lust Box Set

Casual Encounter Box Set

Sinful Desires Box Set

Twisted Affair Box Set

Serving HIM Box Set

About the Author

M. S. Parker is a USA Today Bestselling author and the author of over fifty spicy romance series and novels.

Living part-time in Las Vegas, part-time on Maui, she enjoys sitting by the pool with her laptop writing her next spicy romance.

Growing up all she wanted to be was a dancer, actor and author. So far only the latter has come true but M. S. Parker hasn't retired her dancing shoes just yet. She is still waiting for the call to appear on Dancing With The Stars.

When M. S. isn't writing, she can usually be found reading– oops, scratch that! She is always writing.

For more information:
www.msparker.com
msparkerbooks@gmail.com

Acknowledgments

First, I would like to thank all of my readers. Without you, my books would not exist. I truly appreciate each and every one of you.

A big THANK YOU goes out to all the Facebook fans, street team, beta readers, and advanced reviewers. You are a HUGE part of the success of all my series.

Also thank you to my editor Lynette, my proofreader Nancy, and my wonderful cover designer, Sinisa. You make my ideas and writing look so good.

Printed in Great Britain
by Amazon